As Close As You Are To Me

David Williams

A Wild Wolf Publication

Published by Wild Wolf Publishing in 2014

ISBN: 978-1-907954-39-9

Also available in e-book

www.wildwolfpublishing.com

Acclaim for previous novels by David Williams

For *11:59*

'A taut thriller ... A near-cinematic stylist, the author deftly sustains the tension right up until the final segment... a sterling example of astute character studies melded with highly topical concerns.'
~ **Publishers Weekly**

'I was immediately drawn into the characters' lives and wanted to know what happened next... This is a good read with engaging characters and a modern, topical plot-line. Recommended.'
~ **Bookbag**

For *Mr Stephenson's Regret*

'This richly detailed and meticulously researched storyline breathes life and a palpable sense of intimacy into these historical figures and immerses readers in an England embroiled in political and social upheaval as it teeters on the cusp of the industrial revolution.'
~ **Publishers Weekly**

'The hallmark of any historical novel must surely be that, primarily, it tells an entertaining story whilst at the same time arousing an interest in the period or subject matter so that the reader may be encouraged to carry out some later research. With this novel about the pioneers of the railway age, George and Robert Stephenson, David Williams has succeeded admirably on both counts.'
~ **Historical Novels Review**

This book is dedicated to Paula.
Thank you for being as close as you are to me.

David Williams

CONTENTS

UNCANNY RESEMBLANCE

I know things like this happen all the time, but not like *this*. I can't count the number of times I've said to Karin, 'Doesn't she look like...?' or she might say, 'Who does he remind you of?' But I'll swear this was Ruth to the T. I mean, to the T.

What I can't figure out is my own reaction, or rather non-reaction. Why didn't I jump up and follow her? Catch her, touch her on the arm - 'Excuse me...'

Excuse me, what exactly? What would I, could I say? 'You look exactly like...' 'You're the spitting image of...' (horrible phrase). 'Excuse me, I don't quite know how to say this, but you bear an uncanny resemblance to my dead daughter.'

Course not. Nutter in the park syndrome. And she'd be right to think so. The fact is I give that impression anyway these days. I'm aware I have a sort of forlorn look about me, I can see it in people's eyes. I've even had the odd stranger (well-meaning type, usually some buttoned-up oldish woman) come up to me in a timid sort of way and say, 'You all right, dear?' Something like that. 'You OK? Anything I can do?' Some bloke passed by the other morning, gave us a 'Cheer up, mate, might never happen.' Just a nod, little smile from me, mutual acknowledgement sort of thing. I could have said, 'It already did, pal,' but I didn't.

I've been so locked in on myself, so inactive mentally and physically - maybe that's why I just sat here when Ruth walked by. I should have done something. I could have followed without her noticing - just walk behind, see where she's going, try and get a closer look. What if she saw me, though? Might take me for a stalker, call the police, shout help at the top of her voice. (*Her voice. Would she have a voice, poor dead Ruth?*) I should have done something. Even at the risk of... At least I'd have the moment of her turning around, seeing me. If she *was*... If by any incredible, unbelievable, supernatural chance she really was Ruth I would know when she turned around, not only from her appearance but from her *look*. I mean obviously she would recognize me straightaway. It's been, what, just over a year. I can't have changed that much - she hasn't. As soon as she turned round I would see it in her eyes...

What am I thinking? Ruth has been dead for over a year. A year and four months. But this Ruth... I mean this girl, this... young woman... Who is she? Couldn't possibly be my daughter. *Could not* be my Ruth. Except she is. Was. To me she was. I'm certain of it.

Calm down, think it through once more. Go through it as it happened. I'm sitting here, looking at nothing in particular, inside my own head as ever these days. Park gates to my right, only in view if I turn that way which I don't, but that's the direction she comes from, *must* come from since I would have noticed someone pass directly in front of me. She moves into my peripheral vision as she turns along the path towards the fountain and I look up - immediately there's that sense of her presence, I mean the importance of her, snapping me out of... whatever. Like I've suddenly come to attention. I watch her walk along the path and already my heart's swelling inside big enough to choke me. She's there as clear... in profile first, then her back view as she walks to the square, not hurrying really. She even dips her fingers in the fountain for a second, not stopping, just brushing the surface as she passes. Just as Ruth would. No ghost could... that's a *solid* action, a human one, I mean, a living human. So it's not her. But it *is* her. And she walks on beyond the square, following the path, maybe going out at the Collingwood Road end, but I don't know for certain because from where I am the trees and bushes are in the way.

And I just sit there without moving. Watching her. The best part of a minute, and I never get off my seat, not even when she disappears along the far path. What kind of foolishness is that?

Possibilities. Number one, some sort of waking dream that felt absolutely real at the time. It often happens, doesn't it, in dreams (it does in mine) where you seem wrapped into something happening in front of your eyes and yet you're not really a participant, more an observer. That would explain why I never moved from my position. But I never felt that waking sensation you always get after dreams like that; no sudden jolt back into reality. I suppose my heart rate's back to more or less normal by now, recovering from the immediate shock of seeing her, but that's quite different from waking up after a dream, even a daydream.

Possibility number two - I really have seen a ghost. Well, I've been on this earth forty-three years now. I've never had any sort of ghostly visitations or imaginings, not even just after Ruth... Nightmares about it, yes, but nothing I'd describe as ghostly. Nobody I know whose opinion I respect has ever seen a ghost, or told me they have. I've watched the odd documentary, ghost hunter sort of affairs, always been on the side of the sceptics and scientists; nothing in it as far as I've ever been able to work out. I'm not saying it's impossible - and I am someone who considers that things happen for a reason - but I'd take some convincing about a visit or a sign from a ghost, even if I wanted to believe.

Besides she was just too *there*. Her fingers playing in the fountain, and also now I think of it I'm sure I heard her heels on the path when she was quite near me - in fact that must have been part of what drew my

11

attention. I can't imagine a ghost wearing stilettos, not even short heels, not ones that make a noise anyway.

Which takes me to possibility number three - I saw a young woman who looks startlingly like my daughter. It's the obvious explanation; why am I fighting it? It's not as if the green coat she had on was particularly like any I've ever seen Ruth wearing, nor was there anything about her handbag that was especially distinctive, though it was slung over her shoulder on a strap just about the length Ruth preferred. But while I agree (with myself) that this is by far the likeliest explanation I'm not ready to accept it.

This is my daughter; how could I mistake her? At one point she was less than twenty feet away from me. It's true I didn't see her full face but her profile was exactly...

I've just realised something. Her earring. Silver Maltese Cross earring with rounded ends on the cross-pieces - exactly what Ruth wears. Wore. I haven't even considered it until this moment because her earrings have been so much part of her appearance since... well, since Karin and I picked them out specially for her seventeenth birthday. She loved them, hardly ever took them out. Pierced ears. Maltese Cross earrings with a few links of silver chain so they dangled ever so slightly as she walked. This girl had them - or *one* that I could see from the side - exactly the same. Could I notice that detail from twenty feet? Clearly I did, and yet without particularly taking it in at the time because it was all part of the whole picture, a natural part of her.

OK, the earrings were not made exclusively for Ruth - there must be hundreds, maybe thousands out there identical - but not set against that profile, that cheekbone, that face, under that delicate... her wispy blonde hair. The breeze lifting it slightly and the earring visible. This is, this was my girl.

So, so, so - what's a man to do? Call the police. And say what? No, I don't think so. That whole experience dealing with them last year was just... I'm not going there again, not unless I have to. What I want, of course, is to tell Karin all about it. Easier said... Anyway, I'm going to need more - what? - *evidence*. Otherwise how could I open it all up again for her? It wouldn't be fair, supposing she even gave me the chance.

I walk through the park and out at the Collingwood Road entrance. Which way to turn? After some hesitation I go north, partly because that's not a route I've used before (maybe that's how I missed her in the past) and also because there seem to be more office buildings in this direction - does she work in one of these offices? The chances are good.

12

But which building, which door? Some of these places have twelve storeys and higher. Which of these windows might she be sitting at, if any? I try walking along the street one way, on display as it were to the buildings on the other side of the road, then cross and come back the opposite way. Then down again the same side and up the other. I'm giving her every chance to notice me, wherever she is. Stand for a while at a bus stop, move away when the bus comes. One side of the road has a couple of benches concreted in to the pavement, near to a bin. I try them both at various times over the next couple of hours. Solid seats, hard to the touch. Traffic noise, diesel fumes. This is a real day; I have not been imagining my daughter's appearance.

At lunchtime I hang about for a good while outside the sandwich shops and coffee bars, watching the workers come and go. No sign. Another hour, then it strikes me she could just as likely have turned south from the park entrance, so what to do? I have the bright idea of returning to my original seat near the fountain so that I can be there when the offices close, watch the workers go by on their respective ways home. As I'm waiting I have time to consider that Ruth passed mid-morning after most of the commuters would already be at their desks, so perhaps my work theory is flawed. But I have no other strategy. I wait and watch, watch and wait until it seems half the office staff in the city have passed through the park on their way back to wherever. But no Ruth. It's getting dusk before I decide to wrap it up too, and make my own way home.

What I call home these days is a grubby ground floor flat near the lesser of the two universities, surrounded by students and singles. Needs must. Gladstone Terrace is a long way from Beech Grove, socio-economically speaking. I turn the key and push past various items of mail on the floor which I won't bother checking as none of them will be for me. In the hallway a purple-framed bicycle with a low white saddle that wasn't here when I left this morning. As I'm negotiating my way around it the door across from mine opens and the woman who lives there pops up; smiles an apology. She's obviously been listening out for me.

'Oh, I hope you don't mind,' she says, 'Only I didn't want to chance leaving it outside.'

'OK.'

'I got it off one of those postcards ads in the corner shop.'

'Right.'

'Did you see the bus fares went up again?'

'Yeah, noticed that.' Out of politeness I make a show of surveying the bike, appreciating it. 'It'll pay for itself quite quickly, I imagine. No running costs anyway.'

'I'll need to buy a pump. It doesn't have one at the moment.'

I register the fact with a nod, and in the silence that follows I stand there, stupidly working out in my head what size of pump she would need to fit the space allocated for it on the frame. She'll want a white one to match that seat.

Eventually she squeezes out of the doorway and sidles past me to pick up mail from the doormat. She sifts through, smiling - I think the smile is meant for me, not the mail, a sort of acknowledgement that we are still 'in conversation'. She's about ten years younger than I am probably, tad overweight, hair a bit too red to be natural, clothes from charity shops but tasteful enough in a bohemian sort of way.

'You're not Mr Robson, are you?' she says at last.

'No.'

'No.' She places the letter on the table next to the door. 'Maybe that's one of the students on the first floor. Nice boys.'

'I haven't met them yet. I'm fairly new myself.'

'Yes. At the university?'

'No.'

She holds another letter up, almost as if she wants to pass it to me. I stand my ground. 'I never quite know what to do with these.' She turns it to show the address window. 'The Occupier. Well, which of us is The Occupier? All of us and none of us, I suppose.' She flips the letter on the table with less care than she placed the last one. 'I usually just wait till there's a whole pile of them, then stick em all in the recycling. Well, what can you do?'

'Absolutely.'

She's encouraged by my agreement. 'I'm Jane, by the way.' Then - as if to excuse herself for divulging the information - 'should you be checking the mail...' (There's something of the English teacher about her.) 'Jane Ogden. Or Ms Jane Ogden, or Ms J Ogden. No middle name, just plain Jane.' She pauses, maybe expecting a response, then adds, 'Ogden's such an ugly name. It's a fat name.'

'Not really. I mean, not at all.' She isn't, I'm thinking. Not particularly. 'Alex,' I offer at last. That'll do for now.

'Nice to meet you, Alex.' She extends her hand. Actually, that's my first touch of a woman in months. It's a thought I hold onto as I close the door into my flat.

Longer still since my fingers touched the keys of a piano. There'd be no room for the baby grand in this place even if Karin had allowed me to take it. I only have my imagination now to stroke the notes, fill the room with music. Catch myself doing it sometimes at the computer table. When random characters start popping up on screen, I come to, realising I must have been absently shaping chords, inadvertently brushed the keys. Wrong keyboard, Alex. Mostly though it's just in the back of my brain, lying on the bed. And mostly the Ravel adagio. No, always the Ravel adagio, truth be told. Think I'm a touch OCD.

Drag myself out of that thought, boot up the computer, quick check on my eBay account (pretty dismal sales figures these days) then the usual keyword search on Google - nothing new on Karin and, as ever, nothing at all on Ruth. Like me, Karin doesn't bother with social networking; we're a family that prefers to keep our private lives private. I spend some time looking at images of Maltese Cross earrings. There are some that look the same as Ruth's, but that doesn't make the coincidence less spooky. I wonder what Karin did with them... afterwards. She never told me. Lots of things she never told me, or was prevented from telling me. Lots of things I've had to find out for myself, and still there's the central puzzle, or puzzles - the how and the why. I mean the *exactly* how and why.

I feel I'm in danger of drifting. Fact is, I've been drifting for months now, hardly noticing the days. In the doldrums, out at sea. That's what the doldrums means, I believe, literally. Originally. Somewhere sailing ships got stuck, where they spent day after day just rocking on the waves. That's me, been me. Today has been a breath of wind in the sails. As if Ruth is somehow reminding me of my need to stick to a purpose, follow a course. What I need right now is a plan.

I pull out the printer drawer and rescue a sheet of A4 paper. Find a felt marker pen and write out the headlines of my plan in large capital letters.

TRACE GIRL IN PARK
GET BACK KARIN
SOLVE MYSTERY OF RUTH'S DEATH

I pin the sheet on the back of the door and go back to lie on my bed. Not to sleep, but to think. From my position on the pillow I can still read the words on the paper. I stare at the note while I'm thinking. Almost like I'm waiting for someone to walk through into my room.

II

It begins as a slow-moving mass of traffic - ariel view as though a silent helicopter is tracking the rush hour for the television news. Nothing stands out until the jam frees for no discernible reason, the queues thin, and the perspective narrows to one lane. As gaps stretch between vehicles a white transit van gradually draws the attention, though it is in appearance nondescript; another anonymous working vehicle. Off onto a quieter road and now it's only the van in view below. Trees either side, dappled sunshine on the roof. A closer rear view, dipping under trees to follow the van, chase it even. Fine film of grime on the back door panels. The next shot should be the driver, maybe reflected in the wing mirror. Instead... jump cut - the van brutally parked or crashed, angled in a ditch. A swung-out rear door gravitating to the tilt. One corner of a dust sheet poking out. A hand reaches into a diagonal close-up of the other door, wraps round to wrench it open...

And I wake to a mangled chord. A piano lid crushing down on fingers as they play. Mouth opens - my cry is the chord. Eyes open - the darkness rings. I feel the vibration of the chord as a relentless throbbing in my arm. Shift position. My hand, released from under me, pricks and tingles. I flex and relax it while I lie staring at the dark. Reassembling. Thinking. Some time later, en route to the toilet, I pick up my felt pen and write *white van* under the headlines of my plan on the door.

When I leave the flat mid-morning the purple bike has gone. She's off to work, I guess, wherever that might be. Jane... what was it, Hodgson? Ogden. Plain Jane Ogden. I must be still carrying a vestige of our conversation in my head as I'm about to push open the door of the corner shop, which is what makes me notice the gap in the column of hand-written cards stuck up inside the window. I even find myself checking for other bargains that might be still on offer. No more bikes. What's a stroller? Some sort of pram. 'Pair of classic roller skates, hardly used.' I'm familiar with the euphemism of small ads - classic means out of date. I could roller skate once, after a fashion.

The Asian bloke at the counter gives me a sage nod of recognition that says I've seen you in here before. Another week or two and I'll get the regular customer smile, or does he reserve that for the ladies? Yes, they do sell stamps; a book of twelve first class is fine. I need milk but I don't want to be carrying a full carton around the streets all day.

I use the first stamp from the book just outside the shop, posting my envelope to Karin. Not a letter, just a note really: *Staying off limits, don't worry, but I may have some information regarding Ruth. Please call.* My mobile number below, in case she's lost it, and an *A xx* that I've tried to make jaunty as well as affectionate - a signal of reassurance.

I reach the park on schedule about fifteen minutes before the time I saw Ruth yesterday and sit at the same bench to wait - just checking a notion that she has a regular routine and I might come across her again. It's a little cooler but otherwise it's Groundhog Day - except she doesn't show.

At least waiting gives me a chance to reflect, check I'm on a steady course even if I don't have more than the outline of a map yet. The main thing, apart from a second sighting of Ruth (vital so I can make a proper observation without being distracted by shock like the first time) is being ready for Karin's reaction to my message. I know I said I'd wait for more evidence, but that was before I realised this is a vital window of opportunity - if I don't act quickly it might close on me. Besides, there's still at least twenty-four hours before she reads my note, probably longer considering how poor the postal service is nowadays. Plus I've already got quite a lot to spark her interest.

Don't quite make the hour I'd planned to wait as I become haunted by the idea Ruth could be just around the corner and I'm missing her by staying in one place. I end up rushing past the fountain out of the park as if I'm needed somewhere urgently.

But where exactly? At Collingwood Road I turn to go north again, then spin round and go south instead towards the main drag of shops, trying a different tack. Steadying myself in logic. There's more footfall at this end of town, statistically more chance...

It is much busier here, typical Thursday mix of workers and shoppers, though there's a surprising lack of girls around Ruth's age. Plenty of solo professional types looking very purposeful compared to the shufflings of the elderly women who are shopping together in a vague, meandering sort of way; mixed couples of various ages; youngish women with kids in buggies (strollers?); hard-looking hoodies huddled round as though they're trying to warm their faces off the shared heat of their cigarettes. Outside McDonalds there's a droopy thirty-something in a soft-brimmed cowboy hat trying to sell The Big Issue without much success. He keeps glancing up and down the street as if he's expecting to be collared any moment, or maybe in the hope some rich philanthropic type is going to happen along and buy his entire stock. I stand watching him on the other side of the street, impatient with a new idea but having to work up the courage to go right up and ask him.

'Excuse me, do you work here every day?'

17

'Eh?' He looks suspicious, shifty. His hair is long and lank under the cowboy hat. Rustler stubble.

'Are you generally round here?'

I'm so concerned he'll hit me I can't concentrate on making myself understood. Fortunately he seems to get it.

'This is my pitch, aye.' He thinks I'm making a play for his spot. 'What's it to you?'

'No, just that...' (How can I put this?) 'I'm looking for somebody and I thought you might have seen her, that's all.'

'Oh aye.' Still suspicious.

'Yesterday. Or... or any day, really. Girl about nineteen-twenty. Average height. Shortish blonde hair, quite fine. Pretty. Swedish-looking.'

'Swedish?'

'Half. She doesn't have an accent or anything, if she talked to you. But Swedish appearance if you know what I mean. She might have had a green coat on.'

'What's she to you, like?' (He's seen her!)

'Oh... Sorry, I'm... She's my daughter. Have you seen her?'

'No.'

'Oh.'

'Well, I might have. But she could be any amount of young lasses, couldn't she? Not much of a description. Swedish-looking.'

'She has earrings. Very distinctive earrings. Maltese Cross.'

'I don't go round staring at people's earrings.'

'No, but you might have noticed them... accidentally. I mean, by chance.'

'Never notice earrings. Tattoos, yes.' He gives me a firm look. 'It's not running away if you're nineteen, you know. She's an adult, got a right.'

'She hasn't run away.'

'So why you looking for her? Wait till she visits, man. She'll come in her own time.' I get the feeling this bloke has had experience of counselling somewhere down the line.

'It's complicated.' (Certainly is.) 'I just need to see her.'

'And you say you're her dad.'

'I am.'

'You don't look Swedish to me. Don't sound it neither.'

'No. That's on her mother's side.' I need to move this along before he asks too many questions. 'Listen, would you like to earn fifty pounds?'

'Hey, I'm not that desperate, mate.' He's a big guy when he straightens out of his stoop. Again I'm worried he's going to hit me.

'Not like that. No, I just want you to look out for her, that's all. There's fifty quid in it if you see her and tell me.'

'Fifty?'

'Yeah... And another fifty if I find her as a result.'

'A hundred altogether.'

'That's it.'

There's a long moment while he assesses the situation. As if he's holding me out for inspection, sussing, before he says, 'Tell you the truth, feller, you don't look like you could scrape up a hundred quid. No offence like, but I'm a professional - I can usually tell.'

It's come to something when your social credentials are being questioned by a scruffy Big Issue seller. Do I look that much of a mess?

'Not a problem, honestly. You'll get your money. And you don't really have to do anything, just keep your eyes open. It's a no-brainer.'

'Like a *stakeout*, sorta thing?'

'Exactly.'

He nods; decides. 'Fair enough.'

'Great. Thanks. Do you know what a Maltese Cross looks like?'

For answer he tucks his pile of Big Issues between his knees and rolls up the sleeve of his dirty denim shirt. The whole of his right arm is blue-black with tattoos, and there among the hairs of his forearm is a crude version of a Maltese Cross with a red spot in the centre that may have been meant to represent a ruby but looks like an insect bite. For me, though, it's a sign this was meant to be.

'Fantastic. Do you have a biro? I'll give you my details.'

'Biro?' He gives me a sardonic look then to my surprise whips out a smart phone from his pocket; efficiently punches in my name and number. Any remaining doubt I might have had about my new friend's 'professionalism' disappears when I make to leave and he checks me with a strong tap on the shoulder.

'Hang fire, mate. Got to be worth the price of a Big Issue. Down payment sort of thing.'

Being made to fork out two quid for an unwanted magazine is an unexpected blow. The plain truth is one hundred pounds will be quite a hit on the current Taylor fund but I reckon it's buttons for regular surveillance in the heart of the high street. Having Cody (*That's what I go by* he says, so not his real name I'm guessing) will be like having my own private detective on the case. Undercover. After I stump up and move away from him I notice how he goes back to scanning up and down the pavements with what I take to be renewed interest. This has to be a good investment.

19

The irony of having someone help me look out for the person I'm starting to call the living Ruth is that I feel released to make the trip that has become a pressing need since seeing her - a visit to her place of rest. Which is why, not long after meeting Cody, I take the bus to Deerholme Woodland Park.

It feels weird stepping through an early autumn fall of leaves to the sound of bird song barely thirty minutes from leaving the bustle of the city behind with its office workers, shoppers and street-wise Big Issue sellers. I seem to be the only human here, which is a relief because, strange to say, I would not want to come face to face with my lovely Karin; not in this setting, not yet.

I imagine it would be easier to find the person you're looking for in a traditional graveyard - turn left at the third row and it's the twelfth headstone on your right - but I'm glad Ruth is in a place like this, so rural and peaceful. The idea is that everything returns to its natural state, so there are no rails to divide the plots. No grave markers, none of the usual sort, but many of the trees here are dedicated to loved ones, and some graves have simple bronze plaques, small enough to be unobtrusive and just large enough for the unwary to trip over. It takes a good deal of attentive wandering before I see Ruth's but I don't mind; almost feel as if she's by my side helping me find her place without urgency like we're out together on a Sunday stroll. We do come across the right plaque eventually, and I bend to read the words... *Ruth Taylor. Taken too soon, forever loved by Karin and Alex.* Not so much an inscription as a private note we're sharing.

Can feel my eyes prick, but I don't collapse or anything, or give in to real tears. *Taken too soon Forever loved.* It applies to Karin too. I cling to that as well as to the insane idea that Ruth is somehow still with us. For the first time it comes to me that maybe she has returned to help us get back together. Maybe Ruth has shown herself to Karin as well, in which case my note to her must surely strike some sort of chord - make Karin realise that whatever it is has to do with all three of us.

I take out my mobile. Release the catch. Squat to take a close-up of the words. Faintest of clicks in the silence of the park. Like a kiss.

There's a definite movement behind my left shoulder, a kind of rustle, makes me catch my breath. I stand but don't turn, not straight away; keep my head down almost in expectation of a touch on the elbow, a gentle squeeze. It doesn't come. When I do look round there's no-one near, no-one anywhere in sight between the trees or on the tracks of

20

flattened grass. Maybe it was just a bird among the branches. Or a squirrel - I saw a couple of grey ones scampering about last time I was here.

In the building near the main gates, where they hold services before the burials, is a Book of Life. I spend some time leafing through the pages for Ruth's entry, pausing every so often when my eye is caught by what other people have had to say about their own loved ones. Most are fairly maudlin, which I guess is understandable; others factual, a bit dull; a few quite funny in their way, like some guy called Terry who's here according to this because he'd do anything to get out of washing the dishes. I wouldn't mind an entry like that - no harm in it, just aiming to capture something of their personality, their character. I'm trying to recall exactly what we said about Ruth, what tone we used, and it's only when I've delved much further back into the book than I'd expect to that I remember we didn't take up the option of an entry. A pity in some respects, but that's typical Karin - she tends to put the shutters up. Actually, we're both quite private in that way.

Being a private sort of person, I must admit I don't particularly encourage friendships, not casual ones, so this evening when the doorbell sounds a loud *brr-ring!* in my room it's not just unexpected - it's pretty near heart-stopping.

I've got my suitcase open on the floor as I'm going through some of my artefacts, preparing them for a new eBay auction to boost the depleted bank balance. The sound has me taut, motionless on my knees as if I'd had a gun poked between my shoulders. I'm blank - not able to compute who this could be - until the bell rings again, which frees me to close the lid of my suitcase and stow it back under the bed. Who can be ringing this late, and why *my* flat, not one of the others? Too late for Jehovah's Witnesses, or even for tat-sellers claiming to be art students working their way through college. Now there's a voice echoing around the hallway. I steal across to my door and listen carefully, an ear pressed against the panel.

'Alex. Are you there? Alex?'

Female. Not Karin surely, she won't have my letter yet and besides I didn't give her the address. Not... Ruth? Insane. Like Cathy's ghost tapping at the window in *Wuthering Heights.*

I open my door a fraction - no-one in the hallway. The voice is coming through the house letterbox.

'Alex? Is that you? Can you let me in?' Pleading.

I put the latch on my own door and pad across to the outside one, feeling small in my socks. I can see fingers holding up the letterbox flap,

21

and a grateful glint of recognition in the eyes as I approach. I open the door to Jane the bike woman on her knees and now in compromising proximity to the fly of my jeans, a position made even more ludicrous by the fact that she is wearing a yellow cycling helmet. I can just make out her bike below in the dusk, leaning against the scrubby hedge at the foot of the steps.

'I lost my keys.'

She looks ready to cry. I help her to her feet.

'Thanks, Alex. I'm really sorry to disturb you. I didn't know what else to do.'

We wander through the hallway in an awkward daze of friendly unfamiliarity, and stop to stare helplessly at her closed apartment door.

'This one as well?'

Jane nods, gives a sort of contrite smile as if she's putting me out, which in a way she is by getting me involved. Stupidly I push at the door as though I were expecting it to open to my touch. It doesn't.

'I've got the wrong kind of bag, that's the problem. It's a rucksack I need.'

She's not carrying any sort of bag. Reads my quizzical look and explains.

'No, it got in the way, so I left it and stuffed everything in my pockets instead. Big mistake.'

Jane's fingers go on a tour of her open jacket, taking out and returning her purse from one place, her phone from another. She pulls at the opening of her right trouser pocket, one of those little square ones cut just under the hip. 'I think I put them in here, but it's not really deep enough. They must have fallen out onto the road somewhere.'

'Have you retraced your steps? Well, not steps, your ride...'

'I've been all the way back along the route, and back again - that's why I'm so late. Nothing.'

We continue standing there, out of ideas, until I look up to catch her watching me, and realise I've had my eyes fixed on the front of her cream trousers where her pocket is. My roots prickle but she smiles as if to say it's OK and after another second says aloud, 'Tell you the truth, I could kill for a cup of tea. It's been hours.'

I glance past her at my half-closed door, picturing my shambles of an apartment. 'Mmm, I'm completely out of milk at the moment,' (which is true) and almost leave it there but she looks so helpless I find myself adding, 'If you wait till I get my shoes we can walk over to The Grapes for a quick drink and maybe work out what's best for you to do next.'

22

This is only the second time I've been in The Grapes. The other was when I read somewhere that an old acquaintance from my music days was due to be on a Sky Arts programme, so I came along hoping to get it on the pub tv. Trouble was it clashed with some European football or international or something - whatever, they wouldn't let me change channels so I just had a sulky half and left.

I'm glad Jane left her helmet with her bike as it looked a bit nerdy on her (I'm one to talk). Not that she'd keep it on in the pub, I dare say. As it is, she looks more like she belongs here than I do, certainly nearer in age to the students that make up most of the clientele, and more relaxed than she was back at the house. I notice the cup of tea she was thirsting for has suddenly turned into a Southern Comfort and lemonade, but I suppose she took her cue from me ordering Guinness. It would have been cheaper to go down to the corner shop for milk, but on the whole I'd rather she was here than in my room.

'So what are we going to do, then?' (Why did I say *we*? This is not my problem. Mam always used to say I'm too polite to people. *You'd let them walk all over you*.)

'Don't know. Bit stuck really.'

'Have you reported it?'

'What, to the police? Do you think that would do any good?'

'Probably not. Only somebody might have found your keys and handed them in.'

She thinks about this. 'You know, I'm not even sure where the police station is. Is there a little one round here, or just a main one in the city centre?'

'No idea.' (I know the one near Beech Grove but that's a long way out.)

'Suppose if anybody picked them up they'd take them to the nearest one, if they know where it is. Course it would help if I knew where I dropped them.'

'If you knew where you dropped them you'd be able to go back and pick em up yourself.'

'Good point.' She laughs at this even though it wasn't meant to be funny, and she's still smiling after she's sipped from her glass. She even casts around the pub as if she were looking for somebody to share the joke with, but she could be invisible for the notice anyone else is taking of her. (What a contrast to Karin, I'm thinking, who draws attention whenever we're sitting in a public place, though she's never loud or particularly demonstrative. It's that radiance she has; people just can't help stealing little looks. Women even - a little envious, maybe. As for the

23

men, that doesn't make me jealous, just proud she's mine and not theirs.) Jane settles into her seat again. Strikes me she's in no hurry now that's she's comfortable, but then she's not buying the drinks. I'm the one left to come up with ideas as well, and I do have another thought, an obvious one.

'Have you informed the landlord?'

'Mr Chatterjee? No, do I need to?'

'Well, he has all the keys. He could let you in.'

I can almost see the light go on in her head - she genuinely hadn't considered this. I guess I was wrong thinking, English teacher; she hasn't got the brains for it.

'Oh, he could, couldn't he?' She reaches into her pocket for her mobile, and starts to scroll through her contacts, then looks up at me. 'Not too late, is it? It's well after office hours.'

'He'll be used to people ringing day or night, I should think. Occupational hazard for landlords.'

She locates his number and calls it, then (as people nearly always do in pubs) stands up and walks towards the main exit with the phone in her ear, straining for an answer or maybe just a signal. She disappears through the doorway and I'm left contemplating the table. I'm pleased to see she's not through her drink yet. I'll try to make mine last until she's sorted. In fact it's not long at all before she's back, shrugging.

'No answer. Just rang and rang, then the O2 woman came on.'

'Did you leave a message?'

'No, I'll try him again in a bit.'

And she settles back comfy in her place. She's obviously used to socialising in pubs, so how come she doesn't have any friends she can turn to in an emergency like this? Actually, I haven't explored that avenue.

'Is there a friend you can call, maybe, help out?'

'Not really. Not round here. I'm not from round here. I mean originally.'

'Nobody at work?'

'No, work's just work. We don't really... you know. Anyway, I haven't been there that long.'

'Right.' A pause that I'm forced to fill. 'So, what is it you do?' As soon as I ask I wish I hadn't, not for what she'll say but because I know she'll return the question and I really don't feel like talking about it. Well, it's done now.

'Data processing,' she says. 'I work for a data processing agency. Exciting, eh? Right now we've started on a big project with the NHS.

24

That's why I was recruited, actually. New start for me as well. It's a short term contract, but I'm told if this goes well the sky's the limit.' She laughs and gives the back of her red hair a little tug which pulls her head to one side. 'Honestly, that's exactly what Greg said to me... my boss, that is, Greg... the day he appointed me he said, *Jane, this could be a breakthrough opportunity. If we get this right the sky's the limit for all of us.* And as if he thought I might not get what *all of us* meant, he says, dead serious, *That means you, me, everybody.* Oh, bless.' She giggles. 'What I want to know is, how high can the sky be in data processing?'

'Cloud computing.'

'Eh?'

'That's where they keep data these days, isn't it, in the clouds somewhere.'

'I don't know about that. Greg's in the clouds, I can tell you that. The rest of us are very terra firma. Stuck in the mud, most of them. You can't get much *firma* than that.' She laughs at her own joke (quite a good one, to be fair) and takes a bigger slosh out of her glass before she leans forward, open-faced, and says, 'What about you, Alex? What do you do to knock em dead?'

There we go, I knew this was coming. Blah-blah. I answer reluctantly, hoping she won't bother to press the point. 'Oh, just sales at the moment. I mainly just sell things.'

'Really?' She seems genuinely surprised. 'Salesman, eh? Salesperson. I wouldn't... Who do you work for?'

'Just me. Just myself.'

'You work for yourself? You mean you've got your own business?'

'Sort of.'

'Wow. Impressive.'

'Not really. Not at all.' I can see she's not about to let this go. 'It's just a temporary thing. I'm a musician. Used to be.'

'Musician. God, how cool is that.' Jane is alert and in inspection mode now, as if a spotlight has suddenly turned on to me. 'Yeah, I can see... I must admit when you said sales... So what sort of musician? What do you play?'

'I used to play piano. Piano and keyboard.'

'Not anymore?'

'I had an accident.' She nods sympathetically, willing me to go on. ' I damaged my right hand, well my wrist. Quite badly.'

'Oh no. What happened?'

In the beat before I answer is the rip of glass, the shocking blood spurt. So much blood.

25

'I fell through a table.'

Jane clutches her hand to her mouth - I can't tell if she's aghast or trying to stop giggling, her eyes so bright. 'Oh, my god,' she says behind her fingers.

'A glass coffee table. I didn't realise it was there, just stumbled over it backwards and next thing I'm sprawled on the floor with broken glass under me and blood gushing out my wrist. M&Ms scattered all over.'

'M&Ms?'

'They were in a bowl on the table. We were in the green room after a gig. Last gig of the tour.'

Jane's hand moves to her hair and she pulls at it again, then twists it in her fingers as we continue talking. Her expression is a strange mix of concern and curiosity, almost delight at hearing my story. She has to be fed with more detail about the initial panic, the attempts at first aid, the ambulance arriving, my stay in hospital. She takes all this in eagerly before she settles back into her seat with her drink, watching me so intently it becomes an embarrassment. I look away, and I'm relieved to find that still no-one in the pub is taking a blind bit of notice - I was half-expecting an audience, or at least a few nosy glances, but nothing. The interest is all from Jane.

'So you were in a band?'

'Yes and no. I've played in several bands, big names some of them, but I've never been *in a band*. I'm always the guy behind the stack.'

'I have no idea what you're talking about.'

'Exactly - you're not meant to. We're the guys with no identity. But if you look carefully at a lot of big concerts, stadium gigs especially, you might see the odd head bobbing up and down behind the speakers, somebody quietly playing away in the background. We're there to fill in the music for the band. We do the fiddly bits.'

'Like a session man?'

'Sort of, yeah. I do that as well. *Did.*'

'Oh, what a shame.' Jane's forehead knits in sympathy. 'And is that it? Will you ever be able to play again?'

'Not to a professional standard, I shouldn't think so. I've had a couple of operations, but I've still only got about eighty percent movement in my fingers - not enough for what I need to do.'

'You should get some sort of insurance, surely.'

'Oh, that's still dragging on. Been over two years now and it might be another two before I see a penny.'

I drain my glass, and become conscious of Jane watching me do it; don't immediately cotton on to the idea that it's my damaged hand she's

26

interested in. Somewhere between snooping and voyeurism. Her own hands are clutched round her glass. I notice she bites her fingernails, and I must have smiled involuntarily, catching myself inspecting her the way she's inspecting me.

'What?'

'Nothing.'

Her glass has been empty a while and I assume she's been waiting for me to finish my drink in the hope we can have another. I'm shamed into offering, and even more shamed when she insists it's her round. After she plonks down the refills she goes off to try Mr Chatterjee again, and comes back to report progress.

'He's in Dudley, apparently.'

'What's he doing in Dudley?'

'Never got round to asking him. The point is he can't get back until tomorrow morning.'

'Ah.' I apply myself to my drink while I consider the implications of this. Jane re-settles herself opposite, and again seems to be waiting for me to come up with solutions, though she has one of Mr Chatterjee's to offer when I press her for more details of their conversation.

'He says if I need to I can smash a window to get in, and he'll have it repaired tomorrow.'

'OK then, let's do that.'

'But he'll have to send me the bill, he says.'

'Well, that's only fair...'

'And he can't be accountable if I get a break-in in the meantime.'

'Well, if you don't leave the house you'll be safe enough.'

'Safe? I'll feel anything but safe sleeping with a broken window next to me. I won't be able to sleep a wink.

I'm too polite to point out the contradiction in what she just said, and in any case I can sense she's getting upset again. It crosses my mind she could find an available hotel room, late though it is, but if she's as short as funds as I am... I watch her fingers working through her hair as she stares down into her glass, and I'm surprised to hear myself say, 'Let's go and give your doors and windows the once-over - you never know, there might be a way in yet. And if not... well, there's always my place.'

Jane smiles into her glass, and her blush matches mine.

III

When I wake up Jane's no longer in my bed. Neither am I, but I can see it once I lever myself off the sofa. I'm still in my sleeping bag so I feel like a kid getting up from a fall in the sack race. There was a polite dance around the sleeping arrangements last night. I'm not quite sure what Jane was expecting, if she had any expectations at all, but she was first to offer to sleep on the sofa then I said *don't be daft you take my bed*, and there was a bit of shilly-shally about that, and I ended up on the sofa after some more rigmarole about undressing (lights off, lights on, you turn your back I turn mine, toilet arrangements etc, all very silly and adult at the same time) until we finally settled down into our different places. Lucky I still had my sleeping bag from my camping phase. I heard her sigh a few times, quite loud sighs in the darkness, but whether that was some kind of signal, whether she wanted company or what I don't know - to be honest there was part of me... then I was thinking Karin would never forgive (I always have this strange thing about her *knowing* somehow, like she's this presence) and the next thing I'm aware of is waking up here in this sleeping bag full of Guinness farts and nobody in the bed.

Just as I'm wondering if she's gone outside to wait for Mr Chatterjee the toilet flushes and a couple of minutes later Jane comes out of the en-suite. She's wearing last night's tee-shirt over her knickers and she reacts a little when she sees me awake, mouths a *sorry* as if she's not supposed to be there and tiptoes quickly across to my bed to drape the duvet over her bare legs - not before I notice she has quite a pert backside, a bit of spare flesh at the top of her thighs but not wobbly. There's a blueish mark, maybe a birthmark, like a fading bruise just below her panty line that is weirdly attractive. Sorry, Karin. Trust me, there's no competition.

'How was the bed?' I try to sound everyday.

'OK, thanks.' She moves to straighten it up a touch, still half-wrapped around the duvet. 'I've just realised I had both the pillows - I should have given you one.'

(Is that a deliberate *double entendre*? No.) 'The cushion was fine. Anyway those pillows are so flat you need both.'

'Mine's the same. Next door I mean.'

I stand up clumsily in my sleeping bag. My boxers are lying in a heap next to the sofa. It's an awkward moment.

'Excuse me, I'll just...' Hoist up the sleeping bag so my feet are at the bottom corners, then shuffle across to the drawers for a clean pair of boxers; jeans and shirt from the floor. 'I'll just dress in here, so you can...'

28

and through into the en-suite. I lock the door and immediately regret it - it's like saying I don't trust you not to burst in and ogle me while I'm having a piss.

I take my time washing and dressing so that I don't accidentally catch her half-in-and-half-out of her underwear or anything. When I finally emerge (*ta-raa!*) the first thing I notice is the bed's made better than I ever do it. Jane is standing by the door, fully dressed and with her coat on, as if she's waiting for me to let her out. But that's not what she's doing. She's reading.

TRACE GIRL IN PARK
GET BACK KARIN
SOLVE MYSTERY OF RUTH'S DEATH
And underneath, *white van.*

Damn, I should have had the nous last night to quietly take that off the door - a few pints and my commonsense goes down the plughole. I didn't even remember the note was there.

Jane turns to me half-laughing, quite excited. 'What's this?'

'Oh, nothing really.'

'Nothing? Sounds like some murder mystery - girls dying and disappearing, obviously a revenge thing going on.'

'What revenge?'

'GET BACK KARIN.'

'No, that means... Not get back *on*, just get back, like, get her back to... me, for example. I mean that's the sense of it.'

'Right.' Jane looks at the list again as if she has to decipher the new meaning. 'So Karin's your... ex?' and before I can answer, 'And who was Ruth?'

'They're... nobody, they're...' (I grab onto her own idea) '...characters.' (Brilliant.) 'Just some ideas for a story I'm writing. Thinking of writing.'

Jane cocks her head at the list like a robin. The hair-pulling thing again. 'I thought you were a musician. Or some sort of salesman. So now you're a writer.' She has that look like she's glad she didn't make the mistake of going to bed with me. Or maybe that she wished she had.

'No, not a writer. Just... well, it's a money-making idea, that's all. You get millions if you write a bestseller, don't you? Just thought I'd jot a few ideas down. Stuck them up there for... inspiration. I haven't actually written anything yet. Might never happen.'

'Ah.' She nods her head, colours a little as she makes eye contact. 'Sorry, I'm a bit of a nosy parker. Sorry.'

'It's fine.'

Jane glances back at the list. 'You should, you know. Sounds intriguing. What's the white van got to do with it?'

'Mmm, don't know yet. Not sure.'

'I bet it's abduction.'

'Probably.'

She smiles, open-faced once more. 'Well I'd read it, anyway.'

'What? Oh, the book. Thanks. I'll sign it for you. Personally.'

'Mmm. Could be worth thousands one day.'

'Better finish it first.'

She looks past me at my room, imagining my working there. Takes in my laptop on the IKEA desk. Right next to it, the bed she just made. She smiles.

'Honestly though, thanks for putting me up last night. And for putting *up* with me. Sorry you had to sleep on the sofa.'

'I've crashed on worse places. It was fine. You don't have to keep saying sorry all the time.'

'Sorry.' Realises what she's just said and mock-slaps herself. 'Saved my life anyway.'

'No problem. What time is Mr Chatterjee supposed to be coming?'

'Oh Christ, yes.' Jane grabs her phone from her pocket and at first I'm thinking it's to ring Mr Chatterjee, but it's to check the time. 'Oops, should have been twenty minutes ago. Hope I haven't missed him.'

She opens my door and we both look out into the hallway, empty except for Jane's bike.

'He would come in, wouldn't he?' she says.

'It's his house.'

Jane walks across the hallway to her own door, tries the handle - it's still locked. She listens at the door, knocks timidly and waits, then shakes her head at me.

'How long's he going to be?' As if she expected me to know.

'No idea. If he's had to get back from Dudley... Traffic's always terrible on the M6, especially on a Friday.'

'Only...' Her eyes are on the bike. 'I've got to go to work.'

'Couldn't you ring them, tell em you'll be a bit late?'

'Not really.' She looks anxious. 'Thing is, I was late yesterday 'cause I miscalculated how long it would take me to ride all the way. Greg wasn't particularly chuffed.'

I know what she's after, and softhead gives in. 'Look, get yourself away. I'll hang about for Mr Chatterjee coming.'

'Oh, I couldn't put you to that trouble...'

'It's no trouble. I wasn't really planning to go out anyway.'

30

'Ah, thanks Alex.' She takes the couple of steps across the hallway, clutches my shirt sleeve and pulls herself up to kiss me on the cheek, actually half on the mouth which may or may have not been by accident. Only platonic as far as I'm concerned anyway, though she's a nice enough girl. Why I'm getting involved with her business I really can't fathom, but I suppose it gives me something to do while I'm waiting for other things to develop.

Actually if Jane had waited just ten minutes longer she would have seen Mr Chatterjee in person. I've just booted up my laptop in preparation for listing the latest items on eBay when I feel the slight draught at my bare ankles that tell me someone's opened the front door quite quickly. I don't move immediately in case it's just one of the students leaving, but soon enough I hear him calling out in the hallway and tapping at her door.

'Missus Jane? Missus Jane, are you there now? Please, if you are uncovered, I am about to open your door and come in. It's Mr Chatterjee merely. No cause for alarming yourself.'

I open my own door and approach him as he's searching for the right key from a large bunch he carries. Mr Chatterjee is a tiny man in his sixties with hands to match, which makes the bunch look absurdly oversized. The way he bustles about he's like an Asian version of the White Rabbit. He even has a waistcoat.

'Jane had to go to work, Mr Chatterjee. She asked me to look out for you.'

'She locked herself out, stupid woman,' he announces man to man, safe in the knowledge his female tenant can't hear him. 'I will have to be fixing the glass now.' The key found, he opens Jane's door with some impatience and scuttles towards the front window. I linger at her doorway to explain.

'No, no, Mr Chatterjee, Jane didn't want to break in, she didn't feel safe. She... made an alternative arrangement. She does still need new keys though, if you could leave them with me.'

He turns back and eyes me with a certain suspicion. His short grey beard has what appears to be a tobacco stain just above the chin. His suit has the rumpled look of a man who has slept in it, or driven in it from Dudley, or both.

'Alex Taylor,' I offer. 'Flat 2,' to remind him.

'Taylor. Flat 2.' He seems about to dispute this, staring at my unshod feet as if for proof of an impostor, then sharply up at my face. 'Flat 2. You made an *amendment*.' He pronounces the word like he's reading it from a dictionary. 'Your direct debit...'

31

'That's right. Just a slight change in my financial circumstances. I hope that didn't cause...'

'As long as you pay up.' His features relax. 'Who is caring as long as you pay up prompto? Eh?' And he giggles as if he's made a good joke, so I guess the question was rhetorical. He takes a turn around Jane's room, bobbing up on his toes while he studies the ceiling and cornices, then down on his knees to check for.... wear in the carpet? mouse holes? who knows. He straightens up again; points past me to the hallway. 'Flat 2.'

I lead him into my room (hoping that none of the *amendments* I've made to the fittings are in obvious breach of the tenancy agreement) and watch him go through the same gymnastic routine as he did in Jane's to a jingling percussion accompaniment from his giant bunch of keys. He must have been satisfied as he comes up with a smirk and mutters to himself, 'Very good value. Chatterjee properties, always very good value. The best, eh?'

He's about to leave on this note of self-congratulation and I have to remind him, 'Er, Jane's new keys?' Mr Chatterjee switches his own impressive collection from one hand to the other so that he can fish from his inside pocket a sealed envelope, presumably containing Jane's spares. He checks the inscription carefully as though he might be secreting a dozen alternatives in the pocket, then dangles the envelope in front of me rather than handing it over directly.

'Twelve pound to pay, please.'

'Excuse me?'

'Twelve pound. I am telling Missus Jane last night.'

'She didn't mention it.'

'I am mentioning it.'

Clearly he's not about to leave without the cash. I have to raid my stamp money to pay him. Mr Chatterjee does not offer a receipt.

Alone again, I decide to fix myself a coffee before I get back to my computer. When I open the fridge I remember - no milk. Walking to the corner shop and back will cost me at least another twenty minutes. I waste the best part of twenty minutes working up the will to do it. I'm checking around for my shoes when my attention is caught by the envelope containing Jane's new house keys. She wouldn't begrudge me a thimbleful of milk supposing she knew she was lending it. Besides, I've just paid good money for those keys, and they haven't been tested in the lock yet. Three good arguments for hopping across the hallway instead of trailing to the shop. I pick up the envelope, tear it open to get at the keys, grab my mug from the sink unit and go.

Being at the front, Jane's apartment is bigger and airier than mine, with a proper bay window. Smells fresher too. She does have milk in her fridge - unfortunately it's not been opened and I have to decide whether to take the risk of her remembering she hasn't broken the seal. Not that I'm naturally cautious, but I am somebody who doesn't particularly like to leave tracks if I can help it. I've already worked out that Jane's a fairly tidy person, but on the other hand she seems a bit of a scatterbrain so she probably won't notice. I decide to chance it - how big a deal is borrowing milk, anyway? Besides, she owes me. I break open the seal, pour enough in my mug for one cup of coffee and replace the bottle exactly where I found it in the drawer of the fridge. What to do with the strip of broken seal? I could dump it back in my room, but if I were a detective trying to solve the mystery of the opened milk bottle I'd be even more suspicious if I couldn't find that bit of broken plastic in the immediate vicinity. Got to be consistent. I look around for a litter bin.

Next to Jane's bed there's one of those straw waste paper baskets with a carrier bag lining. It's on the same side as the fridge so I reckon it would be the natural place for the plastic scrap, but as an extra precaution I make sure it's hidden under a used blister pack that's already in there. Jane will only see the seal if she's specifically looking for it. (Clever.) I have to crouch down by the bed to place the plastic properly, and as I do that I can't help noticing something pinkish-purple tucked under her pillow. I must admit my first thought is, sex toy. Curiosity gets the better of me. I lift the pillow (which by the way is nowhere near as flat as mine) and see that the pink object is not a dildo after all; it's a page-per-day diary.

Who could resist taking a peek at somebody's diary when they're not around? I take note of exactly where I'd need to replace it before I pick it up as gently as an unexploded bomb. There's a lace bookmark fixed to the spine, and the diary falls open at the page it's marking - Jane's latest entry. That was Wednesday - no entry for yesterday obviously as she couldn't get into her room. Wednesday was when we spoke to each other properly for the first time, though we have been known to exchange the odd nod and smile passing in the hallway. In my eagerness to read what she might have written about me I nearly make the mistake of sitting down on the bed, just check myself before I make any telltale creases, and walk across instead to read by the light coming through the window.

The first couple of paragraphs seem to be about people at work - blah blah - then picking up the bike she's bought - *quite excited* - then worrying about parking it in the hallway without checking that's OK with the guy opposite; right, that's me...

Spent about 1 hour watching by the window and when i finaly saw him coming in popped out to see him with my fingers' crossed praying he wasnt going to be the type to make a fuss. Luckily he was fine about it and we spent sometime chatting about pumps etc. Quite 'brainy' i'd say but not put-downy, definately not. Not what youd call a chatterbox but i make up for him in that dept. and anyway i quite like the strong silent type. Well, not so sure about the strong in Alex's case (thats his name) he's got quite a stringy whippet look about him as far as I can tell with his clothes on (down, Jane!) which might not be a bad thing. A. is that bit older than me, but not what youd call a huge gap. Experienced? Watch this space. Pretty sure we'll hit it off actualy, some of the signals he was giving out. Have to see, wont we?

Some of the signals I was giving out! What's the woman on? Boot very much on the other foot, missy. I read through the entry again. Spelling a bit off, random apostrophes like everybody seems to do these days, and don't ask me what the small *i* is about - some sort of girly affectation. Hornier than I'd reckoned on - I'm surprised now that *wasn't* a sex toy she had under her pillow - probably keeps it handy in those drawers the other side of the bed.

Wonder if she has anything else to say about me in earlier entries. I leave the lace bookmark primly in place while I flick through, scanning for any mention. Get stupidly embarrassed when I come across a reference to *my period* - the other-sexness of it brings me up sharp with shame for snooping into intimate details, and I glance through the window in a sudden flush as if someone's caught me out doing it. And there... call it coincidence if you like or something else, I don't know - but there at that very moment is a white van cruising slowly down the road, just a couple of yards from the house.

Such a shock - I bang the diary shut, step back from view. My heart's racing. It looked... I press back into the side wall for a minute, maybe more. Don't dare move to check if the van is stopped or returning, but I stay aware of the daylight coming through the window, watching for any passing shadow. I can feel my chest beat where I'm holding the diary to me, the clench of my fingers around the book. Only when a clammy slip of sweat between my palm and the back cover becomes too obvious to ignore do I make a move. Slide down the wall to the floor, snake my way to the sheepskin rug at the far side of the bed, and there I rub the diary back and forward, trying to remove any sweat marks before I replace it in its exact spot under Jane's pillow. Still on my knees I lift my mug from the top of the fridge, keeping it level for the milk, shuffle to the door and open it a crack. Listen for movement in the hallway.

Nothing. I pull myself up to a standing position between door and wall, check the latch will lock when I pull the door closed, and leave, moving as smartly and quietly as I can between Jane's room and mine.

It's impossible to work now. I don't get round to making the coffee that I promised myself. Lie on my bed thinking and thinking about this white van. Remembering the day I saw it, or one like it - Ruth's last day. I didn't even have the chance to say goodbye to her.

Karin had driven herself to the dance studio earlier than usual - a planning meeting I think - said she'd be with me mid-afternoon. I went off on a walk; just popped into the village for a paper and a take-out breakfast - tea and a muffin, that sort of thing. I remember coming back, stopping to lean against a tree in the morning sunshine, just across from our home. A doughnut, that's what it was - I remember biting into it looking over to ours, thinking how nice the house looked with its white gates picked out by the sun, and the hedges trim (not that I ever did them myself, I have to admit). When Ruth came out.

She was not one to look particularly flustered (so much of her mother about her) and way too cool to run unless she was dressed for it, but I could tell she was late by the way she negotiated the three steps down to the drive, and the brisk rattle of the gate when she got to street level. She had on the least amount of school uniform she could get away with - she was only weeks away from leaving, or would have been... and she appeared quite the young woman already, but one that was late for school. I didn't want to delay her any more by rushing across to say goodbye - just stood and watched her go, followed her with my eyes as she clicked her way past the other big houses in our road, and I suppose I was thinking, *that's our girl*. I really was quite proud of her. *We* were proud of her.

And it's only because I was watching Ruth's progress down the street that I noticed the van at all. Well, perhaps I might have - ours isn't a through road and vehicles, especially commercial-looking vehicles, are relatively scarce - but there was nothing special about it, just an ordinary white transit. Except it was driving very slowly. And I wouldn't have noticed that but for the fact it blocked my view of Ruth walking. It came from somewhere to my left, passed our gates, and on past Ruth so that I lost sight of her for what seemed like several seconds. It must have reached the corner shortly before she did because my memory is that I saw her turn left. Unless that's me unconsciously filling in the blanks because I know that's the way she always went - whichever, I do recall that the van turned left, along the same road as Ruth. They disappeared more or less together. Which would have been unremarkable, something I would quite easily have forgotten - in fact *had* forgotten to all intents and purposes, even in the immediate shock of what happened to her - until very recently indeed. As if Ruth, coming back, is trying to tell me something, trying to jog my memory.

That afternoon I was at the piano. Not playing properly, of course, since my fall, not much more than prodding keys, testing myself on how far I could do scales, little runs... even tried a couple of bars of my favourite Ravel. I was due for my second operation and feeling more optimistic than I had been for a while. Karin was pottering about the house. She'd made me a cup of coffee which she'd set down near the piano on the low table next to Ruth's photo. The sun had moved across and was shining very agreeably through the front window. It was bliss really - just seemed to sum up everything we were at that time in our lives, notwithstanding my accident. That feeling I'd had since the morning - my sense of how fortunate I was to have this home, this beautiful family - was still with me. Everything calm. Serene.

I started tentatively to sketch out a tune I'd had in my head for a while. *Karin's Song.* That was my title for it, or would be when it was finished. Not complicated - necessarily within the limits of what is now my range - but evocative. In my imagination at least the tune captured her essence, in particular her natural grace and movement. My idea was to say nothing to Karin about the piece until I'd fully worked it up. I wanted it complete and thoroughly rehearsed so I could play without effort - in fact with all the grace the music signified. At the right time - maybe her birthday or our wedding anniversary - I would play it for her, note perfect, expressing everything within me for Karin. A sincere gift of love from my heart to hers.

The house phone rang. I may have called out to Karin to answer it - she'd do it anyway, not wanting to disturb me - and I heard her pick up at the foot of the stairs. I stopped playing to listen. Her telephone voice, trying to suppress her Swedish accent - it always made me smile the way she did that. Then, abruptly, her voice changed. 'No,' she said, very hollow. Then again, 'No!' and this time I could hear the panic in her voice. 'No, what road... how... how could she be?'

I stood up, left the piano. Her panic had spread to me - it was like a wave, though I didn't know the cause. I just knew my wife was distraught, had to go to her. In the doorway of the front room I stopped for a second, arrested by the sight of Karin, one hand holding on to the banister post, the other clutching the phone, and her eyes wild and round as I'd never seen them. She seemed to look through me and I heard her

36

cry out, 'How could my girl be dead? How could my Ruth be dead?' Then the tears brimmed over, streaking her beautiful face.

Like being hit with a hammer - I reeled with it. A double blow. My daughter. My wife. I could make no sense of it then, had no *sense* of anything at that moment, just the instinct to reach out to Karin, to comfort her, to comfort us both. Three steps across the hallway and I had her in my arms, enveloping her, stroking her hair, cradling her head into my shoulder. But there was no quieting her. In that same instant she lost it completely. A wail - not just a wail, a long scream from the base of her, which I will never get out of my mind as long as I live. Followed by a sort of fit. A wracking, sobbing fit, with her slipping down onto her knees and her arms flailing in all directions, the phone spilling out of her hands and skidding across the floor. I could hardly cling on to her. It was as if part of her wanted to die right there, and part wanted to beat on the world for what it had done to our little girl. I was heaving with emotion as well, but at the same time trying as hard as I could to hold everything in, trying to restore some calm around her. It was no good - it was all too much for both of us. Everything was broken. Everything. I've been trying to fix it ever since.

To be honest I might have lain on top of my bed all day and all night if I hadn't to listen for Jane coming back to give her her new keys. As it is there's one false alarm when I hear a rattle at the front door around the hour I'm expecting her return. I drag myself out into the hallway only to see one of the students turning at the top of the stair - it must have been him, not her. Later there's more movement coming from the hallway but I stay put, assuming that's another of the students since Jane wouldn't have been able to let herself in through the front.

So I get quite a surprise when I take another peek out of my room and find her purple bike parked at the wall next to my door. Trying to compute this, I'm thinking she must have come in along with one of the others, but where is she now, since she can't get into her own room? Hitting on one of them upstairs maybe. No, that's a mean thought. Without expectation I knock at the door of her apartment, and here's a second surprise - she opens it.

'Oh, hi Alex. How are you?'

'OK. I thought... How did you get in?'

'How did I get in?' For a moment it's as if she's in denial over the last twelve hours of our lives, then she catches up. 'Oh, I found my keys.' She widens her eyes, giggles. 'You know what? They weren't lost after all. I'd left them at the office.' She laughs again, and combs both hands

37

through the back of her hair, making her breasts lift and exposing a portion of midriff under her lemon tee-shirt. An image of her in this morning's knickers as she continues. 'As soon as I saw them I remembered I'd taken my keys out my pocket and put them in my desk drawer 'cause they were digging in to me while I was typing yesterday.' Her right hand goes down to the place, prodding with her fingers. 'What am I like?'

'Oh, well. Least you found them.'

'Yes. And...' She half-disappears behind her open door as she reaches up and unhooks something to show me. It's a small black nylon rucksack.

'Quite neat, don't you think?'

'Smart, yeah. That's you sorted.'

She nods and we smile stupidly at each other as if we've got to the end of some mini-adventure. I wait for her to break eye contact so I can move away politely, but before I do Jane pushes her door further open. 'Would you like to come in for coffee?'

I think about the broken seal on her milk bottle. What if she starts interrogating me? 'No, I don't think so.' Maybe too abrupt - she seems a bit put out. 'No, I mean that's really nice of you, but I've got so much work to do.'

'Started on the book?'

'What? No. Just work work, you know.'

'Maybe next time then, eh?'

'Absolutely.'

'Pop round anytime you like.'

'I will.'

Jane doesn't close her door until I'm opening mine, keeping her eyes on me like on a feast. I give her a wave which now I think about it might have looked more like a dismissal. Hope she doesn't think so. Nothing wrong with her - I just need my personal space. She never even asked about her new keys. Well, I'm the mug who paid for them so they're more mine than hers, arguably. Think I'll hang on to em. That spare front door key might come in handy.

IV

Tuesday lunchtime something amazing happens. Cody calls.

When the number comes up on my mobile I don't recognize it, but immediately my scalp tingles with shock and excitement. Not that I'm expecting Cody - to be frank I'd almost forgotten him - instead I'm thinking, Karin. Maybe she has a new number, maybe she wants to talk to me about my letter, about Ruth. I'm disappointed at first when the voice turns out be male until I realise who it is and tune in to what he has to say.

'Alright, chief. I think I've seen her.'

'Who, Ruth? No!'

'That the name, Ruth? Not a Swedish name, is it?' He tries it out. 'Ruth.'

I'm too buzzed to beat myself up for blurting out her name. 'You've seen her? Really?'

'Oh aye.'

'Where?'

'Well...' He pauses, then says, very sly, 'Information is power. Ever heard that expression, pal? Information is power, know what I mean?'

'Why don't you just tell me where you saw her?'

'I will. But there's the little matter of fifty quid first. *Show me the money* as Arnie used to say.'

'You'll get your money. And it was Tom Cruise.'

'Not in my book.' (Eh?) 'Anyway, show up here, show me the money and I'll show you what I've got.

'*Show* me?'

'On camera.'

'I'll be with you in an hour.'

On the bus a fever of excitement has me tapping the seat rail in front, jiggling my toes - so much that the woman in the seat across the aisle sneaks a sideways glance as if she's afraid I'm going to wet myself. I try to calm down after that, helped by creeping doubts about Cody's reliability. He could be making it up, saying anything to get his hands on the cash. But he claims he has photographic evidence - is that just to make sure I turn up? If it's true, though, what then? What does that say about Ruth's *thereness*? You can't photograph a ghost, they reckon. Could Cody even see a ghost that is, as it were, *my* ghost?

I remember a play reading we did in school years ago where the teacher made me read the part of Banquo's ghost. The class thought this was hilarious because this same teacher used to call me *the boy who wasn't there* - supposedly I never looked like I was paying attention and never had a word to say if he asked a question. Actually, if *he'd* been paying attention, instead of parading his ego in front of the class half the time, he'd see I was actually paying attention even if I wasn't looking at him in awestruck wonder (mostly it was the girls that did that - he was allegedly good-looking). I might have been staring at the classroom wall but sometimes that's what you do when you're *thinking*. Though I admit that some of the time I was playing music in my head. Anyway the other reason this was apparently hilarious is that Banquo's ghost isn't a speaking part. He appears at a feast and sits at an empty chair. Only Macbeth, who has killed him, can see the ghost. Presumably this is meant to represent Macbeth's guilty conscience. Everybody else at the feast thinks Macbeth has gone mad, ranting to an empty chair. The lad who was reading the part (Philip Aldrich, very good actor actually, went on to drama school though he's never been in anything I've ever seen) had to look at me and point whenever he got to the speeches concerning Banquo's ghost. As a lesson it was a complete waste of time because everybody just fell about laughing, including the teacher. The only people who weren't laughing were me and this kid playing Macbeth who, give him his due, was putting everything into his part. So was I. I was trying to be a ghost.

So, anyway, Cody has seen Ruth and from what he said has been able to take a picture of her. Ergo, she's no ghost, she's a living human being. Not Ruth, then. Or she *is* a ghost and what people say about not being able to photograph ghosts is bollocks. Well, first I need to check Cody's evidence.

He's standing with his copies of The Big Issue in the same place as that first time I saw him, still with his cowboy hat on and his denims. Before I approach I decide on the spur of the moment to test his observation skills and his memory for faces. I park myself on the opposite side of the street in full view for nearly five minutes, but he never acknowledges me once though he's constantly scanning for punters. I mention this when I eventually come up and speak with him. Cody is totally unfazed.

'Yeah, clocked ya, but I didn't want to blow the gaff.'

'What?'

'Step into my office.'

'Eh?'

He takes me to a bench five yards away. It's currently occupied by a couple of hoodies bunking off school, but they slope off once Cody has treated them to his menacing stare. He sits down, plonks his copies of the Big Issue to one side of him and motions me to join him on the other.

'Did you bring the cash?'

'First things first. What have you got to tell me?'

'Like I said. I've seen her. The girl with the Maltese earring.'

'Where? Tell me exactly.'

'OK.' Cody stands up, indicates his usual pitch position. 'I'm here.' Swings his arm slightly to the left and nearer the road. 'First eyeball there, just before she walks by.' (*Eyeball.* Cody is playing screen detective.)

'How do you know it's her?'

'Swedish-looking. I've trained my eyes for young girls with long, soft blonde hair. Not a bad gig, know what I mean?' He grins wolfishly. I can see a gap in his teeth where the cheek's pulled back. Wish I hadn't told him her name. 'So then I'm like in radar mode, tracking her.' He demonstrates. 'And here's the clincher.'

'The earrings?'

'Got it in one. Maltese Cross earring in her left ear. Clear as day.' He takes his seat again, satisfied with a job well done.

'Did you speak to her?'

'Not in the job description, man. What did you want me to say? *Your dad's looking for you, he's worried, phone home.* I didn't even know her name until today. You should have told me. I could have called out, *Ruth!* See if she turned.'

He's right. Wish I *had* told him her name. What else do I need to know? 'Was she alone?'

'Ah, good question, good question. There was a guy, some tall guy, just behind her. She was really close to him, might have been together, but maybe not. You know, there wasn't much room on the pavement. But you see that crossing?' I turn to watch where he's pointing. 'They both waited at the lights, then crossed the road and both took that same cut off the street. He stayed a little bit behind her. Coincidence or no? Pay your money, take your choice. Never spoke, but they looked like they might have been together.'

'How old was he, this guy?'

'I'll show ya.'

My nerves are on vibrate again as Cody pulls out his smart phone. He punches a couple of buttons, stares intently at me, hiding the screen from view, and says in a cod Arnie Schwarzenegger accent (it's *Tom Cruise* bonehead), 'Show... me... the money.'

I drag out the wad of five tens I've been carrying in my pocket and hold it under his nose, clutching it as tight as he is holding onto his phone. 'Show me the picture.'

Cody turns the screen towards me. My vision adjusts to take in the image, such as it is. There's an out-of-focus side-to-back view of a young blonde woman waiting at the pedestrian crossing. Could easily be Ruth, but it's impossible to be sure. On a scale of one to a hundred, maybe just over fifty. As far as I can tell from the collar she has a similar coat on from the girl in the park, but is it the same? From this angle her hair is covering her right ear. I'm excited and mildly disappointed at the same time.

'Is that the best you could do?'

Cody raises his finger, ham acting. 'I have another one.'

He turns the phone towards himself briefly, swipes the screen and returns it to me. In long view the girl is crossing the road at the lights. There is a tall guy behind her looking straight ahead, mid-twenties maybe, dark casual jacket. I study 'Ruth's' clothes in this view - looks very like *the* coat, and she is carrying a shoulder bag at the same length as last time. My certainty scale tops sixty, seventy. I reach out and swipe the screen right to left, going back to the original picture. I can feel my teeth on my bottom lip, chest swelling like the start of an anxiety attack. My voice is half-strangled, can hardly get it out. 'Why didn't you get a proper shot of her face?'

Cody, huffed, snatches his phone back. 'What d'you expect us to do, go running after her like the paparazzi? There was a cop car parked up in that loading bay, for Christ's sake. Could've been done for sexual harassment, stalking, all sorts. Jesus!'

'Sorry, sorry.' I stretch my hands out in apology, palms down. The wad falls from my fingers and my attempt to placate him turns into a scramble between us for my cash. I get there first, worsening Cody's mood.

'Listen pal, that's mine by rights. Kept my end of the bargain.'

'You'll get your money. I'm just... thinking.'

I stand up, looking out to the part of the road where Ruth crossed, tracing her route through the cut. 'That way's the university, isn't it?' I'm pretty sure in my own mind, but I'm partly trying to distract Cody from his temper.

'Central Library,' he says, reluctantly at first, before pride in his familiarity with the city gets the better of him, and he starts to expand on it, pointing up past the cut. 'There's a couple of university buildings behind the library, but there's different departments all over. Union bar's that way, I've been in there a time or two. Multi-storey car park to the left.'

'She didn't... doesn't drive.'

'Her boyfriend might.'

'Boyfriend?'

'The guy she was with.'

'I don't think they were together.'

'Ha! Hate to break it to you, Daddy-o, but girls grow up. Wanna lay a bet on it?'

'No.'

The truth is, I don't know what to think now. The more I find out the more confused I become. I appeal to Cody. 'Do you really think it was her?'

'How the fuck should I know?' To the point, if nothing else.

'I mean, from my description.'

'Your description doesn't mean jack shit. Swedish-looking. Blonde. Maltese Cross earrings. Yeah, she had all them. Fits your description. Give us the money.'

'It's quite likely to be her though, isn't it? I mean, I think it is.'

'Well, if I had a photograph I could tell you for definite. You haven't really thought this through, have you? You didn't tell us her name, and you didn't supply us with a mug shot. Pretty basic stuff.'

'I haven't...' Started to say *I haven't got a photo* then changed it. Brain flip. 'So, if I showed you a picture you could tell me for definite?'

'One hundred and twenty percent. I maybe didn't get that clear a shot with the camera, but I had a good long look at her. Only you'd better be quick about it 'cause my brain cells are dying at a rate of a million a minute. Apparently.'

'OK.' My mind is racing. 'I'll call you as soon as I've got it,' and turn to go.

'*Aa*-aa.' He does the money-rubbing thing with his thumb and forefinger. 'Fifty quid, mush.'

If I give him the money now, what hold do I have on him for the future? As if he was reading my mind Cody supplies the answer. 'Remember you owe me another fifty if you find her. I can help you do that.'

He gets his money. Now I've got to get Ruth's photo and get back to him before his brain cells die.

I'm back home. My real home that is, in Beech Grove. Two slight problems - I'm outside the house, not inside, and not currently in

43

possession of a key. Karin is almost certainly at work (no car on the drive) and frankly even if she was home the time isn't right for me to ring the bell and ask her to let me in. Soon, but not yet. There are some things we need to sort out first, some misunderstandings to correct, some barriers to remove that are blocking our route to what we both want - to be together again. What we need, it seems to me, is an unlocking of minds. In some way that I don't yet fully understand, Ruth is the key.

At present a house key would be helpful. Standing out here makes me appreciate how Jane must have felt (if she really did mislay her keys... but let's concentrate on this issue at the moment). I can see no way to get in at the front with all the windows shut; besides, I'm in full view of the road. I need to move to the rear of the house, explore the possibilities without the risk of being spotted by our nosy neighbours.

I feel less nervous in the relative privacy of the back garden and patio area. A touch sentimental too when I see a couple of garden chairs still left out next to the brick barbecue range - reminders of a lost summer. I have to refocus on the task in hand. At first glance the windows and patio doors all seem to be firmly locked, though closer inspection reveals the patio door key dangling from the inside keyhole. It would take a brick through the glass to get at it. There must be easier options. Flattening myself against the wall and squinting up I can see that the bathroom window is not flush tight, perhaps just half on the catch. As long as the drainpipe takes my weight, and my gimp arm doesn't hamper me too much, I should be able to climb up and work that catch loose. I need something like a screwdriver or a ruler to poke in the gap. A stick from the garden maybe.

I'm looking around for a suitable alternative for a jemmy when the back door clicks open from the inside. Karin? Dive behind the barbecue range. One knee crushes down on a piece of stray coke or charcoal and it takes all my will to stop crying out with the pain. I tuck out of sight to rub at the knee and listen. The lid of the wheelie bin is opened and an object knocked repeatedly against the side as if Karin is in a foul mood and is taking it out on the bin. It seems unlike her. I risk a peek from behind the range. A woman with her back to me is bent over the bin beating seven bells out of a Dyson cylinder that refuses to give up easily the last remnants of its fluff collection. It's only when she straightens up that I realise she is African, at least ten years older than Karin, wearing the sort of blue collared tunic that you might associate with an auxiliary nurse or, as is obvious in this case, a lowly employee of a large cleaning firm. At the very least it confirms for me that Karin is out - the cleaner wouldn't be making such a racket otherwise.

44

I'm safe where I am until she goes back into the house, but it's possible I might be spotted from inside the patio doors - those doors I was standing in front of so carelessly when I thought the place was empty. Presumably the cleaner has just arrived or was working in another part of the house - it's big enough, fortunately - but I will have to be quick and much more alert when she goes back in.

She either succeeds or gives up on her battle with the Dyson and I soon hear the back door close. No sound of a key turning. I quickly scuttle out from behind the barbecue, across the patio, duck under the kitchen window and press against the wall next to the back door. I wait there a couple of minutes, then inch by inch change position until I can take in the immediate interior through one pane of glass. Nobody in sight, though I can see so little she might be just feet away. I'll have to take the risk.

Slowly I press down the handle, push open the door. Not strictly the kitchen but a wash place attached to it. Close the door quietly behind me, listen. There's a hum in the distance, otherwise nothing. Creep through into the empty kitchen, and on through the back of the hallway towards a choice of doors. An electric cable stretches from its plug next to the phone socket all the way up the stairs. The hum is the muffled drone of the Dyson. So far so good. I know exactly where to find what I need and I can be out of here in less than thirty seconds.

I take the furthest of the two doors into the large front room where the white piano lives. Hesitate slightly, alarmed by the amount of light streaming in through the big window, then dash round the piano - shit, the lid's open, the back of my hand brushes keys - to the coffee table and Ruth's photo.

Except it isn't there. She's moved it, dammit. Of course. She's moved it because she doesn't want to be so cruelly reminded every day of her lovely, smiling lost daughter. Where are you, Ruth? Tell me.

Impulse makes me lift the lid of the piano stool. The picture is not hidden there, just the familiar pile of manuscripts. Another day, another time I might have sifted through, picked one out that took my fancy, closed and sat upon the stool to play...

Where is Ruth's picture? There are prints and paintings but not this or any other photograph on display here or next door in the polished dining room or in the kitchen. I open and close as many drawers and cupboards as I can without undue noise, scanning quickly but not finding what I want.

On the bench under the kitchen cupboards I come across a sheet of paper torn from a pocket Filofax with a handwritten note.

45

Hi Abi Sorry, did we agree Monday is cooker cleaning day? Maybe you could do it today instead? Thanks, Karin x.

Glance across at the cooker which looks as spotless as everything else in the house. Maybe Abi has cleaned it already. I re-read Karin's note, hearing her gentle Scandinavian lilt in my head. Even her reprimands have finesse - *élan*. On impulse I slip Karin's note into my trouser pocket.

Drift back into the hallway, a bit lacking in focus for a minute and uncertain what to do next. The grey flex still leads up the stairs, a little more stretched now. The cleaner must be a distance from the top of the stairs which means I might just be able... without further consideration I slip upstairs on tiptoe. At the stair head I sidle left, away from the cable trail, and into the bedroom opposite.

I'd swear this room was electrified, such is my body's reaction to the scene I've stepped into. A single bed stripped of all covers, just the bare mattress like an accusation. No pictures or decorations on the walls, nothing on the bedside cabinet. Numbed, it takes me a few moments to notice the room is not empty of reminders of Ruth. Stacked neatly in one corner is a modest cache of things, some obviously girly, seemingly ready to be stored or taken away. Once over the initial shock of seeing the stripped bed I pad across for a closer look. There are a few cuddly toys, some felt shapes and a jewellery-making kit, CDs, what seem to be folded posters or prints and - I spot just an edge poking out from the middle of the pile - a photo frame.

I crouch down and carefully ease this out trying not to disturb the rest. It's not the solo portrait of Ruth I've been looking for but she's there, radiant in the picture, maybe a couple of years ago... sitting with a friend on a bench in what looks like some sort of ornamental garden. And there is Karin standing behind the seat, smiling and bending into the picture just above their heads. Even in this snapshot she has the casual grace of a model - no, not a model, her beauty is more natural, and there's not the faintest hint of the contempt you see in all those professional poses. It must have been me with the camera, though I can't immediately place where we are - on a picnic somewhere, I guess, or maybe on holiday.

Picture and frame go into the poacher's pocket of my coat. Straighten up the pile that's already perfectly neat. One more glance at the bed - less forbidding now; I have a strange but warm sensation as if Ruth is present and silently complicit, approving - then I quit the room as softly as I came.

At the stair head the vacuum sounds louder than before. I quicken my step down the stairs, stupidly glance back halfway, and snag my foot under the stretched flex. The plug is ripped from its socket, the Dyson expires with a sigh. A second of shocked paralysis, a curse in her own language from Abi in the bedroom, and I'm off, caution abandoned, down the stairs, out through the nearest exit at the front. Half-fall, half-vault over the three stone steps to the drive, clatter through the white gates and away up the street to safety.

'She looks younger.'

'She is younger. That was taken a couple of years ago. It's the most recent one I could find.'

'Been missing that long, has she?' Cody looks up from the picture to catch my response as if it's important to him. We're in a small back room (it says *SNUG* on the frosted glass) of an unreconstructed pub in a side alley off the sloping street that leads from the city centre to the quayside - Cody's recommended rendezvous. 'Nice quiet place to do business,' he'd said, though hardly discreet since at least four customers in the public bar greeted him by name as we walked in and the barman's welcoming enquiry was *Usual, cowboy? What'll your friend have?* Naturally I had to pay for both, and Cody downed his before we moved into this room; made me order another for him through the little hatch at the back of the bar as some sort of prior condition for settling to business.

Cody tries again. 'How long she been missing?'

'A while.' Not about to give him any more information than he needs. I direct his attention, pointing at the image of Ruth, though the action seems somehow disrespectful of her. 'What do you think? On a scale of one to ten.'

Cody considers. Hands me the photo (now out of its frame) while he searches through his pockets. Finds his phone and scrolls through to the first image of the girl in the street. He compares it with mine, swipes through to the second, back to the first. Takes my picture back from me. I resist the urge to relocate his grubby thumb to the edge of the print. He's ready for his verdict.

'I'd say eight-and-a-half.'

'Eight-and-a-half?'

'Out of ten. Allowing for the age difference.'

'So you're pretty sure it's her.'

'Three-quarters sure.'

'You said eight-and-a-half.'

'All right, more than three-quarters. It's not an exact science, you know. More like... weather forecasting.'

'What?'

'You know, like they say *sixty percent chance of rain*. That sort of thing.'

'But you're more than sixty percent sure.'

'More like ninety percent.'

At one level I recognize how stupid this bartering with statistics is, but it's all I have to hold onto. 'You said if I showed you a photo you could tell me one hundred and twenty percent.'

He passes the photograph over and takes another swig at his drink. 'There's no such thing as one hundred and twenty percent.'

'I know that, smart-arse. But it's what you said.'

'I didn't know you were going to show me a picture of a kid.'

'Hardly a kid. Listen, this would be only a year or so before she...'.

He catches my hesitation. 'What?'

'Left us.'

Cody stares at me again under the brim of his hat, weighing me up. I try not to react, not looking away but at the same time emptying myself of meaning. I can do that under scrutiny. Eventually he says, 'Bottom line is, you owe me another fifty quid.'

'Whoa, cowboy. Not so fast.'

'It's the same girl. One hundred and twenty percent.'

'Supposing she is, that's not the deal.'

'Yeah, it is the deal.'

'When *I* find her as a result of your work. That's when you earn the rest of your money.'

Cody snorts noisily up both barrels of his nostrils, looks around as if for a spittoon to hawk into, then, not finding one, glares back at me. I flinch slightly, genuinely concerned he's about to deposit his phlegm over me, but he swallows it instead. His eyes bulge before he gets his voice back, leans forward to offer husky advice. 'Get yourself up to the university. Ten to one she's a student there.'

I know that's impossible for any number of reasons, but I have to put my objections in terms he can comprehend. 'For a start,' I say, 'there must be twenty thousand students there. Where would I begin?'

'With the first years. The freshers,' he says, reasonably enough.

'Second, it's impossible because... (stay grounded)... I'm her father. She couldn't enrol without me knowing about it. There's the fees for one thing...'

'Maybe somebody else is paying. Or...' he clicks his fingers, Eureka moment... 'No, it's her boyfriend that's the student. She's tagging along with him.' He straightens up, looks lively and interested once more. 'Tell you what...' his new theory has filled him with confidence... 'Leave it with

48

me, Alex. I'll have this totally nailed in a week, and I'll get all three of you together. Then you've got nowhere to hide. No more excuses. Deal or no deal?'

'Deal.'

I try to conjure up this 'getting together' as I walk away from the pub. Me, Cody, some mysterious tall bloke who seems to have stepped into the scene, all gathered round... gathered round who? Ruth's ghost? Bizarre.

Back in my room, sprawled on top of my bed, I catch myself smiling at Karin, reflecting the smile she's giving me from the photo that I'm about to fix once more into its frame. Surprised Cody hadn't mentioned her at all when he was studying the picture. His attention will have been on Ruth, necessarily, but it's Karin who draws the eye, standing behind the bench with her outdoor top unzipped, head slightly askew as she ducks into the shot, open-faced and mischievous as if she's sharing a joke with me, maybe about the likelihood of my cutting the top of her head off - I've never been much of a photographer. Oh yes, now I recall the moment.

I have an idea. Using my mobile I snap a close-up of Karin in the photograph. Tap and scroll through my telephone contacts to find our home entry, edit to add the picture and with a little moving and scaling there she is smiling at me next to her details. Wish I had a separate number for poor Ruth; her mobile. Actually, why not make one, just to store her picture too? It takes less than a minute to add Ruth as a new contact. Insert her close-up. I make up her number from the alpha-numeric value of the letters that spell *heavenscalling*. Add an 0 at the front to make it look like a genuine number and it's *Oheavenscalling*. I can't help smiling at my own daftness as I put the original picture back into its frame. Love to think Ruth would answer if I called that number right now. Almost tempted to try it.

Lying on the bed I scroll alternately between the two numbers on my phone - Karin's and Ruth's - spinning through as if my mobile is a gun and I'm daring myself to play Russian roulette. To Karin's face again and I hold it there, my attention fixed on her smiling eyes. Engaging me from the picture just as she did while I was behind the camera. Sometimes, looking at her, I feel I should check my body for scorch marks; she's like a lightning strike on me. I could call her. I could call her now at home.

Someone's at the door. Not the front door, my own apartment. Someone tapping. I close my phone, hide the photo frame away under my pillow, stand and start smoothing the duvet cover, waiting for whoever it is to go away. Whoever it is knocks again. I slink across to the door, listen behind it for a few seconds, then open up cautiously. It's Jane, squat in slipper socks. She's looking towards the front entrance, turns as she hears my door click.

'Oh, hi Alex.'

'Hi.' Noncommittal.

'Sorry, I... just wondered if you had a smidgeon of milk you could spare?'

She lifts it up like Oliver asking for more - a mug with a design I've seen somewhere recently: the hatched image of an abandoned old teddy bear. I can feel my ears go red. This is her letting me know she knows. I shouldn't have broken the seal off that milk bottle.

'Only, I've run out.' She gives me this knowing smile. 'I'd go to the corner shop, but... well, actually it's just started pelting down.'

(Really? After the beautiful day it's been? Well, maybe I *can* hear rain outside.)

'Fine. No problem. Come in a sec.' Best to act normal. She follows me through, stands in the middle of the room with her mug while I go to the fridge. Our eyes meet when I bring the bottle and she smiles again, indicates the back of the door.

'See you've taken it down.'

'What? Oh, the list. Yeah, I didn't have any more ideas.'

'Pity. I think you were onto a winner there.'

'Well.'

She glances over at my desk, placing me in the act of writing my bestseller. 'So, what have you been doing with yourself today?'

'Oh, you know. Working.'

'Selling?'

'Sort of thing, yeah.' I turn away to put the milk back, shut the fridge door firmly; a signal for her to go, but she stays put.

'Don't mind me asking,' she says. 'Just being nosy again. What sort of stuff do you sell? Anything I'd buy?'

'Oh, no, I shouldn't think so. Well, I don't know, possibly. It's mainly men for some reason, don't know why.'

'Mainly men?'

'Yeah, just through the internet. Internet sales.'

'What? Not *porn* is it?'

'No, course not.' (Why would she say that?) I frown at her, let her know I'm offended. (Just 'cause *she's* got a dildo in her drawer, probably.)

50

Jane gives an embarrassed giggle, fingers to her lips as she says, 'Sorry, I didn't... Just when you said *mainly men.*' Her eyes widen on another thought. 'Oh, it's not... Oops, no, I better not go there.'

'What?'

'Sorry, no, well, to be honest I was going to say *penis enhancement.* You know, like pills for... Sorry, I don't know why I even... Sorry.' She clamps her hand over her mouth, watching my reaction. Close to pushing my button.

'I don't sell pills for *anything.* You think you're living next door to some drug dealer or what? Some scam artist? Sleaze bag?'

'Course not.' Behind her hand.

'Here, look.' I stoop and drag the suitcase out from under my bed. A wee bit too forcefully - she has to step quickly out of the way - but she's got me all worked up about this. Otherwise I wouldn't be showing her. Who does she think she's talking to? Snap the locks open and lift the lid. She bends over with ordinary curiosity, then, fascinated, sits on the bed, places her cup on my bedside table as I kneel to riffle through and pick out some of the more impressive prints and programmes for her to look at, each separately sealed in a protective bag.

'Is this actually...?'

'Yeah, who do you think it is.'

'But he's dead, isn't he?'

'Well, he is now.'

'And is this his real signature?'

'Of course. They all are. It's all genuine memorabilia.'

'And are they all dead?'

'No. Look.' I hand her another publicity shot, also signed. 'Not all dead. But they're nearly all people I worked with.'

'You worked with... Honestly?'

'Yeah, worked with, worked for, whatever. I told you the other day.'

'Yes, but... There's some big names here.'

'That's the point.'

'And have they given you this stuff to sell?'

'I sell it for myself. I've been collecting it for years. So now it's payback time.' I've calmed down by now, soothed by her obvious interest. 'That's how I make my living, or try to, these days.'

'Impressive.'

'Well, it's not easy.'

'I mean I hadn't realised when you said... All these famous people.' She spreads her arms out either side of her, palms sweeping across the duvet cover as she watches me collect up the items and store them carefully in the suitcase. She moves her feet sideways so I can push the case back into position and continues the movement, raising and tucking her legs into a comfortable pose on the bed. Her movement seems to release perfume which wafts across to me. Feel the beginnings of an erection, uncalled for, and adjust accordingly, half-sitting, half-lying on the floor. I'm still mad at her so I suppose this is just an effect of my blood rising or something.

'That really is impressive,' she says again, and I colour up, thinking for a moment she means... but she's still talking about the signed photos. (This talk about penis enhancement has me distracted.) 'Do they ever come round?'

'Who?'

'All these rock stars. Do you see much of them these days?'

'Been a while. My fault. I haven't really kept in touch.'

'You could, though.'

'Oh yeah, course.'

'Wow, I wouldn't mind scrolling through your contacts.' (Not a chance.) 'Are they friends on Facebook?'

'Don't really bother with Facebook. Or Twitter.'

'You keep a low profile.'

'That's it.'

We fall silent for a bit. Jane still has one hand flat on the bed, stroking the duvet cover now and again like a favourite pet. I don't know if she means it to be sexy, but that's the effect it has. Sexy and soothing at the same time. At last she says, 'Can't believe I've slept in this bed. Funny old night, wasn't it?'

Is this a come-on? I don't know what to think about that. Well, part of me does. It is a long time since...

'Are you comfortable down there?' she says. 'You don't look it.' She moves her butt up the bed a touch, pats the cover as though it's hers to pat, inviting me to sit next to her. I'm thinking how best to make the move without showing... when she leans back a little more, disturbing the top pillow, and exposes the rim of the photo frame underneath. Jane is looking my way, hasn't noticed, but for me it's as if Karin has just walked in and caught us at it. I can't hide my confusion.

'Are you all right?' says Jane.

'Oh yeah, it's just... I've suddenly remembered I've got to go out.'

'In that rain?'

'Yeah, well. I've arranged to meet somebody.'

She seems genuinely disappointed. 'Girlfriend?'

'No, a guy... erm, guy called Cody.' (What am I doing giving names out like this? As if I need to establish my credibility. As if I need to make excuses for myself. Get a grip.)

Jane's disappointment edges into frustration. Almost flounces off the bed, grabs her mug. 'Better love you and leave you, then.' As we cross I move discreetly to block her view of the pillow. She lingers at the door, collecting herself. I try not to make it too obvious I'm willing her to go. She does that thing with her hair, cocks her head, sad little girl smile. 'If you're not too late back you could always give me a knock if you like. I'll save some of your milk and make you a bedtime drink.'

'Well, probably be too late, but thanks anyway.'

'No problem. Thanks for this.' She's raises the mug in acknowledgement and disappears back to her place. I stare at the closed door. Does this mean I have to go out now, to keep my story straight? I don't even have a coat that's properly waterproof. But I know Jane will be listening, maybe even checking the window to watch me leave. Jeez, Karin, see what I do for you?

I lift the photo from under the pillow and sit it on my desk. See what I do for you? I search for my boots, reluctantly pull them on. My coat feels skimpier than ever. I turn my coat collar up as I leave the room, just so Karin, watching me out of her picture, gets the message.

V

I see signs everywhere, and I promise I'm not looking out for them - they just happen. Sometimes just the tiniest thing, something you might dismiss or argue away, but not last night. Talk about a sign writ large. Literally.

It was while I was sheltering in a shop doorway from the rain. Not thinking about anything in particular except for wondering when I could risk going back to the flat. Late enough to convince Jane that I really had been meeting somebody, and not so early that she'd still be up and ready to pounce on me. I'd been tempted and passed that test - I didn't want another one. On the other hand I was concerned about some policeman maybe passing by, thinking I was up to no good, wanting to know my business.

I was on the lookout for coppers when I happened to get my eye on it. The sign. There was a tatty-looking church across the street from the shop. Actually, it looked more like an old cinema converted into a church not the other way round as you sometimes see these days. The only reason I knew it was a church was the notice board outside with a big poster and a message printed on - the sort of thing they change every week or whenever they come up with a new angle to persuade you to go in there and prostrate yourself before the altar or whatever it is you're supposed to do when you want to be saved. Well, this message didn't make me want to go in and be saved - but it made me cross the road and stand reading it in the pouring rain because I couldn't believe what I was seeing from the doorway. Could hardly believe when I saw it up close.

It said: *Don't urge me to leave you or to turn back from you. Where you go I will go, and where you stay I will stay. Your people will be my people and your God my God.*

I could read that clearly enough from the doorway. It was the bit underneath that I crossed the road for, the smaller writing that showed where the quote was from. Naturally it was out of the Bible, but I had to get nearer to confirm exactly... And there it was in black and white, or rather in a sort of Mediterranean blue italic font: *Ruth 1:16*.

I still can't get my head round this. I've been awake all night thinking about it. Believe me, I'm not so gullible I'd swallow the idea that some random quote with Ruth's name on it has any significance at all. But it's not random, is it? *Don't urge me to leave you or to turn back from you. Where you go I will go, and where you stay I will stay.* It speaks exactly to the condition. That phrase has been going round in my head as well, and I don't know if

I've made it up or read it in a book somewhere: it speaks exactly to the condition. But how can there be a message from Ruth, dead Ruth, printed up on some poster in front of an old church, and what does she mean by it? Why will she go where I go, stay where I stay? Because she's waiting for something to happen. Waiting for me to do something. *Don't urge me to leave you or turn back from you.* Turn back from where? Somewhere she has to go (heaven?) but she doesn't want to leave, not yet. You read about these things, don't you, in stories, and there's all those films about the spirit of some dead person who refuses to leave this earth until a loved one left behind does something or understands something that's troubling them in some way. But that's not real life, is it? That doesn't happen in real life. Does it? Ruthy?

The second time you showed yourself wasn't to me at all but to Cody - I was miles away. How does that figure? *Your people will be my people.* You said it. I appointed him to be my eyes, and you knew that in some way. That's why you showed yourself to Cody, to prove to me that you weren't just a figment of my imagination. How could you be when he's seen you too. That's clever, Ruth, really clever. You were always a bright girl. You need to keep giving me signs, help me understand. I'm getting that there's something about the circumstances of your death... Is the appearance of the white van another sign from you? I don't know what you can do, what your powers are. But I do know the thing you want is connected with your mother and me, our relationship. You are desperate for us to get back together. I can sense that very strongly.

Once I'm up and about I can feel something different about me. I believe it's coming directly from Ruth, the way she's looking out for me, trying as far as she can to help me move in the right direction - she's given me a greater sense of purpose, a stronger conviction that I can turn my situation around, put things right.

First things first, get on top of mundane business. If I can't even earn enough to eat I can't expect to be in shape for the more important task of reconciliation with Karin. I have a few orders to fill that I've been letting slip recently while I've been overly preoccupied; I pull out my suitcase and with a greater will than I've shown for weeks I knuckle down to it, preparing, sorting and packaging, so that in less than an hour I have four or five items signed, sealed, stamped and ready for the post.

The work is not entirely without distractions as it makes me reflect on Jane's visit last night and her reaction to what I told her about what I do for a living these days. Was she really so impressed, or was she putting on a show to get into my good books generally? What is it exactly she

55

sees in me and, whatever it is, can I use it to my advantage with Karin in some way? Or does she represent a threat to our relationship? Not to my mind, but who can second guess a woman's whys and wherefores? I decide to sneak across and take another look at Jane's diary, see if she's written anything up about last night - suppose in a way it's like checking your answer phone messages - and anyway if I'm right to suspect she knows I've been in her room she probably realises I'm going to read what she has written, probably wants me to.

Nevertheless I am as careful as last time when it comes to lifting Jane's diary from under her pillow. More careful, because today I don't make the mistake of reading it next to the window. I crouch down by her bed and open at the page marked by the lace. Yep, she's bang up to date with her diary writing.

Learnt a lot more about A. tonight in more ways than one. How he makes his money selling signd pictures and other stuff from rock stars off the internet. Not just any random celebs, i mean these are people he actualy knows. His actual ~~freinds~~ friends. Bit of a turn-on mmm, tho' it seem's hard to believe when you see him sitting in a bedsit same as me. But not now i know about his accident and i've even seen his scars. Maybe see more of them very soon, you never know. Thats the other thing foxy little me has brought out of A. tonight (litrally!) - he's definately up for it. Bless, he was even trying to hide his st***ie when i made room for him on the bed. Then he remembered he'd promised to go out and see somebody (a GUY, but not in that way i'm sure). So I sugested he comes round when he gets back and i'm writing this waiting for him now. More later.

P.S. just coming up to 1~~pm~~ am. Hmm, nothing happening. Well, A. did get back shortly after 11. He rushed past the front door pretty quick so i didn't get the chance to realy see him or wave or etc but i heard his door open aswell so definately him. Kept latch off my door and just kind of tucked my toes under the duvet, waiting, but nothing so far. Should i try knocking on his door again? Hussy. Anyway, probs' too late for tonight babe - shame.

Jane, what happened to your resolution? But this is different, i can feel it. M. he is not. No, i could NOT go through that again. But A. wouldn't be that kind of bastard. He's got kind eyes. And not pushy, infact the oppossite. The type to take his time. Am i puting out too much? Need to find out more about him, what hes realy like. Wonder what star sign he is. Please not Leo. Guessing Aquarius which would be fine. Must ask him. Night night diary, night night Alex - better day tommorow.

As I get to the end of the entry I have a strange sensation that someone's reading over my shoulder. For a moment I panic, thinking Jane has crept in and caught me at it, but there's no-one there. All the same, I close the book pretty hurriedly and rush a little to replace it under the pillow so that I worry afterwards whether I put it back in exactly the right spot. My thoughts are churned up and it's not until I'm well on my way to the post office that I calm down sufficiently to reflect on what Jane has written.

She still comes across as horny but at the same time there's something quite childish and immature about her. Not my type at all, never mind if our star signs are in alignment or whatever they're meant to be. (I *am* an Aquarian as it happens but that's all bullshit - it's never even crossed my mind what star sign Karin is.) Who's *M.* I wonder? Obviously someone Jane's had a bad relationship with; is that how she ended up on her own in a flat? Well, Jane, if you're on the rebound don't look for me catching you - I have someone in my life and it's only a matter of time before we're together again.

There's a bus stop near to the post office. With my packages gone, cash drawn out the hole in the wall and nothing pressing for the rest of the day it seems the most natural thing in the world to hop on the next bus into town, then take the short walk to the old Assembly Rooms where Karin has her studio.

I can see into the car park from the other side of the road and it's easy to spot Karin's sunflower MX-5 parked by the low wall. The sight gives me a *frisson* of pleasure - the colour and the elegant lines of the coupé are as seductively feminine as she is, and of course showroom pristine still - while just the car being there reassures me that Karin is nearby. So close.

My urge to enter the building is strong, but the better part of me recognizes the complications - there are issues to resolve and Karin and I need to find time and space without the interference of others to get back on track. I have to be patient. Can't even risk being seen here. I'm smiling now, thinking of the irony: the last time I hung around an office building it was in the hope of being seen by Ruth after her appearance in the park; now I'm trying to melt into the background like a ghost myself. I wish there was some way Karin could privately know I was here, or discover later I've been, just so she'd really appreciate how much I care. Funny, I feel like Ruth right now, working out some way of leaving a sign, some kind of secret message. For your eyes only.

I watch the car from a safe distance. I could write a note, but if I leave it, say, under the windscreen wiper it could easily be picked up and read by somebody else, and if I tuck it somewhere more discreet there's a good chance she won't see it at all. I spend the best part of an hour wrestling with this and with another dilemma; what to do if Karin comes out to the car right now, supposing she's on her own? Do I step further into the shadows or show myself? Wave, or slink away?

She hasn't appeared either alone or in company by the time I resolve to chance it and leave a note. Inevitably, not having planned this visit, I have neither paper nor pen on me. I have to leave my post for a while to explore the shops around the area on the lookout for a stationer or suchlike. Before I come across one I happen on a different type of establishment that provides a rush of sweet serendipity. A Eureka moment that rings in my head like the old-fashioned bell on the door as I enter the shop. Not three hundred yards from Karin's studio is this neat and tiny florist.

'Excuse me,' I ask ultra-politely because it somehow seems the right way to behave, 'Would you be able to supply me at all with just one perfect individual rose?'

Perfect it is. The single red rose held carefully at its stem by a wiper blade of the MX-5. Placed at the perfect angle for Karin to take in the graceful whorl of petals as she unlocks the driver's door or, if she should be in too much of a dream to notice (she can be quite spaced out at times - 'dancing in your head again', I'll say), where she can see it clearly through the windscreen as she settles in her seat. Perfect. So perfect that as soon as I've positioned it I nip back across the low wall and remove myself from the scene entirely. I just want that flower to speak for itself. I can picture Karin, surprised at first, gently freeing it with her slender fingers, maybe glancing round for a moment, wondering, then smelling its perfume, the petals just touching the soft tip of her nose. She will understand. Of course I realise now that walking by the florist was not just a happy accident. Thank you, Ruth.

'Change for a cuppa tea, mate?'

I'd been so distracted I almost tripped over him where he squats on his blanket, half in a doorway, half on the pavement. Quite a young bloke, not that dirty but mealy-looking. Needy. I'm so full of the joys right now I almost hand him a tenner, no questions asked, then a thought strikes.

'You won't spend it on tea though, will you?'

'Maybe.' He shifts his backside on the pavement.

'No, it'll go on drugs. What you on? Charley? Crack?'

'What's it to you?'

'I'm just asking.'

'And I'm just asking for a sub, feller. You can stick your moralising up...'

58

'You don't understand. I'm just wondering...' I crouch right down beside him to whisper, 'Know where I could score some weed?'

It's not something I use regularly, not what you'd call a habit. Used to be just social occasions, winding down after a gig, where your natural high turns nicely mellow as you smoke. Late into the night, shooting the breeze, sharing a few laughs... finding *everything* funny, but never sarcastic, never directed at anybody, just... observational, I suppose, about the general daftness of the world. More giggles than full-on laughs, bubbling up as you talk, swirling around the group. Mostly I would just listen, enjoying the buzz. Catch somebody's eye and they'd kind of nod at you, smiling, then you'd both be nodding away wisely, sharing the moment, laughing together at the absurdity of... life, I guess. Good times.

Must admit I didn't fancy sharing a spliff with the pasty-faced junkie, and certainly not the trainee gangster who slewed up from nowhere on his BMX to deliver the stuff. On the other hand I wanted my good mood to last so I wasn't about to hole myself up in my flat and smoke grass alone like some saddo. Which is why I'm back once more at the burial ground. Being here is the closest I can get to having company at the moment, and remote enough to enjoy a joint outdoors without fear of the law tapping on my shoulder. Not that the dead can be much company, but standing by Ruth's grave makes me feel closer to her. And if she's going to appear again in person surely this is the most likely place. Wish I'd thought to bring flowers, or just another single rose.

Ruth Taylor. Taken too soon, forever loved by Karin and Alex.

A casual passer-by reading the inscription might just see it as cliché - they could have no idea of the heart-rending story behind it or the meaning those words contain for the three of us whose names are here, interwoven with sadness and loss, but joined in love for eternity. I want to take the *forever loved* in with the hit, ruminate on it. Trouble is, moments after I fire up and take my first deep toke I feel guilty for polluting the air over Ruth and I need to move away. In the middle of the park there is a wooden seat under a framework of climbing plants (is it called a *bower?*) where I still have a view of Ruth's plot, so I sit there to continue my joint, summon up some pleasant dreams and memories and, I'll admit, wait for a visitation.

All too soon the joint is gone - those sticks burn quicker than your average roll-up - but the high lingers, helped by an afternoon autumn sun. I spread my arms wide on the back of the seat, cross my ankles and zone out with my eyes half-closed, lips half-open as if I'm offering myself dozily for a wake-up kiss.

My phone rings. Stare at the screen before answering. Don't recognize the number.

'Hello?'

No answer. Is someone there? Sounds like the line's still open, not cut off.

'Hello?'

No-one there. Is that my breathing or someone else's? My listening ear opens into another dimension, ranges across the bandwidth, prospecting for sound. I look out across the park, which undulates slightly in front of my eyes. No-one there. *My love she speaks like silence.* The line goes dead.

I stare at the number until the screen goes blank. Press the button to bring it up again. Press recall. Nothing, then the ringing tone, reaching out, begging for an answer. The tone is abruptly cut off. I call again. Cut off again, on the first ring this time.

I store the number under Karin's name, next to her home number.

Stay another half hour, another forty minutes. My phone does not ring again. Ruth does not appear.

Al fresco burger and fries on the way home. Gladstone Terrace that is, unfortunately, not Beech Grove. Conscientious hesitation outside the flats while I try to work which of the cartons and wrappers are recyclable, then give up and dump them all in the same bin. I find Jane standing with her coat on in the hallway. Like a character in a low budget soap she seems to spring into action just that fraction late as I come through.

'Oh, hi Alex.' Affecting surprise. She smiles and drops her eyes from me as if she's slightly embarrassed about something, riffles through a small wad of mail like a prop in her hands. Her bike helmet looped around her wrist, restricting her movement. I'd have to push past her to get to my room so I stand and wait while she continues sorting the letters. Jane looks up at me again as if it's my cue. She's done something to her hair - am I supposed to remark on this? I'm having difficulty remembering the exact state of play in our relationship. Are we friends now, or just neighbours? Who spoke last to whom and what and when? I'm conscious of fast food traces around my mouth.

'More post for Robson,' she says at last.

'Robson, right.'

'Mmm. Mysterious Mr Robson. Who is he? Why doesn't he pick up his letters?'

'Maybe they're junk.'

60

'Not all of it. Don't look like junk.' She shows me a handwritten white envelope. I study it dutifully. Jane studies me.

'Maybe he moved.'

'Maybe.' Her eyes still on me. 'Maybe I should ask Mr Chatterjee.' (Don't know what she expects me to say.) 'For all I know you could be him. This Mr Robson, I mean.'

'I'm not.'

'For all I know, though. Fact is, I don't even know your second name. You know mine, I don't know yours.'

'It's immaterial.'

'Alex.' She seems wounded by this.

'I'm not being obstructive. Just prefer to keep myself to myself, that's all.'

'Really?'

The way she says *Really?* I can tell she's starting to go off it. Don't know what's up with her, I'm just trying to explain...

'Didn't look like you were keeping yourself to yourself last night,' she goes on. 'Far from it actually.' She sort of flounces towards her door, turns back. 'Well, you can keep it in your pants, far as I'm concerned. Or shove it up your arse.' Spits the words out, real venom in them, but before she gets to the end she's breaking up. *Arse* is just a splutter. She fumbles opening the door with her key as well, so she's still on my side of it at the point she no doubt wants to be slamming it in my face. I wait for her to do that, out of politeness. Where this has all come from I don't know, but if she wants to act the drama queen it's neither here nor there to me.

Truth is, my attitude softens a bit when I reflect on it in my own room. Jane did seem genuinely upset at the end there. I feel sorry for her, but she's brought it on herself. She seems to expect more from me than I've given her reason to. More than I'm prepared to provide. I don't mind passing the time of day with the girl, but I don't want her trespassing on my private life, which is exactly what she's doing as a matter of fact. Next thing she'll be poking about in here to root out more about me than she needs to know.

For safety's sake I look around the apartment for a place I might hole away some of my personal stuff. In the en-suite, where the water works are boxed in, I find an access panel to the plumbing behind. I secrete a few things in the gap there, including the note from Karin I picked up at Beech Grove and another she once left for me on the bench in the kitchen.

61

Thanks, Alex. I love you. x

It gives me a warm feeling to read it again, remembering that shot of pleasure when I first came across it. Just a casual gesture but so typical of her, so tender. I hate to put it in the hole, but in it goes. Mean to include my picture of Karin and Ruth as well, but I can't bring myself to lose sight of them so the photo frame goes back onto my bedside table. I sit staring at it for half an hour or more in a strange sort of mood partly brought on by Jane's outburst. Melancholic - I suppose that's the right word for how I'm feeling.

Shortly before midnight I step across the hallway and listen at Jane's door, don't know why. Maybe checking she hasn't killed herself. I can hear the telly on low, which is reassuring, though there's no particular reason why she would turn the telly off before she commits suicide. While I'm listening a stray thought pops into my head - some article I read which said you're not supposed to say *commit suicide* anymore because it's no longer a crime. There you go. Anyway, the telly goes off after a while so I guess she's still alive in there.

I'm in bed, but not really sleeping. Thinking about my faithfulness to Karin has me remembering the time we were teasing each other, lying in bed like this (but a whole lot more comfortable). I asked her, for a joke, if there was anybody she would kick me out of bed for. She said, 'Of course not,' then she stroked my finger down her chest while she said 'What about you? Anybody you would kick me out of bed for?'

'Only Suze Rotolo,' I said. It was so funny how she grabbed onto me to haul herself up and look straight into my eyes, even though it was far too dark to see properly. I'm smiling now, just thinking about it.

'Who is Suze Rotolo?' she said, suddenly serious.

'Oh well, that's for me to know and you to find out.'

The thing is, when I was a kid I used to sometimes flick through my dad's old record collection. I loved the covers on those old vinyl albums, still do. It wasn't a very large collection - the whole lot fitted into one red plastic record box - and nearly all of it was stuff he'd bought while he was a student, including this one that fascinated me. *The Freewheelin' Bob Dylan.* I'm sure I only tried to play the record once, and my mam shouted at me to turn that racket off, but it was the cover I loved. Bob Dylan is walking down a city street; New York, I suppose. He's very young - it was one of his early LPs - and he has his girlfriend with him. It's obviously cold, and she's tucking into his arm as they walk together, like she's saying, *keep me warm* or maybe just simply *I love you* or even *don't leave me.* There was something about that image that made me want to be Bob Dylan, and to be walking down that street with that girl. When I think about it maybe that was the start of my dreaming about being a professional musician. I found out somehow - probably from the album sleeve - that this girl really was Dylan's girlfriend at the time, and her name was Suze Rotolo; I've always remembered the name.

Karin, of course, had never heard of Suze Rotolo, and thought this was a real girl - I mean, someone I knew. I kept the tease going for quite a while before I told her who she was, and she thumped me on the chest then said, inevitably, 'Does she look like me?'

'Not a bit like you,' I said. 'She's dark haired, different colouring altogether. You're both cool, though. But she's probably dead, so you'll have to do.'

She thumped me again. To please her I said, 'But you do look like somebody on an album cover.'

'Who?'

'The blonde one from Abba.'

'Oh, when I first came to England not a day passed without someone saying that. But now I'm too old and men pass me by in the street without a second glance.'

'I bet they wouldn't kick you out of bed, though' I said, and I brought her close into me, and she showed me why.

I must have fallen asleep on that thought. Some time later - feels like the middle of the night but I don't check my watch - I wake up with a strong sensation that somebody's in my room. I lie with my eyes closed at first, straining to hear, but there's nothing definite. My body's cold and tense under the duvet; my skin tightens where the scar line runs up my arm. Open my eyes gradually, don't move my head at all until I recover enough focus to make out the shape of the ceiling light, then it's a cautious look around for shadows that shouldn't be there. Nothing different. Except (this sounds stupid) there's an air of expectancy as if the room is holding its breath waiting for something to happen.

Once I'm sure nothing's about to grab at me I put my hand out and switch on the lamp. Pull myself up onto one elbow and check around in the lamplight. At first the room looks exactly as it did. I'm about to switch off the lamp and lie back when I spot a folded piece of paper on the floor right by the door. Seems to have been pushed through from the other side. I've never been more conscious of my balls hanging out than when I sneak across to retrieve this note - like I'm expecting some sniper to take a pot shot at them in no-man's-land between the door and my bed. I climb back in sharpish and unfold the paper. It's a handwritten note.

Realy sorry. Its not you, its me. Whats' in a name? A rose by any other name would smell so sweet. xx

The mention of a rose throws me at first, gets me thinking straightaway of Karin. I have to calm down and study the message again before I reach the more obvious conclusion. It's printed in felt pen, which makes the writing look different from her diary, but spelling and punctuation are a giveaway. Not so hot on the quotes either - I'm sure it's 'smell *as* sweet'. Odd coincidence, though, the rose thing.

Or maybe not a coincidence. *Your people will be my people.* Is Jane, like Cody, some sort of instrument for Ruth? Is this Ruth waking me up (her presence in the room?) to see the note, to tell me not to dismiss Jane as just some nosy parker? Maybe warning me that Jane's about to do something drastic, really try to kill herself. Ruth is urging me to stop her.

I climb out of bed and dress hurriedly, shuffle across from my room to Jane's, listen closely at the door. All I can hear is the sound of my own heart. I knock quietly. Knock again.

'Who is it?'

Alive anyway. Doesn't even sound sleepy or particularly miserable. I feel a bit stupid now, rushing over in the middle of the night. For what? Before I can answer, the door opens.

'Oh, hi Alex. It *is* you.'

What does she mean it *is* you? Like she's expecting me.

'I knew it would be. Hoped it would. Come in.'

She turns and walks quite spritely back to her bed, where she sits cross-legged like a pixie, her toes under the duvet cover, welcoming me in. Looking so healthy and cheerful that I almost hate her, as if she's somehow let me down for not being wasted and pathetic as I imagined. Not a victim to rescue on Ruth's call. She's wearing red PJs with (as far as I can tell in the lamplight) little pink hearts all over. I follow into the room, not sure where to put myself. There's a two-seat sofa over by the window but so far away it would be an act of open hostility to sit there. Bed too intimate. I half-park on the end of it, keeping enough distance between us. Wishing I hadn't come.

'I knew you'd come,' she says. 'Sorry about the note. Did I wake you up?'

'Dunno. Something did.'

'Sorry.'

She doesn't look sorry, sitting there smiling. She looks pleased with herself. I'm beginning to think *rose* was a coincidence after all. Nothing to do with Ruth or Karin. Unless this is another test. Not sure what I'm supposed to do next.

'What's in a name?' Jane asks. Rhetorical question. She shrugs her shoulders in a girly, coquettish kind of way. Presses her smile into a sort of apology. Then leans forward with one hand out along the cover, encouraging me. I know what to do next.

'It's *Taylor,*' I say. 'Alex Taylor.'

'That wasn't so hard, eh?' Her eyes positively shimmer. 'Hello Alex Taylor. Pleased to meet you at last.' Excitement in the stretch of her fingers.

'There's something else I should tell you, though. I'm married.'

Jane straightens up. So does her face. 'Really?' She draws her right hand back, crosses it over her left in her lap. She seems lost for words for once, then says, weirdly, 'Very married?'

'What do you mean?'

'Well, you're clearly not with your wife, are you? Less you keep her locked up in a cupboard.'

Don't much care for this sudden change of tone. 'You don't believe me.'

'I didn't say that...'

'Hang on, wait there.'

Without thinking about what I'm doing, piqued by Jane's remark, I nip across to my room, pick up the photo frame, and before she's drawn breath I'm back to show her the proof.

'That's my wife Karin leaning over the seat.'

'Fine, I'm... No need to throw it.' I notice her hand shaking slightly as she settles the frame between her knees. Obviously a big deal for her. Bends over the picture, studying it, her hair obscuring her face, while I close the door that I left open in my hurry to bring the photo through. She stays mute for so long I'm wondering if she's hiding a tear, then, still staring at the photo she says, 'Karin? With an *i?*'

'Yes, it's the Swedish form.' The penny doesn't drop about her knowing the unusual spelling until she looks up to ask directly, 'As in *GET BACK KARIN?*'

She's not forgotten those damn headlines on the back of my door. 'You're not writing a story, then?' she says.

'Not really, no.'

'And which one's *the girl in the park?*' She taps at the glass. 'Looks like they're all sitting in a park.'

'It's my daughter and her friend on the seat.'

65

That burst of energy I had - OK, anger - it's gone as quickly as it came, leaving me deflated, fatigued. How did I get into this at two o' clock in the morning or whatever it is? Jane, though, seems to have perked up again.

'I'm guessing the dorky one's the friend. The blonde girl's the spit of her mother. I can see you in her as well.'

'Thanks.'

'Pretty girl.'

'She was.'

'*Was?*'

(Bugger it, I'm like a knackered boxer, too tired to keep my guard up.)

'She died.'

'Oh, Alex.' Her fingers stretching again. A moan, a bleat. What do I do, Karin? What do you expect me to do? I'm crying here.

'Sorry, I've upset you,' says Jane. Her hand closes over mine. Tear in her eye as well. For Ruth? For me? Who's to know? What's in any woman's mind? It's a mystery.

'A *mystery?*'

(Did I say the word out loud?)

'Oh, that's what you wrote on the door. About a mysterious death. Did you mean your daughter. Was she... *Rose*, was it?'

(*Rose* again.) 'Ruth.'

'Ruth, yes. Sorry. Ruth.' Silence while she seems to save and store the information. Or until she dares to risk asking me. 'What was mysterious about it? About her death?'

'Everything.'

'A mystery illness?'

'No.'

Eyes rounded, Jane draws slightly away from me as she contemplates the other possibility. 'Not murdered?'

'Maybe.' There's no getting away from it. 'Yes.'

'God.' Hand to the mouth. 'You're *joking*.' Realises instantly what a stupid reaction that is (but it is what everybody says), and apologises, over-apologises. 'Sorry, sorry, sorry... What a stupid thing to say. Of course you're not joking, I'm just... sorry.'

'S'alright. Everybody says the same, straight off.'

'No, but just I meant... God, murdered. I mean, how? Who by? Sorry, I haven't got any right to ask... Just so shocked. Can't get my head round it. Never met anybody who... you know.' She trails off, embarrassed by her own inadequacy.

'It's fine. It's cool. Don't worry about it.' Gone too far not to say more. 'Fact is, we don't know who did it. Just random. A random act of violence.'

'My god.'

'Anyway. Just to let you know.'

Jane stares at the photo a long while, maybe to avoid looking at me. Eventually says behind her hair, 'Did you... find the body?'

'What... me personally?'

'No, sorry, I'm... Not getting my words out right. I mean...'

'Oh yeah, she was... found. We were able to... you know. She's in a lovely place.'

Jane smiles up at me, tears shimmering. 'I'm sure she is now.'

Neither of us connecting properly with the other. Jane's misinterpretation distracts, sets off visions of Ruth wandering the earth like Banquo's ghost, and when I correct her I feel guilty of pushing my daughter back into her box. 'I mean she's buried in a nice place, Deerholme Woodland Park.'

'Oh, right. Of course. Where's that?' Just something else to say.

'Not far from town. Off the Darnley road.'

'Oh, yeah. Nice up there.'

'It is.'

Jane nods, looking past me, like she's nursing some secret wisdom. Or trying to conjure up the next platitude. But we have nothing else to say to each other. I was wrong to think Ruth meant this to happen. Should have kept myself to myself. I'm tired.

'I'm tired.'

Instantly Jane is all compassion. 'Of course you are, you must be.' She leans forward on the bed, her hand covering mine once more. 'What a terrible thing for you. Listen, I want you to know I feel it Alex, you do know that don't you, that I feel for you?'

'Thanks.'

'And I'm so sorry I doubted you. Well... not doubted you, just wanted... Anyway.'

'Anyway.'

In the pause that follows I manage to slip my hand out from under hers. Stand up. 'Anyway,' I say again, making a vague gesture toward the door. Jane still looking at me intently, but she says nothing more until I actually start to walk away.

'Alex?'

'Yes.'

'You know I'll do anything to help you, don't you? Anything at all.'

67

'Thanks. Thanks, Jane.' And that's going to be my escape line until I realise that she still has the photo frame cradled between her knees. Her eyes widen slightly when she sees me coming back to her. She shuffles to the far side of the bed, making room, dislodging the photo so it slides off the duvet and I have to make a sharp move to stop it falling onto the floor. That startles Jane.

'Oh.'

'Sorry. Sorry, just...' I show her my catch like a fielder proving himself to the umpire and she says *Oh* again, but more disappointed than surprised. I make my way back across the room but still don't get to leave before she calls out once more.

'Alex?'

'Yeah.'

'You and your wife... Your... Karin. Has this thing come between you in some way? I mean, I know that can happen. I've seen... I mean, tragedies like that. They're bound to upset... the apple cart.'

'The apple cart?'

'I don't mean to pry. Just that I feel for you.'

'Well, it's late.'

'Course. Can we talk tomorrow maybe?'

'Dunno. I've... I got a lot on tomorrow.'

'I see.' Mournful tone, trying to make me feel guilty, then, 'OK, Alex.'

I wait for her to finish with a *goodnight* but she doesn't, so I quietly close the door and go back to my room for some rest at last.

VI

Not comfortable, though. Far from it. I have a weird dream of being inside a parcel on its way to wherever but before it gets to its destination a corner of the wrapping paper is torn off and I can see Jane's eye peering in. Not a good feeling - I wake up briefly with the shock of it, then drift off into a state of restless dozing, like trying to sleep in a moving vehicle, in nameless transit, holding a lid down on my dreams.

Takes a while to rally, reassemble. When the daylight settles behind the curtains I lie, settling with it. What helps is playing my composition in my head. *Karin's Song*. A gentle thing, not technically difficult, but subtle in tone. Touch, rhythm, control. I play and the music plays upon me. Back at the white piano. Sunlight through the window.

I get up refreshed. The morning doze, the free floating, has released my imagination from its night-time anxieties. I'm soothed, but not sedated - in fact, I'm feeling quite energised and positive again. I've decided to create a Karin opportunity or at least put myself in the way of it, which I know is what Ruth wants.

My mind is buzzing with possibilities so when I step out into the hallway it doesn't immediately strike me as unusual that Jane's bike is still parked there so late on a weekday morning. The only reason I think of it at all is that I'm beaten to the front door by one of the students who comes bounding down the stairs three at a time and barges past, bumping my elbow with his bag.

'Sorry...exam... tragically late.'

'Oh, maybe you should borrow...' I'm addressing his disappearing back and pointing at Jane's bike. But he's off already and I'm in a belated double take. Why hasn't Jane taken her bike to work? Has she gone to work? The thought turns to queasiness, a little wave of guilt. Was Jane more badly affected by what I had to say last night than I gave her credit for? Has she called in sick?

Suppose I should knock and check she's OK. I try two or three taps on her door without success, nor is there any response to my calling 'Jane' quietly at the door panel. I could use the spare key to get in, but what if she's lying there and suddenly wakes to me standing by her bed? Worse, she could be sitting on the toilet with the door wide open, or beating seven bells out of her snatch - who knows what women do when they're on their own?

I remember the sense I had in the early hours that Ruth was delivering me to Jane, that she might harm herself otherwise. But then Jane seemed so cheerful when she saw me, so up for it... At least until I told her I was married. Another disappointment, like with *that bastard M* she talks about in her diary. What is her state of mind after last night? She's a hard one to fathom. What's she capable of? She couldn't really have killed herself, could she? Again I consider the key. No, safer to see if I can spot anything through her window from outside.

Next thing I'm out at the front pretending to do some kind of inspection of the brickwork for the benefit of passers-by while risking the odd peek into Jane's room without making it obvious to anyone inside that I'm staring through her window. Not an easy task. Reassuring, though, that her curtains are open, which suggests that if she's in there she's neither sleeping nor doing anything shameful. I get bolder with each sneaky glance so that by the end I'm fully up against the panes as if I'm scrutinising some defect in the window sill, and that allows me at last to get a squint inside. As far as I can see the room is empty of Jane or anyone else.

Do I take the chance of Jane being out to slip into her room again and check her latest diary entry? I'm interested in her interpretation of what went on between us last night - not just her take on what she thinks of as our *relationship* now she knows I'm married, but any thoughts she might have on Karin and *our* relationship, the only one that matters. From the little she said last night Jane seems to understand at some level that Ruth's death has created some sort of wedge between Karin and me. It would be useful to have a woman's point of view on it, and how can I get that otherwise without having her too personally involved? Tempting to read her diary once more. Hmm. If she's not at work she could walk in at any moment. Worth the risk, I'd say.

Thankfully, Jane doesn't burst out from some hiding place after I unlock the door into her room, though I'm alarmed by a little bumping noise as I open the door. It's Jane bike helmet, suspended from the hook on the door panel. Her coat and rucksack are gone. She may not be far away so I'd best be quick reading her diary. But for once it's not under her pillow. This stymies me for a minute. Where can it be? On the other side of the bed is a bog-standard IKEA unit with three drawers, the type with no handles, just a recess where you can slip your fingers in and pull the drawer out. Little socks and knickers in the top one - they cushion my left hand as I hold them in place and explore underneath with my right. Nothing. In the middle drawer, under some tee-shirts, I find the letters addressed to Mr Robson, still sealed (or maybe resealed if she steamed them open). What's her game? A couple of pairs of jeans in the bottom drawer - nothing else that I can find here or anywhere else a hurried search around the room can reveal. If she has hidden her diary she's done

70

it properly. And it can only be from me. There's a trust issue here, never mind what she said in her note. I'm really glad now I squirreled away my stuff. There's no telling what lengths she'll go to just to find out all she can about me.

Coming out of her room it spooks me to see her bike in the passage, as if it's Jane herself standing there, or her guard dog. I'm so jumpy these days. Staring at the thing. She still hasn't bought a pump. This mundane fact anchors me, re-establishes the bike as an inanimate object. Even then I catch myself nodding at it as I pass. *Easy, girl* I almost say. God, I'm stressed out. There are mad people more sane than I am right now.

Karin's car is parked in exactly the same spot by the low wall at the back of the old Assembly Rooms as if it has not moved since yesterday. I'm almost tempted to go and check whether my rose is still in place under the windscreen, except I don't want to risk her catching sight of me from a window - I'd like to be in control of timing my reappearance in her life, and I think it's today, just not quite yet.

When then, and how? Do I call her from here, tell her I'm in the vicinity and ask if she'd care for a spot of lunch? That's what I'd planned when I was thinking this through in bed this morning, but now I'm outside the building it suddenly doesn't seem so simple. She hasn't responded to my note about Ruth. I thought maybe seeing the flower I left would prompt her, but nothing so far. I don't know the full situation, whether she's being prevented from contacting me or if my ringing would compromise her in some way. Text? Too impersonal and not guaranteed an answer. I'm worried though, if I phone, about coming across as weak, hesitant, incoherent. I need her to see me as clear and decisive, sure about our... love, really. What I'd like to do, actually, is just walk straight in there through the studio and, no matter what she's doing, present myself before her. Just the two of us face to face again - no complications, no interference. We wouldn't even need to say anything, we'd just... Everything would fall into place.

Then the doubts rush in. Suppose she's in the middle of a rehearsal, in a meeting... Plus there's all these petty gatekeepers that get in the way. So much fuss and nonsense, so easy to spoil the moment, and before you know we might be back at square one. Too frustrating. I don't know what to do for the best.

After ten minutes or more of dithering I walk along the path that skirts around the back of the Assembly Rooms towards the front. I still have no clear idea what I'm doing but I'm kind of daring myself to pass

71

the front entrance in the vague hope I'll be brave enough to dash in and just... go for it. At the main street corner of the building I hesitate. This surely needs more consideration. Then the strangest thing happens.

Cars that were moving on the road in front of the Assembly Rooms come to an orchestrated stop. In the hush that follows I can hear the repeated pings of a pelican crossing. Someone is crossing to this side, but I can't see at first for a delivery truck in my way. By the time I catch sight of her she has already made the pavement and about to swing to her right, away from me. The world has stopped around her and I have my first unambiguous full-face view since the day I lost her of my lovely Ruth.

'Ruth!'

My cry is a second or two later, with the lights changed, the cars in motion again and Ruth walking away from me. She doesn't hesitate, maybe doesn't hear me above the traffic noise.

'Ruth!'

Louder this time, and I'm following her, but she doesn't stop or turn. I'm just a few feet behind when she skips up the stone steps and without hesitation disappears through the long brown doors of the old Assembly Rooms.

My first clear sight, and it is absolutely her. Even to the Maltese Cross earrings. No room for any lingering doubt. Also not in doubt is that there is something deliberate and purposeful about the signs and signals I've been getting and her appearances in front of me. Otherwise why here, why now?

Ruth, I know what you're doing. You're scaring me, baby, but I totally get it. You're somehow tuned in to my anxiety, and you're leading the way. You want me to take courage, go in there, be with your mother. Now is the time.

A moment to take stock, then I follow Ruth's exact path up the stone steps; they seem to me almost to shimmer in places as though she's left a fairy trail. I'm in a tingling fever of excitement but when I get to the top of the steps something in my peripheral vision causes a chill. From here I have a view of a loading bay a little further along the road, and in that loading bay there sits a dirty white transit van, faced away from me. It's my heightened state of imagination, of course, that has me believing the wing mirrors of the van are tilted to provide an aspect of the steps. What would I expect to find in a loading bay if not a commercial vehicle? Shrug off my paranoia and push through the doors to another trio of steps that lead to the lobby.

The doors to the main function hall are on the ground floor immediately in front of me. I have on occasion in the long and distant played piano on stage here. Karin has her studio on the first floor, accessible by a wide swirl of staircase either side of the lobby. Take the swirl to my right because I fancy that's the way Ruth would have gone, though both sides lead to the same studio reception desk, which is at the moment unattended.

There's piano music, a simple solo piece I don't recognize, playing in the background, probably from a speaker in the studio beyond. Maybe Karin is with a pupil, or even going through some steps herself. My heart, already quickened by the slight exertion of the stairs, drums into the wall of my chest, hampers my breathing. I steady myself with the tips of my fingers on the desk. There's no-one here to stop me; why don't I just go through? Yes I will, once I've regained my balance.

'Can I help?'

A woman, fifty-something, hair tied up in a bun, emerges from a room along the landing. Her arms seem to be full of more A4 sheets than she can feasibly carry - inevitably some slip off the pile as she hurries to attend to me, and I have to help her rescue them.

'Thank you - more haste, less speed. Mammoth photocopying session.'

I can see Karin's signature repeated on some of the papers that the woman piles loosely onto the reception desk. She catches my grin, misinterprets it. 'Sorry, I must look so foolish and disorganized.'

'Not at all.'

'Actually, I *am* rather disorganized at the moment. Fourth day in the job, that's my excuse. I've not done office work for... a few years, now. Anyway, babble-babble, what can I do you for, sir?' Sits herself behind the desk. 'Do *for* you.'

'Er, I'm hoping to catch a word with Karin.'

'Oh. Is it a sales call?' Hint of suspicion in her question.

'No, no. Personal.'

'Aha. Let me just...' Her hand on her computer mouse. 'What name is it?'

I smile at her switch into gatekeeper mode. 'Don't worry,' I tell her. 'I'm Karin's husband.'

The woman glances up, flustered. 'I am sorry, sir. I didn't realise...'

'Not a problem.'

She looks back at her screen and brightens. 'Oh, *Alex*, is it?'

'Yes.' My turn to be suspicious. What's that screen telling her?

'She's obviously expecting you.'

73

'Sorry?'

'I'll just let her know you're here.'

I'm still dazed by this as she vacates her desk and disappears through the doorway behind reception. I stare blankly ahead for a moment then, recovering, nudge the flat monitor of the computer, skewing it enough to lean forward and read the screen display at an angle. It's an electronic calendar, with Karin's name at the top. Someone, presumably the receptionist just now, has highlighted one of the entries for today.

12.30 pm. Alex

What? Oh, Ruth's doing. It has to be. Ghostly fingers on a keyboard.

Next door the music stops. The silence hangs. I straighten up the monitor, straighten up myself, return my gaze to the door, brace myself for Karin's appearance. But it is the receptionist who steps back through.

'I'm really sorry, Mr Taylor, I can't find her. She's not in her office. Must have slipped out while I was at the photocopier.'

The piano music starts up again in the studio behind her.

'Isn't that...?' I start to say.

'No, that's... Frankie, I think her name is. One of the part-timers. She hasn't seen Karin either, but she said she'd normally pop off for lunch around now.'

'Yes, with me.' (I know this is stretching it a little, but I feel a sense of entitlement now that Ruth has ghosted in the appointment.)

'Mmm.' The woman seems genuinely perplexed. (Is she to be trusted?) 'Perhaps she thinks you're meeting her there.'

'Where?'

'Wherever you're having lunch.'

Where indeed. Another thought strikes. 'She would have passed me if she'd gone out.'

'Did you come through the main entrance?'

'Of course.'

'Perhaps Karin went out the back way. The car park's round...'

'Yes, I know.' Wasting time here, I'm already on the move. Along the landing. Down the sweep of stair towards the main exit. Stop. The odd idea strikes that there is a trap for me out front - the white van. Illogical, but... Change direction, turn and run instead through to the function hall. Empty, chairs stacked to the side. I know from previous experience there's access to the car park from a corridor behind the stage. Fortunately it's a fire exit so no lock to bar me, and I'm bursting into the

74

open - just in time to see the sunflower MX-5 slip clear of the car park and vanish into the one-way system.

'Karin!'

Too late. Run helplessly to the street but the car's already out of sight. What's going on? Did she know I was coming? Did she see Ruth's entry in her diary? Left to avoid me? Spirited away? Or am I just unlucky to have missed her? Do I dare to think she'll feel unlucky to have missed *me*? When she returns and the receptionist tells her I came... will she be disappointed? Will she call me, maybe?

Not sure what to do next I wander back up through the car park. The fire exit door yawns open, a reminder of my urgency and the futility of my chase. I try to close it from the outside, part of an effort to regain my composure, but I'd have to go back inside to secure it properly and I don't want to do that, so I give up and leave the door open though it nags at me like an unfinished chore. Down the slope of the car park again. I consider the option of squatting on the low wall to wait for Karin coming back. There's a sandwich shop just across the road, presently with a little queue of office workers to serve. I could join that to kill some time, then eat out here - a valid excuse for loitering in the area, anonymous, just another pen pusher having his lunch in the sunshine.

They are far too efficient in the sandwich shop, working quickly through the queue, and I'm served with tuna sandwich, apple and a finger-burning plastic cup of tea in little over five minutes. Even eating as slowly as I deliberately do - chewing morsel by morsel like someone with digestion OCD and nibbling my apple to the slenderest of cores - I can't make my lunch on the low wall last much longer than half an hour, and still Karin's car hasn't reappeared. I manage to waste another few minutes meticulously cleaning my fingers with the paper napkin provided by the shop and carefully gathering up my debris to deposit in the litter bin at the car park entrance. I wish I hadn't been so fastidious.

Crushed in among the empty crisp bags and coke cans in the bin, its head almost severed from the broken stem, is a single red rose. Execution. I have a strange, fleeting sense as I lean over and stare that there's a guillotine whistling down on me and any second my own decapitated head is going to land with a thud next to the flower. I grasp the sides of the bin and now there's a wave of nausea rising. I have to straighten up and gasp for air to stop vomiting all over the rubbish. Could Karin have done this? Surely not.

I have to walk away, clear my head, try to figure out what's happening here, where I stand, what I can do. This is not my Karin reacting like this. She just wouldn't. Someone's pulling her strings, I know it - it's the same thing that started after Ruth's death when Karin lost control. Of course she did, that's to be expected, and obviously she needed professional help at the time. Been there, got the tee shirt. But a year later? No, there's such a thing as over-protection. She needs to be given an opportunity to adjust, rebuild, come back to what we knew before. Yes, with a changed perspective, naturally, but we were so grounded and that's what she needs right now. That's exactly what Ruth is trying her best to communicate, poor darling, but she's not getting through, or her messages are being blocked, just as mine are. I don't believe Karin was even allowed to see that rose, she knows nothing about it. My letter was almost certainly intercepted. Our meeting prevented. Who was in the car with her - was she even driving? I know now I'll have to be a lot more subtle than this in future. More devious. I need to work out how I can get to see her on her own.

There's no point in my waiting around the car park now. Plan B required. It comes to me, or the germ of it, during a long, meandering walk back to the flat. Ruth may have been involved in conceiving the notion because it emerges through thinking about how, try as she might, she has been unsuccessful in influencing matters from beyond. Sorry, Ruth, but it's true. You are obviously unable to communicate directly with Karin, and if I'm prevented from getting to her myself I need someone who can. The person who pops into my mind is Jane. *You know I'll do anything to help you. Anything at all.* That's what she told me last night. Perhaps she'll agree to act in some way as an intermediary. She might find it easier than I can at the moment to get directly alongside Karin, speak to her on my behalf.

Will she agree, though? Promise or not, she might baulk at being asked to help me get back to Karin. More than a bit of jealousy involved, I imagine. As far as Jane sees it she's got everything to lose and nothing to gain. I'll have to work on this. First thing to do is to regain her trust and provide some assurance that I'm not without feeling for her. It's a little sneaky, but I suppose I need to give her some sort of hope... Hey, if it's false hope so be it - all's fair in love and war.

Having settled on at least a vague plan, and before I return to Gladstone Terrace, I pop in to the local supermarket. Buy a bunch of flowers, not an individual rose, and this time they're for Jane. I choose innocuous white ones, carnations, aiming to prevent her reading anything symbolic into them, and not particularly expensive - she hasn't Karin's class, wouldn't know the difference.

I sneak a glance through Jane's window as I'm negotiating the front door. Can't see her, but that's not proof positive she's out. Her bike is still in the same place in the hallway. Decide to give a little tap at her door on the off chance but I'm not surprised when she doesn't open up - if she has gone to work she's not likely to be home yet. I stand the flowers in water in my bathroom sink to keep them fresh for later, and fire up my laptop intending to do some work.

Except that I find my eBay account has been 'suspended indefinitely'. I can't log in, and when I check my in-box there's an automated email, apparently from the company, claiming I've committed a 'serious breach' of the company's Rules and Policies by 'listing counterfeit goods'. Obviously some mistake has been made somewhere. I'll have to get to the bottom of this - my livelihood, such as it is, depends on it these days. Before I can investigate further my phone rings.

A female voice, hesitant. 'Hello. Er, my piano hasn't been tuned for a good few years now. Does it cost more...?'

'Sorry?'

'I mean, could you give me a quote? Or would you need to look at it first?'

'Who is this?'

'Sorry.' Pause. 'I was hoping to get my piano tuned.'

'What?'

'Doesn't someone at this number tune pianos?'

'No. Where did you...?'

'Sorry, perhaps I wrote it down wrong. Just a card in the corner shop. Sorry to have bothered you.' And she rings off.

In the space of two minutes I've discovered my online account suspended and been asked for a service I don't offer. Am I living in some parallel universe? What did she mean she saw a card in the corner shop? Not *our* corner shop? In a state of dazed curiosity I go along there to investigate. The Asian shopkeeper acknowledges me as I appear in the doorway, steps up to the counter ready to serve, so I nod and smile back at him, pointing at the ads in the window. No milk today.

There are two postcards offering buggies for sale. A half-size snooker table, *slight tear on cloth near black spot, otherwise imaculate.* (Unlike your spelling.) Wanted: WWII German militaria, *best prices paid.* Under Services: baby-sitting; steam cleaning; garden maintenance. (Who has gardens big enough to maintain around here?) No piano tuners. What gnaws at me - and this is the reason I came round to look at these cards as if this were the one place in town to display them - is that the only person with whom I have recently had conversations about *a)* shop corner ads and *b)* my online sales venture is Jane. Adds up. Could she be playing silly buggers - making some spurious complaint to eBay; sticking up small ads with my phone number on them to get people to call me - and if so, why? Could the woman on the phone have been Jane herself? How does she even know my number? I can't recall giving it to her. Has she been snooping? Why? For what possible purpose? Is this her way of smoking out more gen on me? I've already revealed the essentials of my private life (regrettably). What more does she want? The jury's still out on Jane - maybe it would be a mistake to give her flowers.

But if I don't recruit her help, who else can I rely on? Cody? I've heard nothing from him since his boast in the pub that he'd have the Ruth mystery *totally nailed in a week*. I feel confined, claustrophobic. It eventually becomes exhausting being alone, no matter how much you might like your own company. Oh, Karin, Karin, Karin, you're trapped like I am. If only I could release you I'd set us both free.

I have no solid reason to suspect this stupid business today is Jane's doing. Until it proves otherwise I'll go with my plan. First off, I'll give her the flowers, see how she reacts. As long as she seems halfway normal I'll ask her to help me get in direct contact with Karin. One sneaky strategy would be to tell Jane it's to discuss a divorce - that might make her willing. As long as she doesn't say that to Karin.

Back at the house I try knocking at Jane's door again. Still no answer so I retrieve the flowers from my wash basin, prop them up against her door with a note. *Not seen you around today. Can we talk? A.* Wonder about adding an *x* or two but decide against.

It takes me an hour in front of the computer screen before I'm satisfied that I've found the right balance between hurt, indignity and pleading in the draft of my email requesting eBay to restore my seller account. Another hour lying flat on my bed thinking - frankly, worrying about what will happen if they don't. This is my only supportable source of income. It's hard enough as it is to survive while I work on getting back with Karin. What else am I supposed to do? Piano tuning?

The sudden clarity is like fresh water in my face, snapping my eyes open. Of course. Now I realise that Ruth has once again been the agent of a sequence of events that at first struck me as weird but now I see is neither strange nor random. Her purpose is clear - to lead me to a new, inspirational, brilliant idea for my reunion with Karin, just the two of us together, in the best possible surroundings.

VII

Other than some careful preparation there is nothing I can do to execute my plan until late afternoon, so there is no rush up in the morning. I lie in, thinking through contingencies. Or so I kid myself I'm doing - I can't help drifting off at regular intervals, lost in scenes of a future with Karin once again at my side. I can feel the litheness of her body next to me, that delicate, fragrant scent of her, the wisp of hair like a sigh across my shoulder. She moves in closer as I turn, cup my hand under her breast...

There's a rightness to it. How we are meant to be. The whole earth lies with us in that moment, the world holding its breath, not to disturb. Sun with a warm smile on its face. Nature wishing us well. No people at all but the two of us. No-one to spoil our peace, tear her away, crush the petals of the rose.

I have to get up eventually. Open the window in my room to let the air in, probably for the first time since I came here. How long it has seemed to be, especially when I've spent every day thinking maybe this could be the last that I'll have to stay away from her. Well, now the day really is here, as long as it plays out as I've rehearsed it in my head. It's up to me, and I'm ready for it. Just need that little bit of good fortune along the way - and I'm surely due. Anyway you can help, Ruth, would be much appreciated.

To business. Still wearing nothing but my boxers I get my suitcase from under the bed, lay out the various tools and materials needed. I use the screwdriver to take out the access panel in the bathroom where I hid the note I found in Karin's kitchen.

Hi Abi Sorry, did we agree Monday is cooker cleaning day? Maybe you could do it today instead? Thanks, Karin x.

Abi is obviously new to the job, which suits me, and not too meticulous, which might work to my advantage. Just a little convincing accreditation needed - and here I'm playing to one of my strengths. I already have Filofax paper the same as Karin's (I think we even bought it together) and the necessary penmanship with my good hand though, despite my confidence in this area, I can't stop myself shaking with nervous excitement as I end my version of a note with her signature followed by that dainty little *x*. Scrap three botched attempts before I'm satisfied with the result.

A couple of slightly out-of-date yoghurts from the fridge does for my lunch. I'm tempted by a can of lager in there too but I resist, not wanting to risk Abi being put off by even the merest trace of alcohol. Instead I wash thoroughly, shave and spray myself with a good dose of man perfume before suiting up as neatly as my meagre wardrobe allows me to. Dress for success. I'm ready. Everything I've used for my preparation goes back into the case and under the bed except for the note I've prepared, which folds neatly into my trouser pocket, and my old tuning hammer which slips into the deep inside pocket of my coat along with the screwdriver - just another contingency. I consider the photo on the bedside cabinet, decide against taking it with me and store that in the suitcase with the rest of the stuff. I can come back for it later.

About to leave the room when my mobile bips, giving me a start. It's a text message from Cody of all people - I'd almost forgotten his existence, never mind that he has my number.

Got news for ya. Come to my office. BRING THE CASH.

By his 'office' he means the bench next to his Big Issue pitch. What can he possibly have to tell me that I don't already know? Besides, I can't go and see him now - my schedule is for a steady walk to Beech Grove and arrival perfectly on time. Cody can whistle for the rest of his money.

Jane's bike is still parked in the hallway - second day running she hasn't used it for work. Curiously, the flowers I bought her are still propped up against her door with my note attached. Either she's deliberately ignoring them (unlikely) or she didn't return to the house last night. That bouquet being there irritates me for some reason, an unfinished piece of business. What to do? I still have her key in my pocket. With a rush of energy fed by impatience and without proper consideration I step across to unlock her door, sweep up the flowers and take them inside.

Jane's room is empty. Nothing seems to have been disturbed since I looked in yesterday morning. Bike helmet still hanging on the door - no coat or bag. Quick check under her pillow; no diary. The letters to Mr Robson still unopened in her drawer. She must be away for a few days - I'm surprised she didn't mention it.

Bunch of flowers in my left hand; what am I supposed to do with these? I run a little water and place them in her washbasin, propped against the mirror. Caught by my own reflection I sit down for a minute on Jane's bed, staring at myself. Have I changed much over the months? What is Karin going to make of me? Tidied myself up but I definitely look worse than I did a year ago. A visit to the hairdresser might have been a good move. Too late now. My face is peakier, puffier. Too many lonely days eating rubbish and ready meals. And months of misery - it takes its toll. Try smiling. Not like that - that just looks weird. Try interested. Thoughtful. I'll be fine when I see her. She'll light me up.

What am I doing, I can't leave those flowers there, Jane will know I've been in her room. Maybe I should take them with me, give them to Karin. But how does that square with what I say to Abi? Maybe I should just dump them in a bin on the way.

Beyond my reflection a shadow passes across the daylight in the room - what was that? I spring off the bed and move quickly to the window. What? Jane? Ruth? The white van? Christ, it's Mr Chatterjee. He's unlocking the front door.

Did he see me? What if he comes in here? How can I explain being alone in another tenant's bedsit? I can hear him chuntering in the hallway, muttering about Jane's bike. He'll definitely come in here to complain. Well, so what? Why shouldn't I be in my friend's room, just chilling while she's away. I kick my shoes off, lie on the bed. Chill. Watch the door. Struggle out of my coat, still lying down, toss it to the end of the bed. Watch the door.

There's a knock, but it's not on Jane's door, it's on mine across the hall. What's he want with me? I get up again, tiptoe to the door in my socks to listen. He knocks again, doesn't call out. Only waits a few seconds before I hear the jingle of his keys. Bastard's letting himself into my room. Who does he think he is? What's he after?

Across the hallway the door shuts. Has he gone in, or just popped his head in to check, then left? I listen for the front door opening, but it doesn't. Bastard's in my room with the door closed. What's he doing in there?

I strain my ears to listen. Cheek pressed against the panel so long it sticks to the paintwork. I can't hear anything. Time crawls by. I slither down onto my backside and wedge myself into the corner, ear at the door jamb. Still nothing. What's he doing in there?

Is he waiting for me? While I'm crouched here waiting for him to go, is he sitting on my bed waiting for me to come back? Why? I don't owe him anything. Why don't you *fuck off?*

We could be stuck like this for hours. How long has he been here? I glance at my watch surreptitiously as if I think he's listening out with bat ears to pounce on any movement. Christ, is that the time? I'm already behind schedule. Why don't I just go over there, find out what he's after? For some reason I don't want to. Can't put my finger on it but I have a sense that whatever it is is going to disturb my plans in some way. Another interference - I can't be dealing with it. I need to get away.

I'm going to sneak out through the window. Why didn't I think of that before? Very softly I put on my shoes and coat, move towards the

81

window, then have to double back when I remember I need to check Jane's door is locked from the inside, and back to the window.

Which won't damn well open. It's a sash type, like the one in my own room that I pulled up easily enough this morning, but this damn thing won't budge. At first I don't put all my weight into it because I'm afraid of the noise it'll make, but even when I throw all caution aside and heave upward with all my strength I can't get it to shift one centimetre. It's jammed, I guess, with years of being painted over. Either that or it's locked with a key that's probably been missing since the war. Ironic when I consider it was Mr Chatterjee who suggested Jane get into her locked room through the window. Oh, yeah, try it, mate.

I take out the screwdriver from the inside pocket of my coat, wondering about the possibility of scoring a line through the paintwork at the edge of the window frame to loosen it. About to try when I hear a noise from the direction of the hallway. Dive down instinctively and swivel round, my screwdriver pointing at the door against attack. But Jane's door doesn't open - it's a heavier sound at the front entrance. Mr Chatterjee is leaving, a fact I confirm by raising myself on my elbows to see a retreating figure in a black coat through the bottom of the glass. Thank god.

Force myself to wait another five minutes to lessen the risk he might still be in the neighbourhood, but as soon as the five minutes has passed I'm in panic mode. Well behind time now. I should check in my room to see what Mr Chatterjee might have been up to or whether he's left a note, but I have less than no time to waste now. Seeing Jane's bike squatting in the hallway gives me a great idea - I'll borrow it and make up time getting to Beech Grove; Jane's not here to object.

I end up walking (half-jogging) two-thirds of the way to Karin's house. I'd barely gone a mile on the bike when I felt the bump of metal on road under my backside. Off to inspect, and found just what I feared - a flat back tyre, the rubber already starting to crack with my riding on it. And of course no pump. Maybe that was why Jane stopped using her bike. Impossible to carry on, I pushed it along on foot for a few more yards but soon abandoned the bike against a hedge with the vague thought of picking it up later and returning it to Jane. I had other things to think about, and time was against me.

As a result I'm less composed than I wanted to be when I ring Karin's front door bell. It takes a while for Abi to answer - I'm getting desperate, thinking I've missed her, then I see her peeking with a degree of anxiety out of the window. She has some sort of turban arrangement covering most of her hair this time, but I'm pretty sure it's the same woman; same build, same uniform. God, what if it isn't? While I'm working through the implications she disappears from the window. Soon there's a shuffle and shifting of locks as she comes to open the door, or half-opens it. Try to slow my breathing down.

'Yes?'

'Hi, it's Karl. Piano tuner. Sorry I'm a little late. It's Abi, isn't it?' (Hope so.)

She looks confused, taken unawares. 'Yes. Sorry, I'm not understanding.'

'I'm Karin's cousin, Karl, come to tune her piano. Told me she left you a note about it.'

'Note?' Abi turns her head instinctively towards the kitchen, but her hand stays firmly on the handle of the door. 'No, I haven't seen...' Looks back at me. Blank. My move.

'Hmm, strange. Karin definitely said... Well, can I help you look for it? I know where...' Abi stands firm. 'Right, suppose you'll want some ID. Hang on.' I fumble conspicuously about my pockets. Feeling the tuner hammer clink against the screwdriver in my inside pocket, I consider bringing it out as evidence - tool of the trade - but she might misinterpret and panic. My hand closes instead on my mobile. 'Not sure if I've got anything, didn't expect... Oh, hang on...' and as planned I take out the phone, thumb through the contact list to show her. 'Here she is. See, I've got her picture on my mobile. Cousin Karin.'

Abi stares at the image. 'You want me to call her?' she says.

(Christ, no, that's the last thing I want. The picture was just to reassure... Come on, Alex, stay calm.)

'Oh yeah, yeah. Good idea. What time is it? Er, she did say she'd be in an important meeting at her studio this afternoon. But if you really think you need to speak to her personally, I'm sure she'll understand you had to interrupt. Just a pity you missed the note she left. Should I call first and say 'Abi insists on speaking to you personally'? Or do you want to just go for it, tell her yourself?'

Trying to keep my face as neutral as possible. Calling her bluff. She calls mine, holds out her hand for the phone. Damn.

'Hang on, I'll get the number for you.'

Check the screen. Two numbers. If I choose the landline it won't be Karin's studio; the telephone behind Abi will ring. Can I use the distraction to get inside? Then what? The other number is from the silent call I took at the cemetery. Is it even Karin's? Will she answer when she sees my number on her screen? And if she does, what will she say to Abi?

Which number to choose. Russian roulette. Help me, Ruth. I make eye contact with Abi. Smile, as my thumb moves from one number to another. Trusting in Ruth, press randomly. Give Abi the phone.

Abi's ear on the receiver. We wait. The phone in the hall doesn't ring. So it's the mobile. My throat tightens. I can hear the tone repeating at Abi's ear. It stops.

'She does not answer.'

'No. I expect she's still in her meeting. Won't want to be disturbed. She knows it's only me.' Self-deprecation. A trust-me smile for Abi.

She hands back the phone. Weighing me up.

'Come, please. I will take you to the piano.'

Try to hide my relief. 'Oh, don't worry about that.' I close the front door behind us and follow her through the hall. 'I know exactly where everything is. I've been here many times. You must be pretty new, aren't you, Abi? That's why we haven't met before.'

I'm trying to come across casual, familiar, breezy even, but Abi is still uptight. At the entrance to the front room she glances at a mannish watch on her wrist. 'Will your work take long?'

'No, no. Not too long. Actually, could I bother you for a glass of water? I'll get it myself if you want to get on. Just it's very warm today.'

'Please.' She indicates the piano at the far side of the room. 'I will bring water.'

I wait for her to retreat to the back and for the cold tap to start running before I follow, popping my head round the kitchen door. 'Oh, could I borrow your vac for a minute? I usually give the inside of the joanna a bit of a spring clean before I start tinkering.' As I'm speaking my hand goes to my pocket for the folded note which I push halfway under the letter rack on the kitchen unit. All innocent and smiling when Abi turns with the glass of water.

'Thanks. Is that OK about the vacuum cleaner?'

She nods and I take the glass from her. Minutes later while I'm gazing under the top board of the piano cabinet she wheels in a small Dyson, one I recognize and that gives me an absurd rush of pleasure as if it were a long-lost pet. It's the machine my immaculate Karin keeps for small jobs like this. Not, I imagine, the same that Abi would have been using when I broke in to steal Ruth's picture.

'Thanks. Oh, sorry, forget my head if it were loose. Is there a pen I could borrow? I just need to make a little note.'

There are pens next to the letter rack. Abi, unfortunately, also has one in the pocket of her uniform, and that's the one she gives me.

'Ah no, I don't want to take yours.'

84

'It's OK.'

'Thanks. Mmm, and a sheet of paper? Just off a note pad or something. If you don't mind. Sorry to be such a nuisance.'

Abi leaves the room without speaking or even acknowledging this last request. Did she understand me? Maybe she is fed up with this pest of a piano tuner demanding stuff. She doesn't return immediately. I take off my coat, lay it carefully across the arm of the white sofa, plug in the vacuum cleaner and return to the piano to poke about for specks of dust in the cabinet. Thinking frantically in the meantime but I'm out of ideas for what to do next if Abi doesn't come across my forgery.

The noise from the Dyson masks the sound of her return - I almost hit my head on the top board when she touches under my shoulder as I'm stretching into the far recesses of the baby grand.

'Karl, I have the note.'

I emerge from the innards and turn to Abi, expecting she'll give me the blank paper I'd asked for. But what she also has in her hand is my note. *My* note. Or, from her point of view, the note from Karin. And I know she must have read it because her expression is a mixture of generosity and apology. No more suspicion - I'm well and truly in.

The note reads: *Hi Abi I'm expecting my cousin Karl this afternoon - he's going to tune the piano for me. Just let him in and, if you don't mind, provide coffee or whatever as needed. Don't feel you have to hang around if he's still busy when it's time for you to go. He'll probably wait to see me anyway, so just leave him to it. Thanks, Karin x.*

'It was stuck under the... thing,' Abi explains. 'I didn't see. Sorry.'

'That's OK. No harm done. Easy mistake. Karin will be pleased to hear you're so security conscious.'

'No.' She looks concerned. 'Please don't tell.'

'Fine, fine, no problem. It's our little secret, Abi, OK?'

She smiles. 'Would you like coffee?'

'Tea would be nice. Little bit of milk, no sugar. Thanks.'

I find the piano perfectly in tune. Can imagine Karin playing it as she whiles the evenings away alone - no Alex, no Ruth. Practising dance accompaniments, of course, but music for us, too, late at night. Something wistful. Chopin, naturally. Perhaps some Liszt. I stroke the keys lightly with my fingers, visualising Karin's more graceful, slender ones caressing them, coaxing soft sounds from the instrument like a gentle seduction. I try a few notes of the Adagio, playing from memory, even more slowly than the work demands because of my physical

85

limitation, but it suits the mood. Play a little more, eyes closed, concentrating.

'Is there anything else I must do?'

The voice brings me back to the room, though not immediately to the moment. I have the idea Karin is asking, and I consider the question with my eyes still shut, grasping for what she means. When I look up Abi is there in the doorway, dressed in her outdoor coat. Of course, Abi. Her coat looks unseasonably heavy - I wonder if she's only recently arrived in this country, came prepared for the cold she'll have heard about.

'No, no, Abi. I'm good. I'll just finish up here and maybe wait for Karin if she's not going to be too long. Thanks for all your help.'

'So sorry I didn't see...'

'Not a problem.'

I wait for her to move off down the hallway, then shift myself from the piano seat to the bay window to check she's really going. Hugging myself for how well my plans are finally working out.

A shiver of shock; step back. Parked in the roadway directly in front of the house is a white MPV van. I'm hit with a sudden irrational fear that I've been set up - they know I'm here and they've come to get me. Who or what *they* are I have no notion, but panic sets in on a wave of nausea. I need to defend myself - where's that screwdriver? The front door slams - they're already in the house.

But it's only Abi going out. She has a filled carrier bag, presumably of cleaning stuff, and she pauses briefly at the end of the drive for someone inside the van to open the sliding side door. Another woman, also black, who shifts along the seat to let her in. Abi closes the door behind her and settles back into the seat, perhaps catches a glimpse of me looking out from the house as the van moves off.

I've been so calm to this point - why am I letting nerves get the better of me now? Because I've been almost as close before and always something has happened to spoil it. Something beyond bad luck. I know there are forces working against us, Karin and me, though she has not always been able to recognize them for what they are - she's in many ways so trusting, so naive, despite the sophistication she displays to the external world. I know it better than anyone. Nobody knows her better than I do; maybe better even than Karin herself. And I know the odds ranged against us. Ruth knows them too now; that's why she's here, to help redress the balance. Which is why this time it will be different.

I stand by the window a while longer, recovering myself. More than that - affirming my position. I have a right to be here; why should I stay out of view. A neighbour, woman well over pension age, goes by with her

86

little terrier dog. She sees me watching her from the window and I raise my hand slightly, just a little acknowledgement. The woman looks away - it is, I have to admit, that kind of neighbourhood. I return to my piano.

Playing relieves the tedium of waiting. The good news is this practice is giving me some belief I can eventually get back to something like my old self if the third operation on my hand proves successful. I've been thinking, I'm sure Karin won't mind paying for me to go private next time to speed things up; the investment will be worth it if it means I can start playing professionally again. I like the idea of being able to earn my keep - I'm not expecting to be some sort of house husband for the rest of our lives together. (Don't worry Abi, your job is safe.)

What is it now, just into October. I would say by the end of next summer... that's going to be my target. I'll tell Karin. By the end of the summer I'll be ready to start taking things up professionally. Practise every day here while she's at the studio (maybe help out there sometimes if she wants). Get back in contact with people, set things up ready to start again. It's not going to be easy, but living here, having Karin on side, I know it's do-able.

I immerse myself once again in Ravel. Following the dots this time, full concentration. The minutes pass and now I'm hardly aware of them. Miss the sound of her car pulling up onto the drive, but as my fingers lift from the keyboard and follow the last sustained note to a fade I distinctly hear the click of the front door lock. She's here.

Do I go to her immediately? Or do I stay silent, watch for her reaction as she comes into the room and sees me sitting here? I'd like to be playing as she walks in. Not *Karin's Song*, that's for another day. The Ravel, so familiar to us, is the perfect choice. A re-introduction, a reminder. I'll wait a moment - she'll be taking her coat off, maybe her shoes. As soon as I see her I'll start to play. Just as it was before, just as we were before. I have to play this as well as I possibly can. Gentle, gentle on the opening bars.

Where is she? My hands are starting to shake slightly, poised over the keys. Not nerves - I'm excited because she's here, not nervous. Just the strain of waiting to play. My wrists beginning to ache. Come on, Karin.

Where is she? Did I make a mistake? No, I definitely heard the front door open. She's always so quiet about the place. Listen, listen. I let my wrists and shoulders relax, focus on listening for her moving through the house. Has she gone upstairs? Some faint sounds of movement from above. She's changing into more comfortable clothes. The idea makes me smile.

I ease out of my shoes, loosen the tie I'd put on to reassure Abi. Leave the piano seat, shift across to the doorway to listen more closely. Nothing to be heard downstairs. Step through into the hallway. Check the kitchen; empty. I pause at the foot of the stairs. She *is* up there. The moment overwhelms me. It comes to me she knows I'm here. She's waiting for me. My hand trembles on the banister rail. Softly, softly climb the stairs.

Action on the landing. A swish of a coat as she moves to the stair head. Something bumps against the banister rail. She takes the first steps down. Sees me and stops at the turn of the stair. We both stop. Time stops.

Green coat. A suitcase dropped at her feet. It's not Karin, it's Ruth. Shocked. Then furious.

'What the hell do you think you're doing? How dare you! How dare you!'

Rushing down the stairs. Attacking me. Small fists. Real live fists against my chest and shoulders.

'Are you trying to ruin my mother's life? Who the fuck do you think you are? You're ruining my mother's life!'

'Ruth!'

She pushes me hard. I fall backwards. Helpless. Weightless. Thud. Thud. Thud. Crack. Red flash behind my eyes. Black. Dull black. Light, too much light.

She's there, in a mist, above me. There's blood trickling down the back of my collar.

'Ruth.'

'Ruth's dead, you fucking moron. Don't you dare say her name to me. Ruth's dead. I wish it was you!' Sobbing. 'I wish it was you.'

UNWANTED ATTENTION

VIII

I'm surprised I recognized him as easily as I did, even from twenty feet away and just the side view really. Especially considering I'd only seen him maybe two or three times in my life, and it was well over a year since the last time. I suppose that shows how much of an effect he had on us, and I don't mean in a good way. Anyway I'm glad I spotted him when I did because I was about to walk straight by and god knows how I would have reacted if he'd said something or, worse, jumped up at me. Luckily he seemed to be just staring into space and hadn't noticed, so I took a sharp left and went the long way through the square where the fountain is. I was so agitated, certain he was going to look across any second and realise who it was, maybe start chasing after me. But at least on the outside I tried to play it cool, casual. I remember brushing my fingers through the waters in the fountain as I passed, acting like it was a normal day. But I held my breath until I was well away from the park and across the other side of the road. Well away from him.

I'm pretty good at hiding my feelings generally, but officially useless when I'm with my best friend Emily. We met for coffee and she said straightaway. 'Alex, what's up? You look like you've seen a ghost.'

'I wish I had, though. He's real enough, unfortunately. Guess who I've just seen in the park.'

'Well, a guy, obviously. Who?'

'That weirdo.'

'What weirdo?' She took a second to cotton on. 'You mean, thingy? Your mum's bloke?'

'Don't call him that. Do NOT call him that.'

'Sorry. Was it him, though?'

'I'm practically certain. Or his double.'

'God.' She put a hand out across the table and I let her squeeze mine. 'You all right?'

'Yeah.'

'Thought he was supposed to keep well away.'

'I don't know exactly. Maybe it's run out or whatever. Been more than a year.'

'Should've been locked up.'

'I think they put him away somewhere for a bit. Nuthouse probably. Not sure. But he's back, anyway.'

'Have you told her?'

'Not yet.' Truth is, I was in a dilemma about that. My first instinct was to call mum straightaway, then I thought that means bringing him up in her mind again when she's hopefully forgotten all about him. As far as I'm aware he hasn't been in touch or tried to see her for months, so why should I be the one to remind her? On the other hand maybe she needs to be warned he could be back on the scene.

'I don't know what to do for the best.'

'Afraid she'll freak out?'

'To be quite honest, Em, I'm thinking about the possible consequences for me as well. Look what happened last time. What with him and with poor Ruthie dying, and dad dying, that was my gap year lost, changed my plans for uni...'

'You're not blaming Karin, though.'

'Of course not. She never asked me to do any of that. But she needed me, still does. I have to be *available*. And that's totally his fault, not hers.'

It was a horrible day, the day Ruth died, and dad died. The worst day of my life. And how horrendous it must have been for mum. I was at school when I heard, taken out of last lesson. I knew it had to be the worst news even before Mrs Hind came through to the classroom - I could feel her eyes on me through the glass of the door. I looked up and caught her staring right at me, and it was as if she was scared and at the same time teary. And of course I knew then that her appearing at the door had somehow to do with me. And I remember I looked away from her, avoiding eye contact for some reason, looked out of the classroom window. And what kept running through my mind was, *but it's just a normal day. A normal sunny day.*

When I think about it I suppose if it hadn't been sunny dad might not have decided to take Ruth out and all this might not have happened. It's not something he normally did on his visits and actually we didn't either - being totally honest Ruth could be really difficult to handle if she found herself out of her comfort zone; she'd get panicky and go into a sort of paddy, and there'd be no holding her then, she was surprisingly strong. Even in the early days, when she'd come back with us for the odd weekend, sleeping in her old bedroom, familiar territory you'd think, she could cause ructions. Mum and I learned that lesson long ago. All in all it was safer not to go beyond the grounds, close enough for the staff to help if we needed them, which we did a couple of times. Mostly though she was a sweetie in her own not-quite-with-us sort of way. There's a lush photo which a nurse took of us in the gardens on Easter Monday. Ruth, mum and me. That was another lovely fine day. To think, it was only a few months before the accident.

91

The police wondered if she might have thrown a wobbly while they were driving along, distracted dad somehow or maybe even attacked him - they couldn't think of any other reason why the car should have come off the road in broad daylight in good weather. No other vehicle involved as far as they could work out. I don't know. Mum always said dad drove much too fast, but then they dissed each other about most things, like divorced couples do, plus he used to call her Penelope Pitstop, so who's the blackest kettle or whatever the saying is.

Mrs Hind was totally class with me when she took me into her office, though she was finding it hard to keep the tears away herself. Just for my sake - obviously she never knew Ruth personally. Seen my dad a couple of times, I believe. Despite her efforts I was in a complete state, so how mum took the news with that madman around, hanging onto her, I can't even imagine. Must have been an absolute nightmare.

Not that we knew he was a madman until then, of course. We didn't even know him at all. Just the fucking piano tuner. He'd worked on the studio piano a couple of times for mum but I'd only seen him maybe once at the house, when he came the time before. Actually yes, I remember, because I was supposed to be meeting up with Emily and I had to house-sit instead when mum had to go out unexpectedly and she didn't want to cancel this bloke at short notice. She left me a sweet little note. *Thanks, Alex. I love you. x* Typical Karin, always begging favours but always very grateful to you for helping out. She didn't deserve all this hassle. So anyway, I was left in the house alone with him. To think, I made him a cup of tea, offered him biscuits, and him as nicey-nice as pie. Commented on my earrings. Fucking freak.

I say *freak* now but neither of us had any idea he had a thing for mum until the next time, that horrible day. He'd arrived in the afternoon as arranged to tune the piano, but we found out later he'd probably been hanging round outside the house all morning. One of our neighbours going off to work saw somebody leaning against one of the trees across the road, munching on his breakfast as cool as you like. The neighbour went back in to put his burglar alarm on. Another said they were sure they'd seen some guy looking up at the house a couple of weeks before - a bit suspicious, she thought. Typical of our neighbourhood that nobody thought to mention anything to us at the time - of course they were all tea and sympathy for a few days afterwards.

The strange thing is I can't help the thought that mum getting that terrible phone call in some way saved her from something else. I mean, what was he planning to do, alone with her in the house? His reaction to the phone call was the weirdest thing, but supposing it hadn't happened? What might he have done to her in his own sweet time?

What amazed me was that he never went to jail or even had a proper trial or anything. I suppose it was because mum didn't particularly want to press charges - she'd just lost her eldest child and her ex-husband for god's sake - but you'd have thought the police would do something off their own bat, first offence or not. And it was an offence. Terrifying a woman in her own home, that's got to be some sort of crime. Stalking. That's definitely criminal. I think he was given some sort of restraining order but mainly all he got as far as I could see was molly-coddling and people trying to help with his 'problem'. Never mind our problem with him. Not that I'm against people getting help - poor Ruthie, for example - but there should be some sort of punishment for people like him, plus they're maybe beyond help at all, maybe just perverted full stop. Obviously whatever 'help' or treatment or therapy he had did him no good whatsoever if he's back on the scene again. Roaming the streets. Too close, far too close to mum. I tell you, sitting on that park bench, he looked distinctly off it. I had a very bad feeling the moment I clapped eyes on him. I just knew he was going to be trouble.

I didn't ring mum about seeing him in the park. I should have, because then maybe getting his note would not have come as such a shock to her. When I came home at the weekend she had anxiety written all over her face. She showed me the note almost as soon as I walked in.

Staying off limits, don't worry, but I may have some information regarding Ruth. Please call.

'He's back,' she said. Really hollow, like she was at the bottom of a pit.

'Mum, I know.' And I told her what I had seen on the Wednesday. Said sorry. All the colour drained from her face.

'Why doesn't he leave me alone? I am nothing to him. What does he want from me?'

'His number's there. Let me ring him. Tell him to keep away from you. Tell him to keep the fuck away from both of us.'

'Alexandra, please don't swear.'

'He makes me swear. Should have done it before. Maybe we should have both sworn at him. Kicked him. Scratched his fucking eyes out. Maybe then he'd get the message.'

'Give me a hug. I'm sorry, darling.'

'Mum, you've nothing to be sorry about. It has nothing to do with you. Don't keep blaming yourself.' And we hugged tight right there in the hallway. Cried. Before I'd even taken off my coat.

Later, after tea, we were able to talk a little more calmly on the subject. Mum brought it up.

'What can he mean, he has some information concerning Ruth? How could that be?'

'He's a nutter, mum. It doesn't mean anything. He doesn't even know who Ruth was.'

'Do you think he has been snooping around, trying to find things out about the family so he can use it against me? I think his note is a... what do you call it when you threaten people with notes?'

'Blackmail?'

'Blackmail, yes.'

'He's just fishing. Anything to get close to you. You need to take the note to the police, let them deal with it. Don't get involved.'

'But that is getting involved, isn't it, if I call the police.'

'Well, yes, I suppose. Oh, I don't know. Let me think about it. Why don't you leave the note with me, let me deal with it.'

'Alex, you're nineteen years old. You have your studies to worry about. Let's not talk about it anymore. It's nothing. He's nothing.'

'Exactly.' I couldn't help smiling at her. She's trying to be brave. Trying to be nonchalant. Protective. Poor vulnerable mum.

We said no more about it all evening, but when she went up to have a soak in the bath I copied his number from the note into my phone, just in case. In the Name box I typed STRANGER DANGER in capitals. A little sick joke to myself.

We liberated a nice bottle of white wine from the garage fridge and watched a chick-flick together before we went to bed. The wine helped me fall asleep soon enough, but around two in the morning I was woken by the light being turned on at the stairway, then flooding into my bedroom as the door opened.

'What's wrong, mum, can't you sleep?'

She came to sit at the bottom of my bed. 'So sorry, Alex. Is it very late?'

'It doesn't matter.'

'I've been thinking... I can't get it out of my head. Do you think he had anything to do with the accident?'

'Who?'

'My stalker.'

'What? Mum, he was with you at the time. He was tuning our piano.'

'When I got the message he was, yes, but the crash happened long before that.'

'And miles away - he couldn't have been there.'

'Perhaps he tinkered with your father's car before he drove. Maybe that's what caused it.'

'Why would he do that?'

'To get rid of him, to be rid of Charles. So, in his mind, he could have me for himself. That's how they think, don't they, these crazy stalkers?'

'You've been watching too many films, mum. Anyway, you were already... I mean you'd not been with dad for years. This guy wouldn't know him from Adam.'

'Oh, but he does, he does. I mean, he did.' She moved closer to me. 'It was your father who recommended him when I needed someone to tune the studio piano. They used to work together.'

'Really? You mean he's a proper professional musician?'

'Used to be. Like a session man, but he was brought in to help on various live shows. He had an accident. Charles was with him. It was at a wrap party - you know, when they finished a tour or something. I don't know if he was drunk or what he was but he fell through a table. A glass table.'

'Oh, my god.'

'It was terrible, he told me. Blood everywhere. He cut his arm - nerves, arteries, everything. He almost died, you know, through loss of blood.'

'Stop it. You're almost making me feel sorry for him.'

'Well, I did, you know. I felt so sorry for him, because he couldn't play anymore, not professionally, and he was devastated. Completely devastated. Of course he had to do other things to make a living. So that's how he turned up in our lives. I just wanted to do something to help him. Then there was the funny coincidence of having the same first name as you. It felt like a connection. Like fate, I suppose.'

'You didn't fancy him?'

'Oh please, not at all. But I was nice to him. I think maybe I was too nice to him.'

'Too soft.'

'Maybe.'

We fell quiet. For the first time I began to have a notion of this guy as something other than a monster. Somebody real, with a past life.

'Imagine that, though,' I said after a while. 'Crashing through a glass table.'

We looked at each other, and for some reason we both started to giggle. A total fit of the giggles. I had to grab onto to mum to stop her falling off the bed, and she clung onto me tight, wrapping her arms around my back. We were shaking with laughter, holding on, then I noticed something had changed about mum's shaking. More like jerks, rising up from her tummy and her chest. She clung on so tight as if she never wanted to let go, and not laughing now, but sobbing. Real deep sobs.

'Oh, come on mum, come on. We were having some fun for once.'

'I know. I know. But I feel so guilty.'

'I've told you, you should never blame yourself for what he...'

'Guilty about Ruth. She should have stayed here with us. I should never have let her go into that place. She would still be here now.'

'Mum, you know it was impossible to care for Ruth here. It just became impossible.'

'If I'd given up work, looked after her full time.'

'She was past looking after. You know that. We've been through this.'

'I know. I know. But I miss her, Alex. I miss her so much.'

I put my open palm to the back of her head, patting her like a fretful child while she had her cry out. Once she quietened I broke away a little, holding her arms, studying her. Waiting for her to smile again.

'Come on,' I said. 'I'll snuggle in with you. There's more room in your bed.'

She nodded. And she allowed me to lead her across the landing, holding hands all the way. Poor mum.

I think I turned a bit paranoid - is that the expression? I felt as if someone was stalking me as well as mum. As if I was being watched, followed down the street. For example, when I was walking from halls to uni on Tuesday morning there was this lanky guy just a few steps behind me nearly all the way. When I crossed the street he crossed the street. He was probably just a student like me, going to a lecture, but it freaked me out; I felt like turning back for a few steps to see what he would do then, but I didn't because at the same time I realised I was being foolish. Then there was this man selling The Big Issue outside McDonalds. He seemed to be staring at me as I walked past, and I'd swear to god I saw him pointing his phone at me while I was waiting for the green man, as if he was taking a picture. Stupid maybe, but that's what it looked like to me. Paranoid.

The effect was to trap me inside myself. The whole idea of me living in halls during the week instead of travelling from home every day was so I could get involved with the social side of uni, take the chance to meet new people while I would still be close enough to mum for both of us to feel we were there for each other. But Fresher's Week had come and gone without me getting much involved at all, and now I felt even less like going out because of the stress and this weird feeling that both mum and I were being watched, followed, perved over. Em was still more or less the only person I was seeing socially, and she wasn't even at the university. It was depressing.

I felt guilty feeling sorry for myself when it was mum I was supposed to be looking out for. Especially when we found out that the real stalker was definitely back in action. She rang from the studio late Wednesday afternoon, just as I was about to go into a tutorial. I could tell she was upset as soon as we said our hellos.

'What is it?'

'I think he's outside. Or he's been around sometime today.'

'God, have you seen him?'

'No. I went down to the car to pick up some leaflets that I'd left in the boot, and there was a flower stuck under my windscreen wiper.'

'A flower?'

'A red rose. My heart almost stopped when I saw it. Just a flower for goodness sake, what is wrong with me?'

'No, it's terrible.'

'I ripped it out and threw it in the bin. It made me feel sick. I had to wash my hands afterwards as if I'd been touching something dirty.'

'Do you think he's still there?'

'I'm not sure. I don't believe so. I looked up and down the street and there was no sign. Or he's hiding. I keep looking out of the windows.'

'Have you called the police?'

'No.'

'Mum.'

'I don't want any fuss, especially not at work. It's bad for business. Could you imagine my girls turning up to dance if they think there's a pervert hanging around outside?'

She had a point.

'What about the staff? What have you said to them?'

'Nothing. Well, you know it's Barbara's first week on the job, and Frankie's so young. I don't want to stress them out. Don't worry, I'm fine. I just wanted to tell you. Sorry, I shouldn't...'

'I'll cut my tutorial. I'll come over there now.'

'Don't be silly, there's no need. I don't want to disturb what you're doing there, it's important for you.'

'Well, I'll come and stay over at the house tonight. Oh, damn...'

'What?'

'I promised Em I'd go to a concert with her tonight. She's had the tickets for months. I'll call her, see if there's someone else she can go with.'

'No, no,' mum insisted. 'Don't change anything for me. Listen, Alex, I've told you, you've got your own life to lead. You're young, this is an important time for you. I'm not having you giving up any more of yourself for my sake - you've already lost so much this past year. Go to your concert, I'll be absolutely fine. I'm a grown woman, you know.' She gave a little chuckle to reassure me, but the tension was plain as plain in her voice.

'What are you going to do about him though, mum? This could escalate, you know that.'

'I don't know what to do, I'll have to think about it. Let's talk things over when we can get together again.'

'I'm free tomorrow afternoon. Do you want to meet for lunch?'

'Yes, yes, that would be good. Would you be able to come over here about twelve-thirty? Maybe we could drive across to Deerholme, spend some moments with Ruthie too, some quiet time. Would you like that?'

'Course, yeah. I'll see you then, mum. And listen, make sure you leave work before it gets dark tonight. And check all the locks at the house.'

'I will.' She paused, then added, 'You know, I don't think he's violent, Alex. Just... disturbed. And very confused.'

'That's not what you said last weekend. You thought he'd tampered with dad's car.'

'Oh, that was me being over-dramatic. I'm a little paranoid, that's all.'

'Me too. I've been thinking the very same thing.'

'Well, *chill out* tonight, then.' The phrase didn't really suit her, especially in that Swedish way she said it. 'Give my love to Emily.'

'I will, mum. Bye, and *please* take care.'

I waited for her to ring off, and afterwards lingered uncertainly in the concrete stairwell where I'd stopped to take the call. I gazed blankly down at my screen. What could I possibly do to help? Started scrolling through the names on my phone looking, actually, to see whether I'd stored a number for any of the police or other professionals we'd been in contact with a while back. I came across *his* entry - STRANGER DANGER. Without really meaning to, and certainly with no thought of what on earth I was going to say, I pressed the call button. It seemed at first there wasn't going to be a connection. As I waited I could feel nausea rising from the pit of my stomach into the back of my throat. The voice shocked me when it came suddenly into my ear as if from the shadows behind.

'Hello?'

There was a slight slur in the voice as if the man who answered had been shaken awake, or been drinking. Was it him? I couldn't tell for certain. I opened my mouth to say something, warn him off - nothing came out.

'Hello?' He sounded wary, furtive. A suspicious character. I couldn't talk to him, pressed End. Stupid. Stupid.

Silence but for my heart thudding, then the phone rang in my hand, made me jump, echoing in the stairwell. STRANGER DANGER on the screen. Stupid girl. Stupid, stupid girl. I pressed to reject, stuffed the phone in my pocket. It rang again. STRANGER DANGER in my pocket. I felt for the button to stop it. Stop, stop, stop. I shut the damn thing down totally. Stupid girl. I rushed up the steps into the main building, jangly, massively late for my tutorial.

I was no proper company for Emily that night. The band was very good, but I just couldn't get into it. Miles away. At one point Em asked me if I had a crush on the keyboard player. It was only when she said it that I realised I must have been staring at the guy for ages. He was parked at the back of the stage and he seemed so absorbed, mostly looking down, almost as if he was playing for himself. But of course I wasn't really thinking of him at all, I was thinking about you know who. Wondering about his psyche. Wondering what he was going to do next.

I called mum straight after the gig and she assured me she was fine, just getting ready for bed. She'd made sure she left work at the same time as other people going for their cars so she wouldn't be alone in the car park, and she had a good look round before she got in, but there didn't seem to be anyone hanging about. She said the funny thing was when she was driving home she kept looking in her mirror, worried she was being followed, even though she's certain the guy doesn't have a car or didn't when he used to turn up for the piano tuning. That's what anxiety does.

Anxiety - tell me about it. There are just a couple of Metro stops between the university and mum's studio, but the journey there the next day seemed endless. I felt exposed and vulnerable as if it was last thing on a Saturday night not lunchtime on a Thursday. My nerves were so shot when I crossed the road to the Assembly Rooms it seemed as if the beeps on the pelican crossing were a warning to me. A huge truck was waiting for the lights to change and as I stepped onto the pavement there was such a noise from its air brakes I nearly died of fright. I'm sure somebody called out as well, but if they were trying to get my attention I wasn't waiting to find out. I practically ran up the steps to the studio; it was like a sinister game of chase, trying to reach home before someone taps you on the shoulder. Not knowing who or where the chaser is, or whether he's there at all. Running away from the bogeyman.

I'd hoped to compose myself before meeting up with mum but she was already waiting with her coat on behind the reception desk and she whisked me down the back stairs to the car park before I could catch my breath. Guess, like me, she couldn't wait to get away.

We hardly spoke until we were clear of the city. Mum stopped at a lay-by to put a silk scarf on and let the roof down, then we were off again, just a tad over the speed limit. She turned to me and smiled. 'Thelma and Louise,' she said.

'Who?'

'Two women driving away from their troubles. Strong women. Didn't you see the movie?'

'Was that the one where they drove off a cliff at the end?'

'Don't worry darling, we won't do that.'

She felt for my wrist with her left hand. I lifted it to stroke my cheek on the back of her fingers before returning her hand to the steering wheel; a hint she should take care with her driving.

On the whole she managed without too many alarms along the way, at least until we got to the burial ground when she almost collided with a van coming out through the gates, but that was more the van driver's fault than hers, swinging out into the road without looking. I imagine the workers get used to nobody being about much - unless there's a funeral the park is usually pretty deserted.

There was something out of place about mum's car in these surroundings - I suppose because there's a sort of vivacity, even a cheekiness to the MX-5 that seemed inappropriate here. She must have felt this too; not only did she slide the roof back up as soon as we stopped, she also spent a little time before we got out adjusting her scarf in more modest fashion over her head. I wished I had one too, out of respect for Ruth.

I tucked into mum's arm as we walked up the slight hill towards Ruth's plot. We walked slowly, such a contrast from our drive out of the city, and I felt ancient. I imagined doing this for ever, nothing changing around us but our bodies gradually growing older over the years - me morphing into mum, mum into granny. There was a faint breeze but the sun was high and for October the afternoon was warm. If you were looking for somewhere to be buried, or to bury a loved one, you'd choose this place on a day like this - discreetly tended around the area where the burial spots are, on the fringes of the woodland, with the forest beyond still dense and green from its summer foliage - but we've never been here on the harsh midwinter days when the trees turn scary and the wind must whistle through the branches and the icy rain cut into you. A bleak, cold place to be dead then. Brrr.

'Are you cold? You're shivering.'

'No, just... I'm fine. It's lovely today, isn't it?'

'Mmm. I'm glad you could come, Alex. Thank you for doing that.'

'She was my sister.'

'And we both miss her so much.'

We reached the bower at the top of the rise where you can see the park spread around you. 'Do you want to sit here for a minute?' I asked mum. 'Or should we go down to Ruth's straightaway?'

'We don't have so much time if we're going to have lunch too. Let's go and stand with her. I want her to know we're here.'

'I wish you wouldn't do that, mum - it only makes it worse.' I meant her talking about Ruth as if she was conscious of our presence, as if she was still around somehow. Mum got a bit defensive.

'Well, it doesn't make it worse for me. It makes it better.'

'Whatever. I'm just saying...'

She broke away and started walking down the slope a little ahead of me. She had only gone a few steps when she stopped and looked back at me with some anxiety.

'What's that?'

'What?'

I caught her up and she grabbed my hand, our brief disagreement forgotten. We both looked towards Ruth's plot. From thirty metres away we could see something lying by her plaque like an offering.

'Some rubbish blown across from somewhere,' I suggested. 'Got snagged there maybe.'

We approached hand in hand and confirmed what we'd seen; a small bouquet of flowers, a cheap bunch of white carnations like the ones you see by the fruit and veg in supermarkets or sitting in buckets on a

101

garage forecourt. The stems still had the plastic wrapped round, with the price sticker showing. It was obvious the bouquet hadn't blown across from another grave - it was laid with some care directly in front of Ruth's plaque. Anyway, very few of the plots here had flowers laid on them - it's not that kind of place. Certainly something we never did. We never brought flowers. But someone had, and recently; the flowers were still fresh. Mum's body closed into mine.

'It's him.'

'You don't know that.'

'It's him. He mentioned Ruth, remember, in his note.'

'How could he even know she's here?'

'From the notice in the paper, maybe, I don't know. He seems to know everything about us.'

'He doesn't, mum. He knows nothing about us.'

She shuddered. 'Get rid of it.'

'Where?'

'I don't care, but please get rid of it.'

I bent to pick up the flowers, and recognized immediately the same sensation that mum had described when she lifted the rose from the windscreen of her car. Nausea. Disgust. I held the stems at the end of my fingers and carried the bunch at arm's length across the grass in search of the nearest bin.

Lunch was ruined for us after that. We hardly spoke more than a few sentences between us as we ate in a gloomy corner of the pub mum took us to - so listless in our own company that I could easily pick out details of the remarks rattling about among a group of old women gathered around a big table in the middle, all with a compulsion to comment on every aspect of their outing, their choices and the quality of their meal. On a different day, as part of the fun of *our* occasion, mum and I would have made gentle little jokes to each other about their empty relentless chatter, but if mum heard them at all she didn't say so and neither did I. It was as if we were plunged once again into a state of deep mourning for Ruth while at the same time totally oppressed by the dark cloud that was mum's stalker. Not just *mum's* stalker now. Even poor dead Ruth was getting his unwanted attention, and I could sense him so smothering close I could gag on it.

It got worse. When we got back I noticed the fire exit door that led out to the car park was swinging wide open, but the significance of it escaped me until Barbara, mum's new receptionist, greeted her return with a big smile and a question.

'Did he catch up with you?'

'Who ?'

'Your husband.'

'What?'

The look of shock on mum's face took the smile off Barbara's and she continued with much less certainty.

'Oh, just... Well, I understood you were meeting for lunch. He went off after you in a great rush.'

'Barbara. My husband... my *ex*-husband has been dead for more than a year.'

I watched Barbara's expression move from uncertainty to incomprehension.

'But I promise you he was here, stood right where you are now. And look...' She fiddled in a flustery way with her terminal on the reception desk and turned the screen to show us, as if to justify herself. 'You've even got the appointment in your diary.'

We stared at the screen in silence, though I'm sure the noise inside mum's head at that moment must have been as loud as it was in mine. I turned to her and could see her trying to compose herself, trying to stay professional in front of her member of staff. She lifted her eyes from the screen, stood back and grasped my arm above the elbow. Her fingers were stiff with tension but her outward appearance and her voice had regained some calm.

'Barbara, this is my Alex. My daughter.'

'Oh, I'm sorry,' Barbara said, just in the way people do when they hear someone's died, but she had her own calamity in mind. 'I've made a horrible mistake, haven't I?'

'Of course not, don't worry about it.' I could see that even while mum was struggling with her emotions she was calculating how much to tell or not tell her new receptionist about her weird personal situation. She seemed to settle on blanking it. 'Not your problem at all, Barbara. You'd be surprised what some of these sales people will stoop to just to get past the gatekeeper. No, not your fault at all. Now Alex...' turning to me with a bright public face, 'Have you time for coffee before you get back?'

'Mum, you're going to have to let people know,' I hissed at her as soon as we reached her office. 'He's not just a nuisance anymore, he's obviously crazy and probably dangerous.'

'We don't know that.' She put her hand out to reassure me and left it on my wrist, her vulnerability overtaking her show of control. 'I'm trying to work it out, darling, just trying to work out what to do for the best.'

'Well, at the very least you have to tell the police.'

'Yes, yes, I'll do that.'

'Now.'

'OK.'

She sat herself behind her desk and stared blankly at the telephone, looking as forlorn as I'd seen her in months.

'What am I supposed to do?' she said at last. 'Call 999?'

We took the non-emergency route but by the end of it wondered why we'd even bothered. They kept mum hanging on the phone for ages while they found somebody appropriate to take the call. I watched her becoming increasingly agitated as she waited, distracted by the background noise of her class gathering in the studio. When she finally got through to an officer and started giving details it became obvious they were in no hurry to deal with it, especially when she had to admit there had been no actual physical contact. All she was left with it was a promise to look into the guy's current whereabouts and an appointment with a case worker for Friday afternoon.

'That's that then,' she said, putting the phone down. 'So sorry Alex, I have to go and attend to my students.'

'Well, what are you going to do tonight?'

'How do you mean?'

'You can't go back home. He might be waiting for you.'

'Surely not.'

'He turned up here, didn't he? He's getting bolder all the time. Come and stay with me tonight.'

'What, in your tiny little room?' She smiled as she stood and busied herself, collecting material for her class and, I could tell, trying hard to collect herself. 'Where will I sleep, on your floor?'

'I can do that. Or why don't you book into a hotel, just for tonight? There's a Premier Inn right next to our building.'

'I have nothing with me.'

'Look, I'll go and buy you a few toiletries, get some knickers from Marksies - that's all you need. Come on, mum. I don't want you going back home. Not tonight. Not till you've have had a proper talk with the police, get some protection or have him put away or whatever.'

I think it was as much the pressure of her girls waiting in the studio as my persuasion, but I finally got her to agree to book in to the hotel near me. If I left her a tad happier than when I came in it was only because we had some sort of plan, and I could feel I was doing something instead of standing helplessly by, leaving mum to the random vagaries of some nutter.

I woke up from a dream about my dad. One of those weird unconnected dreams (well, I suppose that's what dreams always are) and the only thing I really remembered clearly was the last bit before I woke up. We were at some mad party where everybody seemed to be drunk or stoned out of their minds. I was trying to keep an eye on dad, and suddenly we were outside the building where the party was - like an old theatre or concert hall but in the middle of nowhere. For some reason dad took it into his head to climb the wall of this building. I shouted at him to come down but either he didn't hear me or wouldn't listen, so I followed, thinking somehow that the only way to keep him safe was not to let him out of my sight. We must have been like Spiderman because we could climb this wall without any drainpipe or anything else to hold on to. There was a parapet of little stone crosses at the top and dad disappeared over it. I followed, shouting for him, but when I got to the parapet all I could see in front of me was a glass roof, like a huge greenhouse, with no sign of dad. I supposed he must have carried on right over the roof so I kept climbing to find him. As I climbed I looked down through the glass and I could see the heads of the people milling around at the party, bathed in bright light. They seemed miles away, but I could hear them joking and laughing. It struck me that if their laughter reached a certain pitch it would shatter the glass. I tapped on the glass to warn them, and somebody looked up. I could clearly make out - as if I'd zoomed in on her - one of the old women I'd seen lunching at the pub. She grinned at me, picked up a chicken drumstick from her plate and waved it as if she was inviting me to come and join them. I tapped at the glass again and it started to crack, a long developing crack like a snake slithering across sand. I turned my head, looking for a safe way back, and there was a man clambering across the roof to reach me.

'Dad?'

He had his head down and I couldn't tell in the dark if it was him or not. The hair looked wrong. I didn't know whether to go to him for safety or keep climbing to get away. I lay there paralysed, with the glass splintering under me. The man stood up. Bigger than I'd thought, with muscled shoulders like someone who works out. I was trying to see his face, but just then the glass panel he was standing on broke under him and he fell through the roof. I watched him drop towards the people at the party, who all looked up, surprised. Everybody's attention was on him except the old woman from the pub who stared straight into my eyes, spat out a stream of swear words and threw her chicken leg directly at me.

It flew up and struck the glass. I could feel the panel giving way under my hands and knees, I started to fall through... and woke with the shock.

I don't know how much meaning there is in dreams - mostly they seem to be random jumblings of things you've seen recently, or had on your mind - but reflecting on it afterwards it seemed as if the stalker and dad were somehow mixed up together, and I guessed that must have to do with him coming into mum's place and pretending to be her husband. The muscled shoulders didn't suggest either of them, but I guess in the dream they signified menace, a threat to me, or mum through me. I was a bit surprised that mum didn't feature directly, but I supposed the idea of me looking out for dad came from my trying to protect her. What the old woman from the pub was doing there I had no idea except maybe the fact that I was on the outside looking in - that's how I'd felt when I was watching her and her group that lunchtime. She seemed to be blaming me for something in the dream. Probably my guilty conscience - that horrible feeling I wasn't doing enough to help, maybe even making things worse.

I didn't mention my dream to mum when we met at her hotel for breakfast - she had enough of her own angst about men chasing her without burdening her with mine. She claimed to have slept OK, though she had that haunted look about her eyes she gets when she's stressed, and I noticed that again she chose a table in the corner away from the entrance and the window. She was constantly looking past me while we were talking, which is not like her at all, and I realised she was running a discreet check on everybody who went in and out. Maybe I wasn't the only one having bad dreams.

'You OK?'

'Sure. Fine.'

'What time is your appointment at the police station?'

'Four thirty. Will you come with me?'

'Of course.' I could see the relief on her face. 'But I want to drop by the house first, put some things in an overnight bag for you.'

She sighed. 'Oh, darling, I don't really want to stay here any longer.'

'You don't have to. I spoke to Emily last night - she knows the situation - and her mum called me half an hour later. She wants us to go and spend the weekend at their place.'

'Alex, you shouldn't have. Putting people out like that. It's not my way.'

'She offered. That's what friends are for. You know you would do the same.'

Mum protested a little more, then accepted that's how it would be. The fact is it was a load off her mind to have somewhere safe she could escape to, at least until we could sort something out with the police. She insisted on giving me the taxi fare so I wouldn't have to go home on the bus, and she made me promise to get there before Abi left for the day so I wouldn't be alone in the house. I agreed, though I thought it unlikely he'd be watching the house when he knew mum was at work. I told her I'd go after my morning lectures and meet her back in town in time for our appointment at the police station. Or that was the plan. As it happened I was delayed by a bizarre, really disturbing encounter on the high street. Not with our stalker, though it had to do with him. Very much to do with him.

I left uni directly after lunch and went straight to the taxi rank by the shops. Being a Friday there was a bit of a queue so I was waiting, looking casually about, when I got my eye on the Big Issue seller, the guy in the cowboy hat I'd seen staring at me a few days before. He was doing it again, from way over the other side of the street. What's worse, when he saw he had my attention he gave a sort of 'howdy' salute as if I was an old friend, then tucked his batch of magazines under his arm and started walking across to the rank. Straight towards me. I nearly freaked - it was all I could do to stop myself running away. But I stood my ground, looked daggers at him as if to say, 'Don't you *dare* hit on me.' Until he floored me with his first question.

'It's Ruth, isn't it?'

I was gobsmacked, struck dumb, My hand went instinctively to my throat. He probably thought I was having a heart attack. It felt more like rape.

He said it again. 'Ruth?'

'I... What are you talking about? Who are you?'

'Go by Cody.' Trace of a put-on American accent. Gross. He poked a handshake towards me which morphed into a calm-down signal when he saw me back off. 'Hey, it's cool, I'm on your side.'

'My *side*?'

People in the queue were looking at us, naturally curious. Cody motioned with his head to move away with him. I was on the verge of ordering him to shove it but I wanted to know what the hell he meant. I followed him to a quieter spot in the shadow of a shop wall, keeping plenty distance between us. He carried on spouting nonsense.

'Just want to say straight off, I think your dad's out of order.'

'What?'

107

'Looks to me like you're old enough to look after yourself so if you choose to go your own way he shouldn't interfere. Been there, done that, got the Big Issue tee-shirt.'

'I think you're mistaking me for somebody else.'

'Don't worry girl, I'm not gonna grass on you if you don't want. But your dad asked me to look out for you.'

'My dad's dead.'

'No way. I seen him a few days ago. He just wants to know you're OK, that's all. Maybe talk to you a little, sort a few things out between the two of you.'

I was totally churned up by now, wanted even more to run screaming down the street, but instead I confronted him, tried to put him straight. 'Listen to me. I have no idea who you are, whether you've had some dealings with my family in the past or whatever. So if it's a surprise I'm sorry, but my dad's dead, OK? So is Ruth.'

He smiled and nodded sadly as if he was taking this in. But he wasn't, not in the way I meant it.

'I get where you're coming from. Like I said, I've been there. Did exactly the same when I was your age, or a bit older. Far as I was concerned my folks didn't exist no more. New identity. Cody's not my real name as a matter of fact.'

'Is that right.'

'But you can never walk away. Not really. Not completely. And believe me he's still there for you - Alex - he's still there.'

Another shock. 'How do you know my name?'

'He told me.'

'Who? My dad? Are you putting out as some kind of psychic?'

Cody seemed pleased with this. 'Well, I do have... More of a sixth sense really, but yeah, you could say that. That's how I knew it was you even before I saw the photo. And it wasn't just the earrings, more... the whole thing, really. Psychic, as you say. I'll hold my hand up to that.' And he actually held his hand up. I'm sure he was expecting a high five, but he got the opposite. I took a couple of paces back.

'What you mean, photo? And what's my earrings... I mean, what the fuck's going on here?'

'Come on Ruth,' Cody said. He ambled off a few steps, then turned to me with a sort of swagger at the hips. 'Come on over to my office, I'll level with you on the whole shebang.'

Office? And 'Ruth' again. I trailed after him in a daze across the street where he sat me down on a bench next to a crammed and smelly

108

bin. Some office. But I was a whole lot less concerned about my surroundings than about Cody explaining himself.

'What's this about a photo? Where is it?'

'Well, I can show you the picture I took.' He brought out a smart phone as if he was drawing a gun. He tapped and scrolled along the screen until he found the photo he wanted. It wasn't the sharpest image, but it was definitely me crossing the street, not ten metres from where we sat now. I knew it must have been on Tuesday - I remembered my suspicion that he'd taken a picture then. Also because the tall guy I had imagined following me was there in the shot as well, so close we could have been together. Spooky.

'You some sort of perv? What are you doing taking pictures of me?'

'To prove to your dad I'd seen ya. But the photo I'm on about is the one your dad has of you and your ma. She's Swedish, ain't she?'

'For Christ's sake...'

'What?'

'Let me see this picture.'

'I haven't got it. Your dad just showed it me so I could confirm you and her were the same person. You and you, I mean. Only a couple of years younger.'

'Eh?'

'When it was taken.'

'Describe it to me. You say this was me and my mum. Where was it taken? Inside? Outside? What were we wearing? Describe mum to me. Go on, if you can.'

'Hold fire, Cody's a sharp cookie but he ain't got a fucking photographic memory.' He stared into the distance as he concentrated. 'So. Very fit. Both ways, if you get my drift. Blonde like you, longer hair. The picture was taken outside - a park, maybe. You were all on a bench.'

'*All?*'

'Tell a lie, you and your friend were sitting down and your ma was standing behind you.'

(A friend? Emily?) 'You never said about a friend. A girlfriend? What was she like?'

'Oh, not the looker you are, no contest. Quite puggy really. No offence intended. Very plain anyway. Hunched-up looking - it was like you other two were sunbathing and she was feeling the cold, know what I mean?'

'Oh my god, Ruth.'

'Good girl.' He clapped his hands in delight and almost did a jig on the pavement. 'See, you don't have to deny your existence. Or did you

109

honestly forget who you are for a while? Did you block it out of your mind?'

I was only half-listening to him. I had in my mind now the exact photo he was talking about. Mum had it framed, she liked it so much. Had she given dad a copy? But even if she had, how and where did Cody manage to see it? I looked up at him pacing about his 'office' like a man possessed. Maybe he was possessed. Or a very good con man. Not that good, if he has to sell magazines on the street. Anyway, what was he trying to blag from me? I watched him closely, trying to work him out. Trying to understand the whole mad thing. Cody gave me a broad grin, put his hand on my shoulder.

'Welcome back, Ruth.'

I shrugged him off. 'My name's not Ruth.'

'Shit, Ruth. Keep up.' He seemed really disappointed that he hadn't worked some miracle cure. 'So what do you go by?'

'What? Oh, Alex.'

'Ah, same as your dad. Interesting you should choose that name. From a psychological viewpoint.'

'I didn't *choose* it. And my dad's name wasn't Alex.'

'That's his handle, that's what he told me. Well, we've all got our secrets, eh? Who speaks the truth these days? Only the lonesome cowboy. Here.' He stuck his phone up close. 'Let's take a better picture.'

'Get out of my face. Stop it!'

A couple of passers-by glanced at us when I raised my voice. Cody gave a half-smile at them, managing to look guilty and so-innocent at the same time. *Who, me?* he seemed to be saying. Nobody actually stopped to ask if anything was wrong. I noticed Cody doing a quick recce up and down the street, obviously concerned about the authorities of one kind or another, then he turned his attention back to me.

'Listen, girl, I need the evidence. Your dad owes me fifty quid.'

'What?'

'For finding you.'

'I'm not lost.'

'Where are you living, then? What's your address?'

'Are you for real?'

'It's not for me, it's your dad, he's desperate to see you.'

'How many more times... My father is *dead*.'

Cody shook his head, brought his phone out again. 'Tell you what, I'll call him. So you can tell him that personally.'

110

'Don't play games...' I started to say, but as I watched him scroll through his contacts something clicked inside me. No, not a click. More of a dull thud.

'Show me the number. No, don't call him. Just show me the number you have for him.'

He grinned, hid the screen away from me. 'Information is power,' he said.

'Show me the fucking number!'

More startled looks from passers-by. Another edgy calm-down gesture from Cody. And he turned the phone to show me the name Alex and a number on the display. My hand closed on my own mobile in my pocket. I knew before I checked it that the number I'd stored there was the same.

STRANGER DANGER.

I stood up, flustered and angry. 'Keep away from me.' I started to walk off, turned back. 'You tell him to keep away from me, and my mother. You tell him, hear me?'

'Easy girl, the whole fucking world can hear ya.'

'Good. I want them to know. You tell him if he comes near me again, or her, or sends scum like you after us, I'll kill him with my own bare hands. You copy?'

'I copy. Jeez, Ruth...'

'Don't call me that, you numbskull. Don't call me anything. Just... keep away.'

I rushed without looking across the road. A taxi driver pulling out of the rank braked hard and honked his horn. I was too frazzled to apologise, but as I took my place at the back of the queue the driver stormed out of his cab to bawl at me.

'Sorry, sorry,' I said, more frightened than he could know. As he was giving me his lecture I could see Cody in the background, still fiddling with his phone at the other side of the road. He was texting somebody, and I could guess who. 'Sorry,' I said again to the driver and half-ran out of the queue to get away. Anywhere to get away.

I must have spent half an hour riding aimlessly up and down the escalators in John Lewis, trying to stop my heart from thumping, trying to figure out what to do. I felt safer when I was moving - or slightly less scared - and thought surely it would be easier from there to spot someone following me. Until I realised I was probably making myself more conspicuous. I jumped off, hurried down the stairs to ground level and left the store. Then I rang Emily.

'I need you to go with me to get my stuff.'

'What, now? I'm working, Alex.'

'It's Friday, you can wag it can't you?'

'Not really. What's up?'

'I'm scared on my own. Something else has happened.'

'Ah, hon. Listen, I've got a break coming. Get round here and we'll have coffee; you can tell me about it.'

Of course Em was all ears about Cody and shocked to hear he was actually being paid to track me down.

'This is getting creepier by the minute. What are the police saying?'

'They don't know about that part yet. They're supposed to be checking last known addresses for Mr Weirdo, and they're meeting with us at half past four. Can you stick around with me till then, Em? Please.'

'I don't know. I can't just walk out.'

'Please.'

I was losing her until the phone rang in my pocket. I took it out, stared at the display. Em saw my reaction, looked over my shoulder.

'Oh, my god.'

STRANGER DANGER.

'Don't answer it.'

'I'm not going to. Not even sure he expects me to.'

'Just letting you know he's there.'

'Something like that.'

'Don't fret yourself, Ally. We'll get you and your mum's stuff across to our place straightaway.'

'Thought you said you couldn't leave work.'

'I'll get my coat.'

I didn't dare go back to the taxi rank in the high street, so Em and I walked to the one outside the railway station. She suggested that instead of taking the cab direct to my house we go to hers instead where she could borrow her mum's car to fetch the clothes in. I was secretly glad to find her mother out - I wasn't up to another question and answer session before our big one with the police - and she hadn't taken the car so the two of us could finally get on our way to Beech Grove. I checked the time on my phone.

'Abi will be long gone by now.'

'Who?'

'Our new cleaner. That company can't hang onto people for five minutes.'

112

'They'll pay them peanuts, that's why. I bet she's on about half what I make. You've got your key though, right?'

'Yeah, yeah.'

I was already distracted, thinking about whether I could get everything done in time to meet mum. I didn't want her to be late for her appointment, and I certainly didn't want her hanging about for me. There was a fair chance he'd be outside the studio waiting to see her leave. As we approached Beech Grove I switched to thinking, he couldn't be waiting outside the house, could he?

'Slow down a bit,' I said to Em. 'We need to work out the best way to do this.'

'How do you mean?'

'I think... Drive quite slowly up our street and past the house on this side. Not mega-slow you know, just steady. Yeah, yeah, keep going, keep going. Don't stop at the house.'

While Emily drove I twisted my neck this way and that, checking all the places he could be lurking. Especially under the trees - that's where he was last time. Nobody around.

'OK, OK. Just turn round at the cul-de-sac and come back down again. Sorry about this, Em. Thanks.'

'Not a problem.'

We drove past the trees on the way back to the house. Definitely nobody there, and not a soul on the pavement. I had a passing vision of him loitering outside mum's studio, watching up at the windows, anonymous among the people going by.

'Should I go past again?'

'Sorry, no, no. Just... Don't go up onto the drive. Just stop at the kerb here. Thanks. No, keep the engine running. I'll just run in quickly and get what we need. I'll be two minutes.'

'Do you not want me to come in with you?'

'No, best if you keep a look-out here, if that's OK.'

'Fine.' She paused. 'What do you want me to do if I see him?'

'Panic.' We giggled nervously together. 'No, no, I... Call me on my mobile, yeah?'

'OK.'

'Can you lock these doors from the inside?'

'Yep.'

'Right, then. I'll be two minutes, honest.'

The first thing I thought about when I unlocked the front door was that Abi had gone without putting the burglar alarm on, though not being here that often myself these days I really wasn't sure whether mum would have given her the code. Whatever, that was something I should do before I left even if it meant taking a few more seconds.

I went straight upstairs to pack a few things for mum and me. The small suitcase was on top of the wardrobe in Ruth's old room. I hated going in. One of these days, mum kept promising, she'd steel herself to it - not take the memories of Ruth out of here entirely but to put them in some proper order, and make the room a living space again. But the stripped bed and the pile of Ruth's stuff from years ago in the corner of the room were constant reminders - symbols of sadness. I shuddered, not for the first time that day, before I left the room to get on with what I had to do.

I was desperate not to leave poor Emily sitting outside in the car too long, so my packing was really hurried and disorganized - a bag of toiletries from the bathroom; perfume and make-up; clean underwear and a couple of changes of top for mum; same for me. What else would we need? Nothing. We'd surely sort something out with the police and be back here before the weekend was out. I snapped the case shut and rushed out of my bedroom; banged the case on the banister rail as I turned at the stairs, and... Jesus Christ!

He was there. Standing in the middle of the stairway, looking up. Looking at me. Staring at me. The suitcase dropped out of my hand - fell against my leg, my shaking leg. Jesus!

He had no coat on. No shoes on. You'd think it was his fucking house.

'What the hell do you think you're doing? How dare you! How dare you!'

My anger with him made me hurtle down the stairs, fling myself at him, beat my fists against him.

'Are you trying to ruin my mother's life? Who the fuck do you think you are? You're ruining my mother's life!'

'Ruth!'

Bastard, fucking bastard. I shoved him hard, and almost fell forward, pushing air instead of body. I grabbed at the banister rail to stop myself, felt it shudder with his weight as he crashed against it on the way down. Another thud and a crack as the back of his head hit the radiator at the foot of the stairs.

For a few seconds he didn't move at all. I watched him lying crumpled in a heap on the floor. Had I killed him? Right then I didn't care. He's out of our life, then - honestly, that was my first thought. Then he stirred. Moaned.

'Ruth.'

'Ruth's dead, you fucking moron. Don't you dare say her name to me. Ruth's dead. I wish it was you!' Sobbing now. 'I wish it was you.'

UNDENIABLE EVIDENCE

IX

'You know what the biggest bollocks I've heard today is? That's there's nothing wrong with your brain.'

He's standing there, practically bursting through his blue shirt. A beige tea mug wrapped into his huge right hand. He fills the opening of the cell doorway, leaning on his shoulder as he looks at me on the iron bed like he owns the place. Like he owns me. Whether he said his name when he stopped me to make the arrest, I can't recall. It was such a shock. I'd been vaguely aware of burly blokes like him coming in and out of the ward at various times, talking and laughing at the nurses' station, staring across at my hospital bed the way he's doing now - only cockier now because this is *his* place. Nobody gave me any hint I was to be arrested as soon as the doctors discharged me. Fully expected to go back to the flat, was looking forward to it in a way. A safe haven - somewhere I could sit and think, try and pick up the pieces of what happened, sort things out. I didn't expect this.

'Hear what I'm saying?'

'There's nothing wrong with my brain.'

It's official. They did a scan not long after the ambulance took me in. Just bad bruising and a cut to the back of my head. A clean dressing this morning. I find my fingers straying up to it, fiddling while he watches with a sneer on his face. It's an effort of will to stop doing it, stop revealing my vulnerability.

'Good.' he says. 'Glad to hear you're *compos mentis*.' (He makes it sound like something you put on the garden.) 'So you're up to answering a few questions, then.'

I lean back on the thin pillow, close my eyes. 'Fire away.' Trying to play it cool.

He laughs. 'Not now. Soon.' Says nothing else and when I open my eyes a couple of minutes later he's gone, leaving the cell door wide open. Is this some kind of test?

I close my eyes again. The image of Ruth returns as so often in the past few days. Ruth on the stairs. Except of course not Ruth, which I was so foolish not to realise before. It was only when I heard her voice, heard her call me a *fucking moron* that I knew I'd been set up. Ruth would never use language like that. They could find somebody who looked quite like her (though not identical, once I saw her close up). They could dress her in Ruth's clothes, even get her to wear the same jewellery (the earrings *I* bought her, scheming bastards) but she couldn't match the voice. Not my Ruth, that coarse, cold voice. Crowing over how stupid I'd been.

117

I remember the tattered hoarding outside the church. *Where you go I will go, and where you stay I will stay.* Clear enough if only I'd interpreted it properly.

She was the classic decoy. Leading me away from Karin, not towards her. Heading me off whenever the two of us were about to get close. And finally drawing me into their trap. How could I deceive myself with that helpful-ghost nonsense when the reality was so much more straightforward? Because I *wanted* to believe it - the romantic in me - that's what led me to embrace the irrational and ignore the rational explanation. And it was cleverly done, very cleverly done.

What I've yet to work out is how complicit the police are, if at all, in this conspiracy to keep me away from Karin. Or how much misinformation they might have been fed by others. If I've learned anything from my recent experience it is that I mustn't take things at face value. And I mustn't let emotion and prejudice get in my way of seeing things properly, judging people properly. This bloke that did the arrest seems to have taken a dislike to me but I'm not going to let that colour my reaction to him, or any of them. I'm going to stay on my guard, but as long as they're straightforward with me I'll be straightforward with them. The custody sergeant seemed a good enough sort. He asked me if I wanted to have my solicitor present (what solicitor?) and told me I could make one phone call. I didn't even bother asking if I could ring Karin. Or anybody for that matter. As for a solicitor, why would I need one when I've done absolutely nothing wrong. Unless they count taking a bicycle without the owner's consent - they didn't include that on the charge sheet. Repeat. I've done nothing wrong. That's what I have to hold onto, whatever they've been led to believe.

Burly bloke is back. He's put his jacket on, straightened his tie. Means business. 'Right, Alex. Interview suite.'

Waiting outside the door of the room that he takes me to is a woman, maybe a few years younger than I am, whose mousey hair clearly hasn't felt the tug of a brush in a while. She is carrying her coat over both arms and withdraws one hand from under it as we're introduced. She seems slightly intimidated by the officer, or just by being here.

'Alex, this is Miss - sorry, *Ms* - Peters from Social Services. She'll be your responsible adult in this process.'

'My *what?*'

He ignores the question. Ms Peters gives me a wan smile as we wait for him to sort through his collection of keys to find the one for this door. He has to switch the light on inside as the only window is covered by a heavy blind. Some *suite*. There's an ancient video camera in one corner and some unnecessarily chunky recording equipment on the table next to the wall. He guides me firmly to the chair at the far side of the table facing the camera, indicates a seat off to the side for Ms Peters, and seats himself directly opposite me, with his back to the closed door. Fiddles with the equipment. *Testing, testing.* We watch the levels bob up and down. Stirrings for me of a studio session; but this is very different.

DS Tregarron, that's his name. He says it in his introduction for the tape, then continues, 'There are two other people in the interview room, who are...'

No immediate response - we both assume he's going to fill in our names and has temporarily forgotten them. My 'responsible adult' is first to realise we're supposed to speak.

'Oh, Deborah Ann Peters, Social Services.'

'Alex Taylor... musician.'

'Could you repeat your full name, Alex.'

'Alex Taylor. I don't have a middle name.'

'Just to remind you, you're still under caution You don't have to say anything but it may harm your defence if you fail to mention when questioned something that you later rely on in court. Anything you do say may be given in evidence. You understand that?'

'Yes.'

'What's your address, Alex?'

'11 Beech Grove - well there's a house name, Hambo...'

'That's not the address I have for you.'

'Well, that's where...'

'And according to our records your name is Alex Robson, not Taylor, isn't that right?'

'Robson? No.' I think for a moment. 'That's my professional name. Used to be.'

'What do you mean your *professional* name?'

'The name I used when I worked as a professional musician.' I turn to Ms Peters to explain, surmising DS Tregarron already knows this. 'I used to play the piano professionally, but I had an accident.' Ms Peters smiles sympathetically.

'That's not in doubt,' says Tregarron. 'As far as 11 Beech Grove is concerned, that's the address of the house you broke into last Friday afternoon...'

'I didn't break in anywhere.'

'Entered by deception. It amounts to the same thing.'

119

'Of course it doesn't. I was welcomed into my own home by the cleaner who works there.' To Ms Peters again. 'Her name is Abi. She's African.' Ms Peters nods, smiles again. She's on my side at least.

Tregarron continues. 'An address that was specified on a restraining order served on you some fourteen months ago...'

'Yes, and I never once broke it. Not once. That order's expired now.'

'Would you care to tell us why it was served on you in the first place?'

'It was all a misunderstanding. Certain people got hold of the wrong end of the stick. You see...' I turn to Ms Peters. 'We lost our daughter. She died. It was terrible. My wife had some sort of nervous breakdown. That was what led to all the confusion. Certain people claimed it was for her own protection, but they knew nothing about us. It was just... interference. I wish I could tell you how awful we felt. Can you imagine losing a daughter?'

'No,' says Ms Peters. 'Try not to get upset now.' Leaning across, hand on my shoulder. 'Are you OK to continue?'

She's visibly startled by a loud sigh from Tregarron. Her eyes flick across from my face to his. He lifts his palms from the table. 'Let's move on, shall we?'

Ms Peters and I straighten in our seats like school-children. Tregarron regards us in silence for a moment. The camera behind his shoulder doesn't seem to be in operation - no red light. The two pointers on the illuminated tape display flicker just above zero, picking up the ambience in the room, recording the machine's own low hum. Tregarron seems to soften his style a tad. 'Let me ask you a question, Alex.'

I thought that was the whole point of us being here, but I don't say that aloud. There's nothing to be gained by provoking him.

'Have you ever suffered from any form of mental illness or depression?'

'No.'

'You sure?'

'I'm not depressed. I'm a naturally optimistic person. Despite everything.'

That's true - the one thing that's kept me going through all these months of being separated from Karin is the conviction that we're destined to be together again. Together and happy. It's simple enough - why can't others see that?

'So you've not been under treatment or ever been prescribed anti-depressive drugs, anything of that sort?'

'No.'

'Can we have written permission to check your medical records so we can verify that?'

Ms Peters stirs, makes a small apologetic cough. She blushes when we both look across at her, but she has her say. 'I think... perhaps that's intrusive. At this stage.'

'I'm just trying to establish the facts.'

'Mr Taylor has given you a clear answer.'

'Yeah, same as his other answers.'

He says it like he wants to spit on the floor. For a fat man, DS Tregarron doesn't do jolly. Not a naturally optimistic person. And I'm about to worsen his mood.

'I don't give my permission. At this stage.' (Thanks, Ms Peters. Deborah Ann.)

'All right,' he says, wearily. 'If you're going to play silly buggers. Though I should warn you you're probably throwing away your best line of defence.'

'I haven't done anything wrong.'

'Haven't you, though?'

From an inside pocket of his jacket he pulls out a large plastic bag, places it on the table in between us. 'Can you describe the two objects you see inside this bag?'

I recognize them. 'Yes. There's a screwdriver and a piano tuning hammer.'

'How long is the blade on the screwdriver, would you say?'

'I'm not good at guessing measurements.'

'Have a go.'

'Six inches, maybe.'

'Nearer seven. 175 millimetres in metric, to be exact.'

'Why'd you bother asking, then.'

'That's a long blade, even by your measurement. And this other thing - what did you tell me it was?'

'It's for tuning pianos. It's called a hammer but it's more like a spanner or lever. For adjusting the pins on the strings.'

'Is that right? I don't think I've ever seen one of those before. Quite a nasty-looking instrument, would you agree? I mean, look at the head on that. And that big heavy handle. What sort of wood is it?'

'I have no idea.'

'Oh, I thought you might. I mean, it's yours isn't it? Both these tools are yours?'

'Possibly.'

'Well, they were found in your coat when the ambulance took you from Beech Grove to the hospital. So I think we can safely assume they're yours, eh?'

'Probably. So what?'

'For the purposes of the tape I have shown Mr Robson the tools that he has identified as belonging to him, and that I shall now mark and sign exhibit JT/1.'

We sit in silence while he fills in a label on the bag. I glance sideways at Deborah Ann but her attention is on what DS Tregarron is doing and we fail to make eye contact. Tregarron clicks the top of his pen when he has finished and looks up at me.

'So why did you have these tools in your pocket when you entered 11 Beech Grove? What were you intending to do with them?'

'I was intending to tune the piano. I did tune the piano. Ask Abi.'

'Alex, I don't know much about tuning pianos. When would you use a long screwdriver in an operation like that?'

'You wouldn't.'

'I thought you said that was why it was in your pocket.'

'That's why the tuning hammer was in my pocket.'

'And the screwdriver?'

He's got me there. I can hardly tell him it was my contingency in case Abi wouldn't let me in. Can't let him know I was going to use it to force a window open after she'd gone. Tregarron pounces on my hesitation.

'What were you intending to use the screwdriver for, Alex?'

All I can think to reply at that moment is what I've heard so many suspects in police dramas and documentaries say.

'No comment.'

Tregarron looks, well, cynical. I glance quickly, almost involuntarily, at Deborah Ann. No eye contact. Her brows are knitted. Maybe this is the wrong strategy. On TV usually the people who say *No comment* are as guilty as hell. Fortunately, Tregarron doesn't press the point, moves on to something else.

'You were discovered by a family member halfway up the stairs in the house. What was your intention in going upstairs?'

'I thought Karin was up there.'

'This is Karin Taylor, the householder?'

'Yes.'

'You thought she was in her bedroom?'

'Our bedroom, yes.'

'And you were going up there... to do what?'

122

'Well, to... surprise her.'

'Yes, I imagine it would be a surprise for her, seeing a strange man barge into her bedroom. Quite a shock, I'd say, wouldn't you, Ms Peters?'

'I... It's not appropriate for me to answer.'

'I'm not a stranger to Karin,' I tell him. 'I meant a *pleasant* surprise. Because I haven't been home in a while.'

DS Tregarron sits back in his chair, watching me. Waits for me to look at him, and when I do he shakes his head. I'm not quite sure what he means by it, but it's clear he doesn't have a high opinion of me. He looks across at Deborah Ann, eyebrows raised, seeking corroboration I guess, but she doesn't say anything. I don't think she likes him very much. He leans forward to continue the interview.

'What is your relationship with Karin Taylor?'

'I'm her husband.'

'Is that so?'

'Yes.'

'Not her cousin?

'No.'

'Though you have claimed to be her cousin.'

'I... Not really.'

He reaches into a pocket again, his side pocket this time. Another plastic bag. He flattens it out on the table between us. Inside is the note left for Abi.

'For the tape, would you like to read that aloud for us, Alex? It is Alex, isn't it? Not Karl?'

He grins like a jackal at Deborah Ann, apparently inviting her to appreciate his joke, though I don't expect she's read the note so she will have absolutely no idea what he's talking about. I look down at the words, clear enough through the plastic, and imagine Karin writing them before she leaves for the studio, her favourite pink pearl nail polish at the tips of her graceful fingers.

'Yes, my name is Alex, and no thank you, I would not like to read the note aloud.'

Tregarron sighs theatrically. 'Well, if you want a job done, do it yourself, Jack.' He spins the bag around so the words are the right way up for him to read for the tape, which he does in a sing-song voice, acting up in an attempt to impress Deborah Ann, or just taking the piss.

Hi Abi I'm expecting my cousin Karl this afternoon - he's going to tune the piano for me. Just let him in and, if you don't mind, provide coffee or whatever as needed. Don't feel you have to hang around if he's still busy when it's time for you to go. He'll probably wait to see me anyway, so just leave him to it. Thanks, Karin x.

Back to his normal voice, with a hard edge to it. 'Only it wasn't Karin who wrote that note was it, Alex? It was you.'

'No comment.'

I can't keep saying that. But sometimes the truth is too complicated to explain. Especially to somebody like DS Jack Tregarron. People like him don't have the sensitivity to comprehend. There's no way I can make him understand how I wrote the note *on behalf* of Karin, almost as her medium really, because it was the only way we could work around the barriers to seeing each other. He hasn't a hope of ever grasping the nuance of difference between *my* writing the note and *our* writing the note.

'For the tape, the note I have just read I shall now mark and sign exhibit JT/2.' Tregarron continues talking as he completes the label. 'I have to say, Alex, it's very well done. But then it's not your first effort, is it? From the investigations we've made so far it seems you've had quite a business going on the strength of it. You're quite the little forger.'

He offers the pen to me. 'Could you do mine, Alex? I'd very much like to see it. Here's my signature, look. Here's a piece of paper. Why don't you have a go?'

I fold my arms, stare at him.

'Have a try. Go on.' Insistent. 'Go on.'

In my peripheral vision I notice Deborah shifting in her chair. She's working herself up to speak again.

'That could be regarded as oppressive questioning, Sergeant... er. If you don't mind me saying so.'

'Just part of the process, Ms Peters. If you read your guide notes properly you'll see we have a certain amount of leeway. I'm no way bullying the suspect, just gathering important evidence.'

'Anyway...'

'Anyway, no need to pursue it now. Frankly, we've got quite enough to be getting along with. We can leave your little eBay scam for another day, Alex, but trust me we'll get to it.'

He checks his watch.

'Time for a short break. The time is 14.56 and I'm turning the tape off.'

'Is there a Ladies?' Deborah Ann sounds nervy after daring to interrupt DS Tregarron in full investigation mode. He shows her the way and comes back to me, closing the door behind him.

'Tell you the truth, Alex, the only concern I have right now is deciding which of the charges to leave out, there's that many to choose from. And we've hardly got started yet.'

124

He sits down heavily in his chair, flicks through his notebook. 'See, we've got trespass, burglary, harassment, stalking, deception - well, any amount of fraud - forgery, carrying offensive weapons, going equipped... You pay your money and you take your choice, don't you? Not to mention the 'attempts' eh? Rape? Murder maybe, eh? What are you capable of? That's the question I'm asking, Alex. That's the question I'm asking myself, and you know what my answer is?'

I shake my head.

'A lot. That's where I'm coming from. You might have Deborah Ann Peters fooled, but you don't have me fooled, mister piano man. I've seen people like you who look as if they wouldn't say boo to a goose. And they're the worst kind. And you know how I know you're one of them? 'Cause you're persistent with it. Actually, you've dedicated your fucking life to it.'

We stare at each other like we're in some sort of who'll-blink-first match. Neither of us will. Neither of us do.

'Listen,' he says. 'I'm no trick cyclist, not any sort of *ologist*, but I've got you down as a regular psychopath. With a bit of schizo thrown in. Is that what it says on your medical records?'

I'm saying nothing.

'I could get a court order for access you know, easy as pie. But I don't think I'll bother. From my point of view I'd sooner you were treated as a common or garden criminal - they're all fucking nutters inside anyway, as you're about to find out. I just have to work out what I can make stick, that's all.'

There's a tap on the door - Deborah Ann too timid to walk back into the room on her own account. DS Tregarron stands up to let her in, but before he does he turns back for one last 'unofficial' word of advice.

'It's not looking good for you, Alex, you know that, don't you? Not looking good at all.'

X

Another restraining order, community service and a medical referral. DS Tregarron was furious. Obviously he was going all out for a pretty hefty custodial sentence, but half his stupid charges were quashed straightaway on review, and the magistrate did the rest. It almost restored my faith in British justice, except of course I'm back at square one as far as Karin is concerned - in fact further back than square one. She must be as frustrated as I am, but her hands are tied. She didn't appear in court, so either she couldn't face it, scared of what might happen to me, or more likely she was prevented from coming.

Strange to say, but I'm partly reassured by the revelations of the last few days, if only because it settles a few doubts. For example I couldn't believe that Karin would have thrown my gift of a flower into a litter bin, and I was proved right - it's clear to me now that the girl pretending to be Ruth had done it, just as she made sure she took Karin out of my way when I came to the studio, and either delayed her coming back to the house on Friday night or hid her up in the bedroom while she dealt with me, pushing me down my own damn stairs. Unfortunately there's no going back to Beech Grove in a while unless I take a risk and ignore the terms of the restraining order. At least I can get back to the flat now, start planning what to do, how we're going to work round this. Karin will be relying on me to think of something, and I will.

There are letters and circulars strewed across the doormat that neither Jane nor the students have bothered to sort through. I can't be arsed either for the moment, so I pile everything up on the hall table to look at later. The empty hallway reminds me how I abandoned Jane's bike after I nicked it - god knows if it's still where I left it. I'm not sure what to do about that. Do I knock on her door and fess up, or go back in the hope it's still parked in the same place? If it is I could pretend I've come across it by chance so she'll think it's been pinched and dumped by somebody else. That sounds like a better plan. Anyway I don't want to talk to her right now even if she is in - the first thing I need is a good long shower.

It's even parkier in my flat than normal, and I soon discover why; I forgot to close the window I opened last Friday morning. The temperature has dropped rapidly over the last few days so it's like Siberia in here. I was more comfortable in the police cell. Welcome back, Alex.

And it's a welcome back from Mr Chatterjee - not. On top of my bed is a plain white envelope, unstamped, which turns out to be a notice of eviction from the landlord. He's given me just two weeks from today.

No, not today, the letter is dated October 12th, last Friday. That's the reason he turned up unannounced and let himself in, to give me this. For 'dishonesty' the letter says. It can't be anything to do with what happened at Karin's house because he was here before that all kicked off. What dishonesty can he be talking about? There must be some mistake; I'll have to talk to him. But all I get when I call is the standard voicemail message. That's another problem I'll have to sort out later. They're mounting up.

Now I find the hot water's running stone cold so I can't have a shower unless I'm prepared to be frozen to death. Why am I even bothered about being thrown out of this shitty hole when the hot water system and everything else is so crap? Oh, this isn't Mr Chatterjee's doing as well, is it? He hasn't shut the heating off? I bet that's why he was here such a long time, faffing about. That's surely illegal. I try the light switch - thank god, the electricity is still on - but I can't get the cooker rings to work. He's had the gas turned off. Fuck.

What am I supposed to do now? I'm dirty, and I'm starting to get hungry. Apart from that I've got to try and find my neighbour's bike, track down my landlord. I'm due at the probation office in the morning to be told what bottom-scrubbing work they're going to make me do for my community sentence. Oh, Karin, can't I just come home and drop into your soft embrace? Fill the bath tub with hot water and rose petals and sink into it together. Dry each other on top of the bed with white fluffy towels, then snuggle under the duvet to keep warm. Just simple, ordinary, honest pleasures - why is the world conspiring to stop us enjoying them?

I have a cat-lick of a wash in cold water trying not to get my dressing wet, put on a change of clothes. Transferring things from one jeans pocket to another, I come across Jane's key. I've half a mind to go over there and ask if I can have a shower - after all, she once borrowed my bed. If she's not in I could always use her shower anyway. On second thoughts it would be pretty hard to cover my tracks and she might get quite upset with me about it. Maybe I should try and find her bike first, then ask. Plus I need to find something and somewhere to eat before I starve to death. Hospital meals followed by police station food leave you ravenous and grateful for anything half-decent.

A quarter pounder with cheese and fries washed down with Coke counts as more than half-decent when you're as hungry as me. Not that it was so easy to find a McDonalds that's outside the limits of my restraining order. I wouldn't go into town anyway in case Cody got his eye on me and started demanding his fifty quid. I found loads of missed calls from him on my phone and a message in his rubbish Arnie Schwarzenegger accent with an added touch of Clint Eastwood: *Show me the money punk, or I'll hunt you down.* Which is why I've ended up just off the City East roundabout, next door to a motel. It's not too bad in here, or it would be OK if it wasn't for all the traffic outside. And sirens. In the time it takes to eat my burger (which I admit I'm dawdling over, having nothing else pressing) at least two police cars go past the window with their blue lights flashing, and an ambulance. We just need a fire engine for a full set. In between this action there's the regular grate of lorries changing gear and a constant dull undercurrent of traffic from the ring road that even thick double glazing can't keep out. But the place itself is clean and light, and the staff are positively cheery. A major improvement on what I've been used to recently.

To be honest if I had the money I'd check in to the motel rather than face the cold comfort of the flat, but at the moment I can't even afford as much as one night in the cheapest hotel in town. I only had the quarter pounder in the expectation it will tide me over till lunchtime tomorrow - I'm hoping the probation officer will point me in the direction of benefits and maybe give me advice about accommodation supposing I can't sort things out with Mr Chatterjee. He's still not answering his phone and the battery's all but run out on mine since I listened to Cody's message. Must remember to recharge it before the landlord cuts off the electric as well.

I reckon this place is about two miles from where I dumped Jane's bike. Walking due west from here I should cut across the route from the flat to the house. Actually it will be nearer Beech Grove and probably just into the restricted zone but I'll have to take a chance on that. As long as I don't draw attention to myself I'll be fine; even I'm not paranoid enough to imagine the police are cruising around the area specifically to pick me up. It will be a tedious walk back to the flat if I have to wheel a push bike with a flat tyre, but it will save on the bus fare and, besides, what else do I have to do with my time today. I really want to find this bike because I'm desperate to repair my relationship with Jane. I need all the friends I can get right now. Actually, one friend would be a start.

Three miles would have been a better estimate as it happens, not helped by the fact that, coming from an unfamiliar direction, I'm a bit disorientated. I can't remember exactly which of these streets I left the bike in; spend about quarter of an hour criss-crossing one square mile of estate looking for the spot. All the hedges are trimmed and all the gates are black fretwork, carefully closed - everywhere is bland, neat and samey.

I'm the one who stands out, wandering around like this. Talk about me trying to stay inconspicuous.

As luck would have it a patrol car does pass by though it doesn't slow down. My anxiety about being caught in forbidden territory is just beginning to fade with its disappearance when I spot an old bloke looking suspiciously out at me from his front window. He's as trim as his garden in collar and tie; Rotarian and C of E regular, I'd bet a pound. Is it a coincidence that he has his phone at his ear? I quicken my pace along the street, and as I do a clinking from my inside pocket reminds me of something. I pull out the screwdriver and tuning hammer that were handed back when I was released from police custody, still in their plastic exhibit bag. I'm worried about being stopped and searched with these in my possession ('Going equipped....'). There's a moment of minor panic resolved by discreetly thrusting the bag into some thick shrubbery as I'm passing by another well-fortified garden. Better to lose a couple of tools than give DS Tregarron another opportunity to have a go at pinning something on me.

I've spent too long in this neighbourhood, attracting attention, and I can't find the damn bike anywhere. Well, I suppose it was always a slim chance that nobody would have had it away, flat tyre or not, the length of time it's been parked unattended. Such a prosperous part of town as well - you can't trust anybody. I'll just have to face Jane without it. On consideration there's no necessary connection between me and her bike's disappearance. I'm pretty sure nobody in the house saw me take it. There's no good reason why she should suspect it had anything to do with me, so why even mention it?

No sooner have I come to that conclusion and set off back towards the flat than I come across Jane's bike parked exactly where I left it against a hedge bordering an old people's home. I'd been a hundred yards off target in my search. Amazing that it's still here in full view. Now I have to decide whether to take it back, or leave it dumped where it is, wash my hands of it. On balance it seems to me I'd be in Jane's good books again if I turn up with her bike and explain how I've just happened on it by accident - which in a way is true. I grab the handlebars and manoeuvre the bike round to start pushing it the mile or so home.

Almost immediately two police cars hurtle by one after another on my side of the road, blues and twos at full screech, scaring me half to death. For a couple of seconds I'm stupidly afraid it's me they're after, but like the patrol car earlier they're quickly out of sight. Wonder what all the fuss is about. It's one thing seeing emergency vehicles on the ring road, but this is a residential area, quite unusual. Some excitement somewhere.

For the first time in about a week it starts to rain. Lightly at first, then more heavily. My coat isn't especially waterproof. I drag Jane's bike under the awning of a shop to wait for a while, see if it will ease off. Standing and looking out at the rain reminds me of the night I saw the quotation on the church notice board. It makes me think of ghosts; of Ruth - the real Ruth. I have the first stirrings of an idea. *Where you go I will go.* If I somehow knew when Karin was going to visit Ruth's grave again perhaps I could be there to meet her. A perfect place for just the two of us, away from other people. Away from the blockers and interferers. When though? It's too long to wait for that awful anniversary. What about Christmas, will she visit then? Or Ruth's birthday. She can't help but go to Deerholme on Ruth's birthday. Yes.

The rain doesn't bother me now. Filled with the potential of the new plan I set off walking once more at a brisk pace, hardly conscious of pushing the bike. I'm too busy thinking, concentrating, working out the possibilities. The great thing about this idea is that it will help me over the next few weeks of having no contact with Karin. What I will have is a definite date - a target to work to - and the blank days between will be all part of the strategy; in fact, key to it. The best way to ensure Karin is given some slack to visit Ruth's grave on her birthday without any 'protection' is for me to lie low for now, slip under the radar, let them forget I'm still around. It will be easier to bear knowing that, the more patient I am now, the greater chance of reward later. The sweeter the prize.

Once I've worked through my community sentence and sorted out some form of regular income, and somewhere to stay if Mr Chatterjee can't be persuaded to keep me on, I'm going to live like a monk in a silent order. Best to think of it as a kind of hibernation. Hunker down. Let the pulse drop. Quietly get ready for spring, the season of love.

These thoughts have me preoccupied all the way to Gladstone Terrace. Negotiating Jane's bike round the final corner I don't immediately notice anything out of place in the street. I'm only a few yards from the house when it registers - two police cars parked right outside and a white van - a police van - a little further up the road. A uniformed officer in a high-visibility jacket is standing in the rain outside the front door as if on guard. I'm shocked out of my state of reverie. My first thought is - Tregarron has sent them to arrest me for straying onto the wrong streets. But that's ridiculous. Even if I have been reported it's hardly a hanging offence; it doesn't need this turn-out.

On the other side of the street a couple of neighbours, strangers to me, are doing a bit of rubber-necking from their doorways, obviously intrigued but reluctant to go out in the rain to satisfy their curiosity, or maybe inhibited by the heavy presence of police. I wheel the bike over to speak with the nearest one, a ginger-bearded bloke in faded blue denim.

'What's going off?'

'No idea, pal. Drugs raid, probably.'

I look across. He might be right, yeah. One of the students supplementing his income.

'Have the police been there long?'

'Don't think so. Not when I let the cat in.'

That's a pretty meaningless time frame from my point of view, but I'm guessing the cars would be the two that went by me with their lights flashing about fifteen minutes ago. They were certainly heading in this direction.

'Thanks.'

The man gives up and goes in. The rain is relentless. I have no alternative but to go and speak with the officer out front. I wheel my bike across the street, between the two parked police cars. The PC at the door takes a pace forward, one hand out as if it shoo me off the pavement.

'Excuse me, I live here.'

'Sorry, sir. I can't let you in at the moment.'

'Why not?'

'There's an investigation going on.'

'What sort of investigation?'

'Can't tell you any more, sorry.'

'Well, what am I supposed to do, stand out in the rain?'

'You and me both, I'm afraid.'

I wait aimlessly in front of him, leaning on the bike, and he stares past me, rocking slightly on the balls of his feet, like comic policemen do, until he seems to become aware of it, gets self-conscious and stops. Eventually he says, more by way of conversation than inquiry, 'Been in a fight, have you? What's the other feller like?'

'Me? No, no.' I finger my dressing, which is pretty damp by now. 'Just a fall. Hit my head on some pipes.'

'I see.' Loses interest for a minute, letting his eyes wander up and down the street, then back at me. 'So you live in one of the flats here.'

'Flat 2.'

'Flat 2? Ground floor, that'll be.'

'Yeah, just beyond the front door, so I wouldn't be disturbing anything if you'd just let me in...'

'And what would your name be, sir?'

'Alex. Alex Taylor.' (Had to stop myself saying, *My name would be Alex Taylor*. Too obviously taking the piss.)

'Well, I can't let you in at the moment, Mr Taylor, but don't go far, will you. You might be needed for speaking to in a while.'

'What for?'

'Just to help with inquiries, you know. Nothing to worry about.'

'Is it all right if I go to The Grapes for a bit? Just, this coat lets the rain in. And my bandage is getting wet.'

'I can see that. Yes, that should be OK. But either stay there or come back here, understand? Don't go wandering off.'

I don't intend to - the last thing I want is to attract any more attention just when I've resolved to live under the radar for the next few months. As for helping with their inquiries I don't even know the names of the students upstairs, never mind having any clue about their comings and goings, but I'm not going to make an issue of it. Nor am I going to press the reasonable point that for all our sakes the most convenient place for me to wait is in my own damn flat. No, let them get on with their job as they see fit. I wheel the bike round to face the way I'd come, intending to head off to the pub for a half of their cheapest lager.

'You've got a flat tyre,' says the PC, bringing his acute observational skills to the fore again.

'Yeah.'

'Where's your pump?'

'Oh, I told her she should get one, but she didn't.'

'Told who?'

'The woman whose bike it is. Jane.'

Even beneath the shadow of his helmet I can detect a stiffening of his features, which alarms me. Oh Christ, she didn't report it missing, did she?

'Jane who?'

'Jane... Jane...' For the life of me I can't remember her second name. 'Jane somebody. Two syllables. Sorry, I'm not trying to be... I genuinely... She's a friend of mine. Neighbour friend, you know. She lives just there.' I point to Jane's window, directly past the policeman's head. He follows my finger, then looks again at me, and at the bike.

'And this is hers, you say?'

(Fuck, she *has* reported it. Why didn't I just leave well alone?)

'Yeah, well, I *think* it's Jane's. I just found it up the road a way. So I was bringing it back to her.'

'What do you mean, you *found* it?'

132

'Dumped against a hedge. I remembered she told me she'd lost it, had it pinched. And there it was, just dumped. Kids, probably, doing it for a laugh. They're terrible round here, some of em.'

I'm conscious of starting to ramble, partly through nervousness and partly in the hope he might get bored and give up, but I seem to be having the opposite effect.

'She told you she'd lost it? When was that exactly?'

'You mean when she lost it, or when she told me?'

'Both.'

Christ, I'm just getting deeper into this. 'Oh well, I'm not sure *exactly*. Few days ago she told me... or was it even her who mentioned it? It might have been somebody else, you know, somebody in the house. Couldn't tell you who - I don't really know them, to be honest, the ones upstairs.'

'But this is definitely her bike?'

'Well, I think so. Not definitely, but it looks like hers. And I know it had a flat tyre.. Like I was saying about the pump...'

'That's enough, sir...' He cuts me off, quite firmly, and now I know I'm in trouble. 'Leave the bicycle where it is and stand over here, please.' He points to a place at the railings on the other side of the steps from Jane's window. Why he particularly wants me to stand there I have no idea, but I'm not about to argue. I try to jam one of the bike pedals onto the kerb so that it stays standing on its own but as I'm moving across to the railings the bike topples over between kerb and pavement, fortunately just missing one of the parked police cars. The PC ignores it, watches me take my position and then, still watching me, leans over and raps hard on Jane's window with the gloved knuckles of his right hand. After a while there's some movement behind the glass - I can't see properly from where I am - and the PC motions whoever is inside to come out.

A minute later the front door partly opens. In the gap I can see a man in an all-white cover-all with the hood pulled down. Whatever's going on, this is not about a stolen bike. The man in the white togs waits at the threshold for the PC who goes up the three steps to whisper something to him - obviously about me as they both turn to look while they're talking. They whisper some more, then the PC goes to pick up Jane's bike from the pavement. He manhandles it up the steps and it disappears with the other officer inside. The PC comes down the steps, this time to open the back door of one of the police cars.

'Come along, sir. I need you to sit in here for a minute.'

'What's going on?'

'You wanted to be out of the rain, didn't you? Get in, please, now.'

133

'I'm just asking...' as I walk towards him. The officer 'helps' me into the back seat, pushing my head down past the door frame.

'Just making a few inquiries, that's all. Nothing particular to worry about, we'll soon have you on your way.' He blocks the space in the doorway as he fishes for his notebook beneath his high-visibility waterproof. 'Now then, can you just confirm your name and address for me?'

I give him my current address at the flat rather than my real one at Beech Grove (no need to get into those complications) and I'm preparing myself for more but he has nothing else to ask, just shuts the car door on me and walks back to his place outside the house. He talks into his portable radio briefly, then resumes his guard duty, watching me now as well as what might be going on in the street. I look in all directions through the rain-streaked windows of the police car. Across the road I can see the man in denim at his doorway again. He half-crouches as I watch him. At first I think he's trying to duck out of sight, then realise he's trying to peer into the car. Other neighbours are nosing out of their doors and windows. I turn my head to this side and watch the PC on guard instead.

It seems like hours I'm sat there, but hearing the time later it couldn't have been longer than forty minutes when a plain black BMW turns into the street. It drives slowly past the house, past me in the back of the police car and presumably parks beyond the white police van. I know somebody has got out because the PC in front of the house straightens up as if he's on parade. Soon two men in plain overcoats pass my position at the window on their way to speak with him. There's a big, burly one and a much shorter, slimmer one.

I know who one of them is before he turns to face me. It's the other one though, the thinner one, who steps forward to speak while the PC ushers me out of the car and stands with me on the pavement. I'm twitching with nerves, but the man is quite unruffled, professional, almost friendly.

'Good afternoon, Alex. I think you'll know why we're here. I'm DI Lambert. You know my colleague DS Tregarron. This is my warrant card.' He checks his watch. 'The time is 16.22 and I'm arresting you on suspicion of the murder of Jane Ogden.'

As he continues with the caution my knees buckle. The officer behind steadies me, then grabs my arm firmly above the wrist. I can feel the metal of his handcuffs on my skin, but before he gets any further DS

Tregarron calls out, 'No need for them. He'll come quietly with me, won't you Alex? You won't give me any trouble.'

I stare Tregarron full in the face. The bastard. This is all his fault. All his doing. I hate him.

XI

The same cell. The same bed. Tregarron leaning against the door frame in the same position. Instead of the mug in his hand, now he has some official-looking forms. Everything so far has been bureaucracy, stretched out forever, and the same rigmarole of swabs, fingerprints and medical questionnaires that I've already been through just a couple of days ago. I'm the same person, you fuckwits. The same innocent guy. I've said that out loud repeatedly, but it's as if they're all deaf. They haven't told me anything more about why I'm in here and they haven't asked me any questions about Jane, about where I was on the night of such-and-such. About anything other than the boring stuff they need for their box-ticking. Why not? My arrest is obviously a mistake. I could clear this up in five minutes if they'd only give me the chance. So a woman has been murdered, apparently (I only have their word for that) and they think it's me because I happened to be pushing a bike that belonged to her. Yes. I was innocently bringing it back to the owner, having absolutely no idea she was dead - go figure. I could explain all that and I could quite possibly be helpful to them in tracking down the real killer if they'd only get round to asking what I know of Jane's recent movements instead of having me stagnate in a police cell not having a chance to talk for hour after hour. I'm simmering underneath just with the sheer tedium of it all.

Tregarron straightens himself up and moves towards me, papers in hand, playing affable. 'So Alex, just to let you know, I have a warrant here that empowers us to search your flat in relation to the offence we've talked about. You understand that?'

'Of course. I'm not a half-wit.'

'Good. These are for you - copies of the authorities that allow us to search.'

He thrusts the papers towards me. Not sure whether to take them - he seems so keen that I do - but I suppose I have no choice. I glance at the top page briefly. Form 5095, there you go, some riveting bedtime reading. Then it comes to me, this is why they've not asked any questions yet - they've been waiting to get into my room, hoping to find something they can use against me. There's stuff I don't particularly want them to see but worse than that, what's to stop them planting anything they like in there?

'I don't give my permission.'

'Sorry?'

'I don't give permission for you to search the flat.'

'Is that right? What have you got to hide?'

'Nothing.'

'Well, then.' He smiles. 'Besides, we don't actually need your permission, that's the point. It's all explained in them papers.'

'How do I know what you'll do if I'm not there?'

'We won't cause any damage. Not unless you've hidden something under the floorboards, have you, Alex, nailed up tight? Anyway, it's not as if you own the place - why should you care?'

'I don't mean that. I mean... How do I know you're not going to plant stuff?'

'What stuff?'

'I don't know, something incriminating.'

'And where am I going to get that from? If I've gathered evidence from one place what would be the point of putting it somewhere else? Besides, we'll have an independent witness with us, so you've nothing to worry about.'

'Who?'

'Your landlord.'

'Mr Chatterjee? He doesn't like me.'

'I don't know anyone who does, so what's new?' I give him a stare and he holds his hand up in brief apology then places it on the cover of the bed as he leans forward to say, 'Listen, Alex, I'm the best friend you've got right now, trust me on that. Because regardless of what you think it's not in my interest to put the wrong man in the dock. If you're as innocent as you say it's as much my job to clear that up as it is to find the guilty man, believe me.'

'Well, why don't you and DI whats-his-name interview me now, then? On the record. Get it cleared up, like you say.'

'All in good time, Alex. Tomorrow, probably. I can guarantee if you've got nothing to do with this you'll be out of here in three days max.'

As Tregarron turns to go I glance down at the papers he's left me. Mind-numbing. Impenetrable. I call him back.

'I want a solicitor.'

'No problem. Give me his name and number and we'll arrange it.'

'Don't have one.'

'Well, I'll ask the duty solicitor to talk to you.'

'Is he connected with the police?'

'Course not. Completely independent. Do you want him to come and see you or not?'

'Suppose so. And about tomorrow...'

Tregarron gives me that don't-try-my-patience look, but he waits to see what else I have to say.

'I want her to be with me.'

'Who?'

'Ms Peters. Deborah Ann. My responsible adult.'

'That's Social Services' call, not mine.'

'Ask for her, though. She'll want to come.'

'Fine. Anything else while I'm at it? Somebody to give you a neck massage?'

The way he put it I think he meant strangulation. I lie my head down on the flat pillow and the door clanks shut. The noise of it reverberates around my cell.

The duty solicitor's name is Mr Marks. He doesn't actually tell me whether it's spelt with a *ks* or an *x*. For all I know he could be a direct descendant of Karl or a distant cousin of Groucho, but he doesn't give much away. Judging by his level of charisma, not to mention his stock of wit and repartee, the chances of such a family relationship are slim to none - so I assume it must be Mar*ks*.

He seems more interested in how much cash I have in the bank than he is in my case. 'It's all about means testing now if you want legal aid,' he says.

'Right now I don't have enough money to live on.'

'Well, perversely, that could work out better for you in this predicament. Would you like me to draft an application for funding a barrister?'

'A barrister?'

'To represent you in court.'

He riffles through the papers in his briefcase searching, I guess, for the appropriate form. Another form.

'Why are you talking about going to court already? I haven't even been questioned yet. You do realise I'm totally innocent?'

Marks glances up from his searching, speaks in my general direction over the rim of his specs.

'As things stand currently, Mr er...'

'Taylor.'

'You are legally innocent.'

'There you are, then.'

'Unless and until found legally guilty.'

Marks crosses his arms over his briefcase and continues in a rehearsed and unemotive style that suggests he delivers the same spiel most days. 'What is material is not whether one is innocent or guilty in *fact* but in *law*. The first stage is, are the police and the CPS convinced they have enough evidence to mount a robust prosecution in court? If so, can the Crown then prove beyond reasonable doubt that the defendant committed the crime and that no defences apply?'

'And you think they have enough evidence?'

'I think we should make that working assumption.'

'Yeah, because while I'm stuck here talking to you they're across at my flat planting god knows what to fit me up - that's what it's called, isn't it?'

The solicitor sighs. 'Really Mr Taylor, I don't think it's helpful to your case to start accusing the police of misconduct. In my experience...'

'You're supposed to be on my side, aren't you?'

'I'm here to help with your legal defence and to advise you in this situation. Right now my advice is to let the police get on with their job.'

'And what about tomorrow?'

'Tomorrow we'll deal with their questions.'

'Shouldn't I stay silent?'

'I don't think that would be helpful.'

To who? I almost say, but I stop myself in time. No sense in pissing off Marks as well as Tregarron. But there is one question I'm burning to ask and I do, just as he's gathering up his documents at the end of our meeting.

'Do you think I did it? Do you think I murdered Jane Ogden?'

He stands up, looks at me steadily. 'My opinion, Mr Taylor, supposing I have formed one, is immaterial to my work on your behalf.'

I know that Tregarron must have come back to the station because I heard him shout at somebody along the corridor. 'Get them to put salt and vinegar on mine.' Must be doing a late shift. Thinking up questions for me tomorrow. Wonder if he has a wife at home. Wonder what he's taken from the flat. Better have kept his greasy hands off my photo of Karin - that's got nothing to do with this.

That's him again, singing as he walks past, enjoying the echo off the hard walls. *As the snow flies.* Elvis Presley. It's a miserable song but he sounds happy enough. Surprised he hasn't popped his head round the cell door since he seems to get a kick out of winding me up. Saving it all until the morning, I suppose.

Tregarron may not have bothered to come into my cell, but through the night somebody else does. Every half hour on the dot the door is unlocked and a torch light shone in my face. It's impossible to get any sleep - and I suspect that's the idea. Anything to weaken me, get me confused for when they come to question me. Is this some kind of elaborate plot to have me put inside for good, keep me away from Karin? Tregarron failed the first time, so now they're upping the ante.

It's the same young officer who keeps turning out with the torch. Says nothing, just switches the beam on, swishes once round the room, then full on my face, and off again. Locking the door as noisily he can. By three o' clock I've had enough.

'What the hell do you think you're doing?'

'Not asleep yet, Alex?'

'How can I get to sleep with you barging in with that torch every five minutes?'

'It's every half hour, actually.'

'I know it's every half hour. Why don't you leave me alone?'

'It's regulations. Home Office Detention Code.'

'Fuck the Detention Code.'

'It's to keep you safe. We wouldn't want you self-harming, would we?'

'I'm about ready to harm somebody.'

'Is that a threat?'

'Oh, go away.'

'Are you thirsty? I'll get you a cup of water.'

'Sod your water, just leave me alone.'

'Can't do that, Alex. Sorry. Don't want you dead on my watch.'

'I am dead. Dead fucking tired.'

'Hey, watch your language. And keep your voice down will you, there's people trying to get some sleep in here.'

XII

I must have fallen asleep eventually because the next interruption I'm aware of comes mid-morning - Tregarron himself bursting through in ebullient mood.

'Hands off cocks, on with socks. Eat up, Alex. We've got places to go, people to see.'

The tang of fried bacon fills my cell. I must admit the sandwich Tregarron has brought is the only palatable grub I've been offered since my McDonalds burger, which seems much further off than yesterday. I could have done without the unrequested sugar in my tea but at least it provides a rush that should liven me up ready for the expected interview.

The question session, though, won't be till this afternoon. First, I'm told, I'm to be part of an identity parade. I'm not even given the chance to clean my teeth after my bacon butty; Tregarron and a PC march me out of my cell to the back yard of the police station where there is a van waiting. Just before we leave the building I hear the constable murmur to Tregarron, 'Few paps out there.' Tregarron turns to me.

'You might want to put your coat over your head.'

'What for? I've no reason to hide.'

As we cross the yard to the van I catch a glimpse of a knot of people gathered in the alley at the side of the station. Someone bangs on the side of the van as it drives up the alley to the main road, and a couple of cameras appear and disappear at the window - press photographers jumping up to get a snap of me. How do these people know I'm being held at the station, never mind that I'd be coming out now? I turn from the window to see Tregarron watching me. He grins and winks. Still looking very pleased with himself. I give him a scowl. Spend the rest of the journey with my own thoughts, picking at my teeth to dislodge a stuck piece of bacon.

The so-called Identification Unit is a complex of joined-up portakabins at the back of what turns out to be a police training base - a college for coppers - as I discover when I'm put with the other members of my line-up. Before that I meet with my solicitor Mr Marks who seems a tad more animated than yesterday.

'It's a while since I've been involved in a live line-up. It's usually VIPER these days.'

'VIPER?'

'Stands for Video Identification Parade Electronic Recording - I think that's correct. They make a tape of you full face and profile and set

141

you against similar types from a video database to see if witnesses can pick you out.'

'So why is this different?'

'There are some words to say during this parade, so they can't use the standard database. Nothing to worry about; it makes no difference really. The good thing is they can set things up quickly here using volunteers from among the trainees. Gets it out of the way for us. Here, I have the script for you.'

He hands me a card with the handwritten words *Just these, please. Thank you.*

'That's it?'

'Mmm. A request from one of the witnesses, apparently. Now, let's go and choose our usual suspects.'

The walls of the next portakabin along are straining to contain a roomful of generously proportioned, clean-shaven blokes with neat haircuts. I feel as if I'm joining a queue of rugby union players waiting for a job interview. I'm supposed to pick out nine to stand in the ID parade with me.

'But none of them look like me,' I complain to Marks.

'They don't have to match exactly. The idea is that as far as possible they are similar to the suspect in age, height and general appearance - obviously they're all white men in this case - and position in life.'

Position in life. There's no danger anybody could ever mistake me for a policeman, trainee or otherwise. However, between us Marks and I manage to select nine that are approximately my age and height. At the solicitor's suggestion I switch coats with one of the line-up so am led into yet another portakabin in company with my new rugby mates wearing a slightly oversized crombie and a soiled hospital dressing at the back of my head.

This room is a long, bare narrow space with spotlights fixed in the ceiling and what seems at first to be a sort of panoramic cinema screen on the opposite wall from where we are asked to stand. I'm given my choice of position in the line-up. I say 5 at first (being the number of letters in Karin's name) then I realise that puts me more or less in the middle, so I switch to 8. We are all rehearsed in stepping slightly forward when our number is called, turning right, left and to the front. We are reminded of the words we have to say and asked if we can remember them without the card. Duh. Amazingly, one of our trainee officers, number 4, asks if he can hold his, just in case. Mr Marks speaks up.

'I think it should be either everyone holds cards or no-one.'

He flashes me a quick smile, looking for praise, I guess, for his brilliant intervention on my behalf. Number 4 is persuaded he can remember his lines without the card, and we are ready. We stand silently in our row for at least a minute, as if we're mourning someone's passing, then I notice dim shadows moving behind the screen and I realise it's actually some variation of those one-way mirrors that permit people to observe a room in secret. That's why this space is so narrow; it's a large portakabin divided in half, with the witnesses being brought in to make their identification without the threat of having to meet the suspect face to face. Good for witness protection, but right now I wish I knew who's supposed to have seen me doing what and where.

The spotlights above us turn to full glare and a disembodied voice says through a speaker 'Number 1, please.'

Number 1 steps forward confidently enough, turns right, turns left, looks ahead and says, 'Just these, please. Thank you.' As he steps back on his heels I find myself thinking involuntarily, *It's not him.*

Number 2 is less confident but manages OK. By the time it's Number 3's turn I'm conscious that I'm taking too much interest in how the others are doing. This could be interpreted as suspicious behaviour. I make myself face forward and so miss Number 4's performance, but I note the long hesitation and how he falters on his words. He says *Thanks* instead of *Thank you* but nobody asks him to do it again. Why did I pick this dope for the line-up? He's made it obvious it's not him. But then again, perhaps he's displaying the nervousness of a guilty man. Or maybe too obviously playing the part of daft laddie.

These contradictory thoughts occupy me all the way down the line. All the while trying to work out how I should say the words. Should I stumble like Number 4, or play it cool like Number 1? What's best to do?

'Number 8, please.'

I'm shocked it's my turn so soon. I feel myself rocking on my heels, then step forward with too much propulsion as if I'm being pushed from behind. The glare of the spotlight on me intensifies. Surely they've turned it up deliberately, some sort of signal. Do I turn right first, or left? I turn right, left, face forward. 'Just these, please. Thank you.' Step back. Long breath out. *It's him.*

I remember having a whole conversation with a druggy guitar player I worked with once about Kafka, though I'd never read him and haven't since. I pretended that I had, to big myself up a bit I suppose, and I got away with it, mainly by listening to what this person was saying and sort of reflecting his opinion back to him. I learned quite a lot about Kafka from that conversation. I know how his characters feel isolated, like aliens on a planet they inhabit but can't quite fathom. They find themselves in places that are somehow apart from the real world, manipulated by bureaucrats with their own mysterious agenda so that eventually they become entirely disoriented. Lost.

I'm beginning to feel like a character in a Kafka story. I'm accused of something I have no knowledge of. All I know, assuming it's true, is that Jane died, or was murdered. Or that's what I've been told, though nobody has said how or where or when. For all I know she could still be alive, maybe standing behind that screen watching me with the others, playing a part for the sake of their secret agendas like the girl who pretended to be my Ruth. And who are these *witnesses*? Why am I and these anonymous men being asked to repeat ordinary words that you might say casually in a shop or a restaurant or something? I could understand it if it was *Get down on the floor* or *I have a gun*, something like that. But *Thank you*? Weird. The ordinariness of it makes it stranger.

Marks is no help. Another bureaucrat handing me forms, leading me like the others through more doors to more rooms and corridors. Then there's Tregarron. I've seen his dark side, but now he's grinning, singing, making lewd jokes. He's enjoying his power over me. Likes having the key to my door. He's taunting me, dangling something in front of him that I can't see. Any minute he'll start hissing *My precious* at me like Gollum. Tregarron is a big slimy ball of menace.

They leave me stewing hours more in the cell at the station before I'm taken to the interview room. The good news is that Deborah Ann is waiting with Mr Marks outside the door. She seems genuinely pleased to see me, which is reassuring.

'I'm sorry I couldn't get along to your ID thing this morning. It was such short notice and I had a commitment with another client.'

'No problem. Do you know what they've got me in for?'

'Mmm, you're front page news, I'm afraid.'

She knows and she came anyway. That's brilliant. Her friendliness is shadowed with a look of nervous concern when DI Lambert and DS Tregarron turn up, but she nods at me as we all troop through into the interview suite, her way of saying she's there for me.

It's a lot more cramped in this little room than last time, with the two officers facing me across the table, Mr Marks next to me, and Deborah Ann off to the side. As Lambert leads us through the introductions I notice the video is on record this time, not just the audio tape. Smile for the camera. They have a copper stationed outside the door

144

as well. What do they think I'm going to do - overpower everybody in here and make a run for it?

'So, Alex,' says DI Lambert, 'Perhaps you can begin by telling us about your relationship with Jane Ogden.'

'We don't have a relationship... didn't have. She lived across the hall from me, that's all. Just a neighbour. I hardly knew her really.'

'But you went to the pub together. To The Grapes around the corner.'

'Just the once. She'd lost her house keys and couldn't get in to her flat. I was trying to help her, that's all. Just being a good neighbour.'

'And did you find her keys?'

'She found them herself. Well, turns out she'd left them at work.'

'I see. She went back to her office to look for her keys, did she, after she'd been in The Grapes with you?' He checked a note in his book. 'That would be some time after ten at night.'

'No, she told me the next day she'd found them in her desk drawer.'

'The next day?'

'Yes.'

'So where did she sleep the night before, when she was still locked out? The night she left the pub with you.'

In my peripheral vision I see Debbie's right hand cross over her left in her lap. Absurdly, in the middle of Lambert's questioning, it comes to me that I've never noticed whether she wears a ring on that left hand. Now I can't see it.

'Well?'

'I offered to let her sleep in my room.'

'And did she?'

'Yes.'

'In your bed?'

'Yes.' A glance at Debbie. 'I slept on the sofa.'

Tregarron pipes up. 'I've seen that couch, Alex. It's pretty small for lying on, even for somebody your size. You must have been pretty uncomfortable.'

'I was.'

'Were you not tempted to snuggle in next to Jane?'

'No.'

'Even though the two of you had had a few beers, got on very well together from all accounts? Very cosy together in the pub. Come on, Alex, we're all men here.' He raises his hand from the desk as Debbie looks up. 'Sorry, figure of speech. You know what I mean.'

Lambert is more direct. 'Did you have sex with Jane Ogden that night?'

'No.'

'But you did on other occasions.'

'No.' I look deliberately at Tregarron. 'I'm a married man.'

Beside me Mr Marks coughs discreetly. DI Lambert leans forward.

'Say again?'

'I'm a married man.'

'We may come back to that. Meanwhile DS Tregarron has something to show you. Jack?'

Tregarron reaches behind him to pluck something from a pile of material on the table below the video camera. It's an object in a clear plastic evidence bag like the ones he was using last time I was here.

'Recognize this, Alex?' he says.

'It's a key, a door key.'

'Yours?'

'Possibly, I don't know.'

'Well, it was in the pocket of the jeans you had on when you were arrested yesterday, so it's likely to be yours, right?'

'Probably.'

Tregarron holds up the bag to the camera. 'For the purposes of the tape I'm showing to Mr Robson a bag holding a key which I have marked as Exhibit IL/1.' He lowers the bag and dangles it directly in front of my eyes. 'We'd all expect it to be your key. That's the logical conclusion.' He places the bag on the table. 'Except I have tried this key in the door of your flat and it doesn't fit. It doesn't unlock the front door either. So whose door do you think that key might open, Alex?'

'Probably Jane's.'

'Why do you say so?'

'I just think it might be.'

'Well, I can confirm that, because I tried the key in Jane's door and, hey presto, it opened unto me.'

He glances at Deborah Ann with a twitch of a smile. DI Lambert uses the end of his biro to pull the bag towards him as he picks up the questioning. 'Can you explain why you are in possession of the key to Jane Ogden's flat?'

'Not really.'

'Well, it seems to me there are only three possible explanations. One: Jane Ogden gave you that key because she was comfortable with you using it to go in and out of her room, which strongly supports the idea that the two of you were in an intimate relationship. Or two: you

146

came into possession of the key without her knowledge during her lifetime. Or three: you came into possession of the key after Jane's death. Which is it, Alex?'

'None of these.'

'Explain.'

'I collected the key on Jane's behalf from the landlord.'

'Mr Chatterjee?'

'Along with a new front door key. Ask him if you like.'

'So why did you still have it yesterday?'

'She found her old keys in the meantime and... I suppose we just forgot.'

Tregarron mutters something. Mr Marks speaks for the first time. 'Sorry, I missed that.'

'I said, accidentally on purpose.' He looks a bit sheepishly at DI Lambert, then straightens up in his chair to address me. 'Your Mr Chatterjee, by the way...'

'He's not *my* Mr Chatterjee.'

'Is under the distinct impression that you were in a relationship with Jane Ogden. So are the other tenants in the building. They've seen you coming and going, in and out of each other's rooms at all hours, apparently.'

'Just being neighbourly.'

'Doesn't square with your earlier statement that you hardly knew her.'

DI Lambert taps at the bag holding the key. 'Have you ever used this key to enter Ms Ogden's room, with or without her knowledge?'

'Can't remember.'

'Come on, Alex.'

'Only to borrow a bottle of milk.'

Lambert laughs - at the banality of it I suppose - but I'm just telling the truth, more or less.

'That's common practice with you, is it, breaking into people's property to get what you want?'

'I didn't break in.'

Tregarron interrupts. 'But it *is* your common practice, isn't it, Alex? We know that from the last time you were with us.'

I'm surprised and pleased to hear Mr Marks at this point. 'You know that won't be admissible in court.' Well done, Marksy, you're doing your job.

'We can bring in bad character evidence where the judge allows it's relevant. Besides, we just need to show the jury what we've found during

147

our search of Alex's room. I'm talking about this, for example.' He reaches behind for another, heavier, evidence bag which he almost throws down on the table between us.

'Don't break the frame, you prick.'

Never mind the look he gives me for swearing at him, I'm furious about his stupid carelessness. 'That's my stuff you're chucking about.'

'Is it, though? Where did you get this photo, Alex?'

'It's mine. I took it myself.'

'Yeah, you took it from a house you burgled in Beech Grove.'

He has me more wound up about this than anything said so far about Jane. 'It's a family photo, you've no right to have it. Got nothing to do with this.'

'Family photo, is it. Can you tell me who's in the picture?'

'My wife Karin, my daughter Ruth and a friend, I can't remember her name.'

'Which one's Ruth? Point her out for me.'

'The blonde girl, the pretty one.' I appeal to Deborah Anne. 'You remember I told you about my poor Ruth.'

Tregarron grabs the frame in its bag and seems to address the group in the photo as he says, 'For the tape Mr Robson has just wrongly identified, as Ruth, a girl named Alexandra or Alex Taylor, who is a member of the family that lives at the property from which we believe this photograph marked IL/2 to be stolen.'-

'What are you talking about? What the hell are you saying?' I turn again to Debbie. 'I don't even know what's going on. They're trying to confuse me.'

She half rises from her chair, says anxiously to DI Lambert, 'I do think you're upsetting him unnecessarily. There are issues of vulnerability here.'

Tregarron scowls, but before he gets the chance to say anything more Mr Marks puts in, 'Actually, gentlemen, I was going to ask for a time out at this point. If I could take the opportunity for a word with my client I think it might be helpful for all concerned.'

Back in my cell the solicitor makes some notes on a lined yellow pad and checks through some documents from his briefcase before he speaks to me.

'How do you think it's going so far, Alex?'

'Oh hunky dory, I can tell they believe I didn't do it. Probably let me out by supper time.'

My irony seems to be lost on him, or maybe he's just trained to react to every situation with a blank expression. If someone told him the world was going to end in five minutes he'd probably make a note in his pad, then check his watch before he sat back to wait for Armageddon.

'It seems we do have one major issue here,' he says.

'What's that?'

'Your insistence on the Taylor identity, and this whole business about your association with the family. You see, without it I'm sure we can get the court to rule your previous... behaviour inadmissible - you're hardly a serial offender and there was no violence involved. But if you adduce the evidence to yourself...'

'Add... what?'

'If you deliberately draw attention to this persona you have adopted then the prosecution will have every justification in bringing up these other matters on the grounds of necessary background information and clarification. If the jury learns you're living under an assumed name and are a convicted stalker...'

'I'm not a stalker.'

'Perhaps not, but you see, you're not really helping matters at the moment. All I'm saying is that the ordinary men and women who are given this great responsibility to act as jurors can surely accept you as one among them, part of their community: an ordinary single man, a self-employed piano tuner named Alex Robson - which is in fact your status *de facto* and *de jure* - if you accept it yourself. Without 'Alex Taylor' it appears to me the police have relatively little on which they can charge you. It's all fairly circumstantial as far as I'm concerned.'

'Is that it? Are you done?'

'That's my advice. What do you have to say to it?'

'I say, read my lips. I am Alex Taylor.'

And as Mr Marks closes his briefcase in resignation I can picture myself, one of a host of gladiators all calling out in chorus, *I am Alex Taylor.*

'Jack and me have been looking through the photos in your phone,' says DI Lambert. We've all reassembled in the interview suite and Tregarron has announced a time check for the tape.

Jack and I, I'm thinking (my mam was always keen on grammar, drilled it into me), but what I say aloud is, 'Have you. Don't mind me.'

He has my mobile on the table in front of him. When he picks it up he wipes his thumb over the screen as if making a point about how grimy it is, then works his way through menus and images as he talks.

149

'You haven't taken very many pictures, I notice, not like some people who are always snapping away, so the ones you do take must be quite important to you.'

'Never really thought about it.'

'This one, for instance, that's a strange sort of photo to keep on your phone, isn't it?' He turns the display towards me. 'Describe that image for me, Alex.'

'It's a plaque.'

'What sort of plaque?'

'Well, actually a grave marker. Not a tombstone. It's Ruth's grave, you can see that from the words on the plate.'

'Ruth who?'

'Are you trying to be funny?' I have a go at bringing Deborah Ann into play, my *responsible adult*. 'That's not fair, is it Debbie, disrespectful. That's my Ruthie's grave.' She acknowledges me with a smile, but doesn't say anything. Lambert continues.

'It's a simple enough question. Ruth who?'

'Ruth Taylor.'

'And Ruth is buried where?'

'Deerholme Woodland Park.'

'A place you know well.'

'I've been there. Obviously.'

'Recently.'

'A week or so ago. I took that picture then - I'm sure you'll already have checked the date.'

'The main bus driver on the route picked you out from the ID parade this morning. There's not that many get off the bus at the cemetery, so he tends to remember the odd repeat visitor. He tells us you've been at Deerholme at least twice in the past ten days, probably more. What keeps you going back, Alex?'

'To see Ruth, I've told you. To see her grave, I mean.'

'Does death have some kind of fascination for you?'

'Fuck off.' Then 'Sorry' to Debbie.

'It was thoughtful of you to bring flowers,' says Lambert.

'What?'

Tregarron joins in. 'Oh, he likes to buy flowers for the ladies, don't you, Alex? A red rose under the windscreen, that's his signature.'

'White carnations in this case,' Lambert says. 'Mind you, I'm not sure they appreciate bouquets at these green burial places. Especially not wrapped in cellophane. Not environmentally friendly. They don't like you leaving them on the graves.'

150

I'm struggling to catch up with this. 'I've never put flowers on Ruth's grave.'

'Yes, you did, last Thursday morning. I can even tell you where you bought them and who served you. Louise at the cigarette counter in Morrisons. She picked you out from the ID parade as well. Remembers you especially for two reasons. Because she thought, at last the saddo has a girlfriend.' He glances quickly at Debbie. 'Louise's words, not mine. And because you said, *Just these, please* which made her think, *Just these please, Louise.* Also you left the sticker and the barcode on the cellophane at the cemetery so we could tie it all up nicely, thank you. Oh, that's the other thing you said to Louise. *Thank you.* Very polite, she told us.'

This is not right, this is not right. I have to think about this. I *did* buy some flowers at Morrisons last Thursday on the way back from Karin's studio, but they were for Jane, not Ruth. Not sure I can tell them that - it will fuel their suspicions about our supposed relationship. But why are they making a big deal of this anyway? What has Ruth got to do with Jane? Is this just another piece in the jigsaw picture they're creating of me as some weird loner? While I'm still deciding what to say about the flowers DI Lambert changes tack.

'When was the last time you saw Jane Ogden?'

'I don't remember.'

'Try. Think about it very carefully. This is vitally important.'

'Well, OK it will have been... last Wednesday.'

'October 10th. A week today.'

'Is it Wednesday today?'

'Time flies when you're enjoying yourself,' from Tregarron. I ignore him.

'Yes, it was last Wednesday evening. I'd just come in and she was in the hallway looking through her post.'

'Presumably you spoke to each other.'

'Just passed the time of day, you know, the way you do.'

'That's all?'

'Yes.'

'So you didn't have an argument? A row?'

'A lovers' tiff.' That's Tregarron again.

'No. Why should we?'

Lambert checks his notes. 'Do you know Shaun Bailey?'

'Never heard of him.'

'He's one of the students who lives upstairs from you. Last Wednesday evening he was on his way out to meet some friends. He was coming down the stairs, only he stopped because he heard a row going on in the hallway. Didn't want to embarrass you by walking in on it. But he heard what went on clearly enough. Jane was particularly upset at you, according to Mr Bailey. Can you remember what she said?'

'I have no idea what you're talking about.'

'Shaun can remember, because the language was quite colourful.' Lambert refers to his notebook, reads what written there. 'She said, *You weren't keeping it to yourself last night, far from it. But you can keep it in your pants as far as I'm concerned, or shove it up your arse.* Does that jog your memory, Alex?'

'Maybe she was talking to somebody else.'

'I don't think so. When he heard Jane's door slam Shaun Bailey carried on down the stairs, just in time to see you disappearing into your room. No-one else was in the hallway and no-one left through the front door. So there you are. That's a very significant conversation, if that's we can call it, Alex, do you know why?'

'Because in your warped minds you think I was so upset by her shouting at me that I killed her for it. What a load of bollocks.'

'Interesting interpretation, but the significance goes beyond that. The point is that to our knowledge this was the last anyone saw or heard anything of Jane Ogden before she disappeared. With one tiny exception. Mr Bailey returned late from seeing his friends, at a time when the whole household seemed to be quiet and sleeping. But just before 2 am, when he was anxious to get some sleep himself because he had a trial exam in the morning, he was disturbed by distinct sounds of movement between the two rooms below - doors opening and closing, muffled voices, that sort of thing. As you know, the only two rooms downstairs are yours and Jane's. Would you care to tell us what the two of you were doing in the early hours of Thursday morning?'

'I was asleep. I couldn't tell you what Jane was doing or who with.'

I can't sit here and let the noose tighten round me like this. I know that was the night I told Jane about being married to Karin, but I also know they'll jump to all sorts of wrong conclusions if I admit it. Hate myself for lying, but what else can I do? Worse, in my desperation I try to shift attention to somebody else who's probably as innocent as I am.

'What about this guy Shaun Bailey? You seem to be accepting his word over mine. How do you know he didn't go down and bump Jane off? Why don't you bring him in for questioning?'

'I can assure you, Mr Bailey has been interviewed at length as has the other tenant Marc Donald. Both sat timed papers under exam conditions on Thursday morning and they have a number of witnesses to vouch for their movements at other relevant times. But perhaps the most telling thing against you, Alex, is where Jane Ogden's body was eventually found. Of course you already know that.'

'I know nothing, I've told you. I don't know when or where or how Jane died. I didn't know she *was* dead or even missing until you told me yesterday afternoon that you were arresting me for her murder. The whole thing has been a complete shock to me.'

'All right then, for the record. Jane Ogden disappeared, as far as we can tell, sometime after 2am on Thursday October 11th though she had scheduled time off from work that day and was not expected in the office. She was not officially reported missing until Monday October 15th after her mother contacted her work because she had not heard from Jane over the weekend as usual and she was not answering her phone. The search for Jane at that stage was low level, not much more than a note on file in the immediate aftermath of the report; she was an independent adult not thought to be in trouble so if she chose to go off and do her own thing for a few days that was hardly abnormal. All that changed early yesterday morning, Tuesday October 16th, when a retired couple out walking their dog in the woods had the misfortune to come across a young woman's body partly hidden by shrubbery. The body was well off the main track - it was the putrid smell that alerted them. The discovery was made in the uncultivated area of the forest that forms part of Deerholme Woodland Park. Identification in her coat pocket soon established that this was the body of the missing woman Jane Ogden. Can you confirm that you've taken all this in, Alex, or would you like me to go through it again?'

I can't answer him immediately. Having some kind of brain freeze. I really do need a moment to let this sink in. Poor Jane really is dead. And she died in the wood near the cemetery. My god, that's why they're so keen to place me there. But what was she doing so far away from home? Why there? Jesus, she was visiting Ruth's grave. She was checking up on my story. Or maybe she was genuinely moved by it, wanted to pay her respects. What were you thinking about, Jane? What was your state of mind?'

'Alex?'

'Maybe she killed herself,' I say out loud.

'Sorry?'

'A lot of people go to places like woods, somewhere quiet, to end it all.'

'I can assure you this was not suicide, but why would you even think she'd contemplate it? Was she unhappy?'

'I don't know.'

153

What can I say to all this? I can clear up the mystery of Jane being in the area, but I can't do it without pointing a finger directly at myself. It's suspicion piled on suspicion. My mind's in a turmoil, thinking about dates, times, when I last saw Jane, when I found her room empty, what I was doing over the days she was missing. Then it comes to me in a great wave of relief. Karin's my alibi, and so are the police themselves.

'I couldn't have done it.'

'Why not?' says Lambert.

'She went missing on Thursday, right?'

'We can't account for her movements on Thursday.'

'And her body was discovered early yesterday morning.'

'Correct.'

'Well, last Thursday morning I was outside Karin Taylor's dance studio. At 12.30 I went inside and spoke to her receptionist. You know this, but check again with her if you want. Organize another ID parade and she'll pick me out. Also I bought a tuna sandwich at the deli outside her office and ate it there in full view of everyone. I went to the supermarket on the way home and later I went to the corner shop - the shopkeeper there waved at me. He knows me; why don't you ask him too? The rest of the evening I was at my computer - there's bound to be some record of that at Google or whatever. As for Friday, you know I went to Beech Grove and ended up in hospital over the weekend, and you know where I was the rest of the time, until late Tuesday morning - in a cell at this station, then at the magistrates' court. So not much time to commit a murder in the meantime.'

'No,' says DI Lambert coolly as if he'd already considered all this. 'But time enough.'

'When? Tell me when.'

'Well, we're still waiting for the full pathologist's report, but first examination of the body and evidence from the scene makes it certain that Jane was killed several days before she was discovered, and that she was murdered at or near the place she was found. Our working assumption is that she was killed on Thursday, or Friday morning at the latest.'

'Well, then.'

'We know you visited the cemetery on Thursday morning and frankly, Alex, we believe that, for whatever reason, Jane was with you, either willingly or unwillingly, and that you killed her there and then.'

'I've just told you I was outside Karin's studio in town on Thursday morning, and I have a witness.'

'You have a witness that places you at the studio around 12.30pm. As you know perfectly well from your journeys, as remote as it seems it takes less than half an hour by bus from the cemetery to the town centre; quicker if you have another form of transport, taxi for example. Time to kill Jane and be back in town before lunch.'

'That's ridiculous - I'd be covered in blood.'

Lambert and Tregarron exchange glances. 'Who said there was blood involved?' from Tregarron.

'Well... it's a murder. There's bound to be blood.'

'Not necessarily,' Lambert says. 'Not necessarily at all. Interesting.'

I can feel the whole room tense up, and a shiver goes through me. Deborah Ann is looking down at her fingers again. Why did I imagine there'd be blood? Why did I say that? I can feel another notch tighten.

'Besides,' Lambert continues, 'As I'm sure you know there's a stream running through the woods, and there are public conveniences attached to the main cemetery building, so the killer will have had an opportunity to wash himself if, as you say, there was blood involved.'

He pauses to make a note, though I don't know why since my stupid statement has already been recorded on tape for all concerned to misinterpret to their hearts' content. I wish I could take it back, but it's done now. Why did I say I'd be covered in blood? DI Lambert finishes his note and looks steadily at me.

'You know what I would do, Alex, if I were a murderer? First, I would get as far away as possible from the murder scene as quick as I could. Then I would make damn sure that everybody knew I was in quite another place, far away. I would aim to do something other people wouldn't forget in a hurry. It's an interesting piece of timing, isn't it, that you have managed to stay well away from Karin Taylor for over a year, yet at just around the time of Jane Ogden's disappearance and subsequent murder you turn up in a very public manner at her office, and later her home, and even contrive to get yourself locked away. Mmm.'

'That's ridiculous. That's just... ridiculous.' But I'm already playing it over in my mind as if I was on the jury, one of those 'ordinary men' that my solicitor talked about. That ordinary man in my head is saying *guilty*. I've no choice; I've got to tell them more about Jane and me.

'Listen, I did buy flowers at Morrisons, white carnations, but they were for Jane, not for Ruth's grave.'

Lambert nods, willing me to go on.

'I remember the girl on the counter - Louise, was it? - pretty, dark-haired girl. I went to her till instead of one of the checkouts because I only had the flowers to pay for. But honestly Mr Lambert, she's mistaken

155

about the time. I bought the flowers just after lunch, not in the morning. I'm probably on CCTV somewhere, have you checked that?'

Tregarron says, 'You think we've been sitting on our arses? There's no working camera in that part of the store, and so far you haven't shown up on any of the tapes we've been through.'

I'm not sure if that's a good thing for me or not. Too jangled to think logically at this stage. Lambert's eyes haven't left my face since I started this explanation. It's unnerving.

'Why did you buy Jane flowers?'

'We'd had a bit of a misunderstanding the day before. Not an argument, nothing like a row, just a misunderstanding that we cleared up later.'

'So you took these carnations home and gave them to Jane.'

' I meant to, but she wasn't in, or at least she wasn't answering her door.'

'What did you do with the flowers?'

'I kept them in my room until I thought she'd be home from work, then I tried knocking at her door again. Still no answer so I left them with a note next to her door where she could see them when she came in. They were still in the same place on Friday morning.'

The image of the flowers in their cellophane propped against Jane's door stirs another flicker of hope for me.

'Surely the students will have seen the flowers when they were coming in and out through the hallway. They're bound to have done.'

Lambert is impassive. 'Sorry to disappoint you, Alex. The two of them went out on a bender after their exam. Didn't come back home at all on Thursday - touched lucky with a couple of girls they met at a club.'

'Have you...?'

'Yes, we've checked with the girls.'

'Damn. Ah but no, though, it's all right.' (Of course, of course it's all right. Thank god.) 'I remember what I did with the flowers. I put them in Jane's room on Friday morning. In her sink in some water.'

'So you let yourself into her room?'

'Yes, I... I suddenly remembered I had the key Mr Chatterjee gave me. So I let myself in to drop off the flowers. Plus I was a bit worried about her by then to be honest, because I noticed she hadn't taken her bike to work like she usually did. So it was sort of to check on her as well.'

'You were worried about her?'

'Sort of.'

'What reason did you have to be worried?'

'No particular reason.'

156

'But worried enough to unlock her room to check... what?'

'That she wasn't ill or anything. But mainly to leave her the flowers.'

'You realise our men have been right through Jane's flat since yesterday.'

'I know, I saw them. Did they find some flowers?'

'Tell you what they did find,' says Tregarron. 'Your fingerprints all over the place. And some letters addressed to you. We already know you'd been in the room on several occasions, so don't think you're getting any Brownie points for finally admitting it. But flowers, no. Not a single petal.'

He says this as if he's getting one over me, but I'm delighted to hear it.

'Well, there you are, then?'

'What?'

'That proves Jane came back to the flat some time on Friday, or maybe even later. She must have picked up the flowers then, and I think it was her that took them to the cemetery. She must have gone to visit Ruth's grave.'

'Why would she do that?' says DI Lambert. 'She had no connection with the family at all. She would have known nothing of Ruth's grave, and as a newcomer to the area it's unlikely she would even have been aware of a cemetery up that way.'

'Well, she did, because I told her. When we were sort of making up, if you want to call it that, on Wednesday night, or rather early Thursday morning when the guy upstairs heard us; that's what I was explaining to her. I told her all about it, all about my family and Ruth's death and everything. I think she was upset, then sympathetic. Definitely sympathetic. That's how I'll always remember her.'

Lambert sits back in his chair. Says nothing for a moment, still looking at me, then leans forward again. 'Well, that's quite an impressive story, Alex, and part of it does help to explain why Jane Ogden went to or allowed herself to be taken to Deerholme, so thank you for that. Only one problem with your version. Not only does Louise at Morrisons insist that you bought the flowers on Thursday morning, but the witnesses who came forward to tell us about the flowers being on Ruth's grave saw them there Thursday lunchtime. Not Friday. Not any other day. Thursday.'

'It's impossible.'

'It's right.'

I close my eyes and my forehead drops into the palm of my good hand. My right arm is clutching my body in and supporting my left elbow. To them it's the dejection of a guilty man, but I'm not finished yet; I'm frantically checking facts in my mind, going over and over them. Where I was, what I was doing, who I saw, where and when - anything I might bring up to prove I wasn't in those woods at the time they say. I remember that Thursday morning I went into Jane's room. Her bike helmet bumped on the door as it opened. Her coat was gone from the hook, so was her rucksack. I was looking for her diary; it wasn't there. Did she take it with her when she went to see Ruth's grave? Maybe she'd written down the address I gave her after we talked. I wonder if she'd filled the page in for Wednesday, written down what we talked about, how we were. It was late by the time I left her room - maybe she took the book on Thursday to catch up on her entry. I can imagine her sitting writing in the park, in the bower where I'd sat smoking weed. She must have had her diary. That would be why she took her rucksack, even though she wasn't on her bike. Dare I mention the diary? If they found it, would that help me, or make things worse? It couldn't be any worse. I lift my head.

'What was in her rucksack?'

Tregarron and Lambert look at each other in surprise. Tregarron purses his lips slightly; his fat neck moves inside his collar. I've caught them out somehow.

'Jane's rucksack was gone from her room. I noticed that on... on Friday morning when I took in the flowers.'

'We haven't recovered a rucksack,' says Lambert. 'Nor a purse, nor a phone, house keys...'

'They'll all be in her rucksack. Little black nylon rucksack, she'd only just bought it. Bet her diary's in there as well.'

More looks between the two officers. This is obviously all news to them. I carry on.

'She kept a diary, I've seen it in her room a few times. But it wasn't there last time. I know because I looked all over for it.'

'Why were you looking for her diary?'

(OK, time to fess up.) 'I wanted to see what she'd written about me.'

Tregarron straightens up in his chair. 'Can you describe this diary for us?' Almost politely for once. Maybe he's at last starting to realise I could be a helpful witness instead of their suspect.

'Sure, it's about the size of a standard Filofax. It's a page-a-day one. Pink cover. It has like a lace bookmark thing fixed inside the spine.'

Tregarron stands up as if he's about to leave the room, but instead he moves across to the table under the video camera, fishes about for something under a pile of exhibit bags, and turns back to show me.

158

'A bit like this, you mean?'

Inside the exhibit bag that he's holding between two fingers is a book-shaped object about the size of a Filofax. The pink looks darker than I remembered it - in fact it's decidedly grubby in the plastic bag - but I'm certain it's Jane's diary.

'Where has it been, in the stream?'

'No, it was nowhere near Jane's body when we found it. It was in a toilet cistern. *Your* toilet cistern.'

Before I have time to react, DI Lambert follows up. 'And just in case the water in the cistern wasn't enough to make it unreadable you tore every page out first, didn't you, Alex? I'm guessing you carefully flushed them down the toilet one by one.'

My first instinct is to lift from my seat and punch him. Instead I turn to Marks beside me and all but scream in his ear, 'I *told* you this would happen.'

'What?'

'They've set me up.'

Tregarron, still standing, looks as if he wants to launch himself at me. He moves halfway round the table, making Deborah Ann flinch as he brushes past her, 'I've never set anybody up in my life.'

'Well, somebody has. It wasn't me put that in the cistern, and you're the only ones that have been in my room since. You and Mr Chatterjee.' His name comes into my mouth before I compute it, but then it seems to make perfect sense. 'It must have been Chatterjee. He's got keys for my room and Jane's. I bet it was him that took the flowers out as well.'

'Why would he do that?' says Lambert.

'To point the finger at me. He doesn't like me, he's trying to get me out. In fact, how do you know he isn't the killer? It's as likely him as me.'

'Absolutely not.' Lambert is about to say something else about Mr Chatterjee, but before he does Tregarron, still visibly fuming, leans over and whispers something in his ear. Lambert nods and Tregarron leaves the room. 'For the tape DS Tregarron has temporarily left the interview suite to collect something from the incident room. The diary identified by Mr Robson as that belonging to the deceased Jane Ogden is the exhibit marked IL/3.'

I look across at Deborah Ann. She makes eye contact, gives a little nod. She believes me if nobody else does. Lambert taps his biro for attention.

'Listen very carefully. To accuse the police of tampering with or planting evidence is a serious allegation and if you really want to make a complaint of that nature it will be dealt with formally, independently and at the appropriate time. But let me say this, Alex. If in our wildest dreams I or DS Tregarron considered planting evidence on a suspect we would certainly not do it in a way that would destroy the very evidence we needed.' He picks up the exhibit bag from the table where Tregarron dropped it and shows me the sorry state of the diary, then replaces it. 'As for Mr Chatterjee I am not saying for one minute he is ruled out of our investigation. Nobody is ruled out until we are absolutely sure of our man, but I am looking at you, Alex, and I have to tell you I am strongly of the opinion that I'm looking in the right direction. Of course it's ultimately for the court to decide.'

Tregarron re-enters the room with what I first take to be a sheaf of papers in his hand. Lambert gestures with an open palm towards him, almost as if he's giving him the stage, and the detective sergeant takes his cue.

'I was going to spare you these, Alex, but I don't think you deserve it. You need to wake up to what you've done.'

With barely controlled anger he flips each sheet with thumb and forefinger from his sheaf, sends them spinning onto the surface of the table in front of me. Lambert, the magician's assistant, traps them with his fingers, preventing some from revolving right off the table and making sure they all face the right way for me to get the full effect. Now I recognize them as photographs but it takes a few seconds for my brain to catch up with what I'm looking at.

In tidying up the display Lambert has separated them into two distinct sets. The ones to my left are shot among trees, long grass and wild fern - obviously the denser woodland above Deerholme cemetery. Featured in the pictures, at various angles and distances, is what in some might be interpreted as a fly-tipped pile of old clothes and sagging bags left lying in thick weeds next to the base of a tree trunk, with some vile wetness oozing out of them. It's only in a few of the close-up shots that I can see features that are recognizably human, but in no way recognizably Jane. The body skin is limp and dark, so almost black that I nearly say, 'This can't be Jane, she's white' until I realise it must be the decomposing process that turned it that dark colour, and that caused the disgusting slime under the nose and over the mouth, where there might also be maggots but I have to look away without inspecting the mess more closely.

Turning my head brings the set of images on my right into focus. These pictures must have been taken in the mortuary or some antiseptic room set aside for the purpose. Jane on a slab. Parts of Jane in close-up. Jane naked but somehow not looking quite naked because of the

160

discolouration and the strange texture of her skin, like it's been daubed for some primitive native ceremony and seared with fire. And poked and pricked with sharp sticks. Her open hands, her forearms, her neck, her chest - all with a haphazard pattern of wounds. Not lacerations like the glass scars on my right wrist and arm; these are smaller, almost neater wounds, incisions, stabs not slashes.

'You terrified her,' says Tregarron. 'She tried to run away from you. We've seen the twigs and branches broken off where she tried to fight her way through to get away, and where you chased and caught up with her. And she tried so hard to stop you while you attacked her. Look at all those defensive wounds on her hands and her arms. She must have been screaming, begging you to stop. But you just kept thrusting away and thrusting away. Till you stuck one right through into her heart.'

'A stab wound through the pericardial sac,' says Lambert. 'Not the definite cause of death, the last we heard, but I think we can safely assume it caused massive internal bleeding. At least it wouldn't have taken long.'

'But not instantly, eh, Alex.' Tregarron sits down and leans towards me. 'Did you wait till you were sure of her, or did you leave her there struggling for life while you went to clean yourself up and get the hell out?'

He jabs his forefinger at the mortuary pictures.

'You know, I think DI Lambert's been too kind to you when he says you went rushing to Karin's to give yourself an alibi. When I look at these pictures what I see is what we call overkill. There's so much emotional rage in those blows that I don't believe would be quietened with the one killing. I think you went looking for Karin Taylor to satisfy your bloodlust.'

I feel breathless under this bombardment, can hardly get my words out. 'Why? Why would I want to kill Karin? What reason what I have to kill Jane Ogden?'

Tregarron bends right over the desk to hiss at me, 'People like you don't need reasons. And don't think what you did makes you special. I've told you before, Alex, I have you down for just your average psychopath.'

I twist my neck to avoid him and make a mute appeal to Deborah Ann. Her whole face colours when she sees me looking, and she casts her eyes down. She's lost the nerve to confront him under this onslaught.

Tregarron leans back slightly. He picks out one of the images at random, brings it close to my face. 'What do you notice about these wounds, Alex?'

'I don't know.'

'Can't you see the little rectangular punctures? See those squared-off ends? What kind of weapon would you imagine makes wounds like these?'

'I have no idea.'

He replaces the photograph in its space on the table, sits back to look at me. 'All right, let me you ask you another question. What's happened to the tools we returned when you were discharged from the magistrates' court?'

I have no answer to this.

'You remember your tuning hammer and your screwdriver. Where are they? Because I've been looking everywhere for them. They're not in your flat, not in your suitcase, not even in the toilet cistern or behind the panelling in the bathroom where you hid some of your other stuff. They weren't on you when we brought you in. So where are they, Alex? Where are they?'

'I... I stuffed them in somebody's hedge.'

'You what?'

'They're in a hedge somewhere, I don't know.'

'Why did you do that?'

'I thought I was going to be arrested. I didn't want them to be found on me. Listen, it's not what you're thinking. It's... oh. Could I please go to the toilet, I think I'm going to be sick.'

DI Lambert's voice sounds detached and cool following Tregarron's outburst and my choked replies.

'The images of the deceased shown to Mr Robson by DS Tregarron will be collated and marked as Exhibit IL/4. The time is 20.18 and I am switching the tape off as this interview is terminated.'

Mr Marks is waiting for me in my cell. Deborah Ann has had to rush off - late for dinner with her mother.

'What happens now?' I ask him.

'You'll go to the magistrates' court tomorrow, then you'll be on remand until your trial starts at the Crown Court.'

'What if the magistrate throws it out? You said it was just circumstantial evidence.'

'You know that's not going to happen, Alex.'

'Can I get bail, then?'

'No chance.'

'So is remand the same as prison?'

'For you, effectively, yes.'

'How long for?'

'Six to nine months, typically. Could be up to a year.'

'A year? A year in prison before I even go to trial?'

'Better get used to it, Alex. That's all I'm saying.'

My immediate thought is not for me, but how Karin will cope. The solicitor asks if I would like to make a statement, which I refuse, and he leaves. It's not long before DS Tregarron pops his head round the door, ubiquitous mug in hand. He's almost companionable now in contrast to his performance in the interview room.

'The lads asked me to say thanks for all the overtime you've given them in the last couple of days.'

I don't think he expects an answer. He swills tea from his mug, then takes a long look at me, like he did the first time I was here. Like he owns me.

'We'll get that bandage seen to before your appearance in court. Want you to look your best, don't we?'

I stare straight ahead.

'Want anything to eat, Alex, or will you just throw it all up?'

'No thanks.'

I lie back on the bunk, expecting him to go away, but the time waiting for the cell door to shut is endless and unnerving. Eventually I lift my head again and he's still there, watching. He has a triumphant smile on him, like he's just beaten me at chess.

'I've been thinking,' he says. 'Thinking about the irony of it all.'

He waits for me to bite. When I don't he supplies the rest of it anyway.

'Been thinking about how the flowers on Ruth's grave were what tied you into being at the cemetery. What's so ironic it's almost funny is that the witness who came forward to tell us she saw them there on Thursday morning was the *real* Alex Taylor.'

I turn over and face the white tiles on the wall. A few seconds later the cell door closes and locks

UNWILLING WITNESS

XIII

Mum and I couldn't believe it when our stalker got off just about scot-free after conning his way into the house like he did. Sergeant Tregarron had asked us if we wanted to go to court on the Tuesday to see him sent down on remand, but neither of us could face listening to him pile on the lies for the magistrate, so we just asked to be kept informed. Mum stayed off work and I bunked off lectures for the day because I knew she would be totally stressed out. It was me who took the phone call.

'Are you ready for this?' the sergeant said. 'Community service.'

'No.'

'And a non-molestation order. Restraining order, in other words.'

'You mean he's not going to prison?'

'I'm sorry to say that's exactly what I mean. I know, I know. I'm flabbergasted as well. I'm sorry, Alex. Honestly, I thought we had it sewn up.'

Mum came out of the lounge and stood like a ghost at the foot of the stairs. She knew from my response what had happened, or rather hadn't happened. She spoke almost in a whisper. 'He's out on the streets again?' I checked with Sergeant Tregarron.

'I've just now seen him off the premises. The only thing I will say is he's not allowed within two kilometres of the house or your mum's studio.'

'But he could ignore that. What's to stop him coming round here right now? Not a piece of paper, I can tell you.'

'Well, in fairness he did more or less keep out of the way last time, but look, I'm not going to leave you hanging high and dry. Here's what I'm going to do. There's a lovely WPC here called Heather Nolan and I'm going to send her round this very day to have a little chat with you, see what might be done to boost your security, that sort of thing.'

'If you're talking alarms we've got those already, so that's a waste of time.' I was a bit short with him, but I was so pissed off and disappointed about it all.

'No, I mean real police presence, at least in the short term, and Heather can discuss possibilities with you going forward. Listen, I'm with you, love, believe me. I'll make no bones about it - I'm sure as sure this man's dangerous. In fact in my book he's a regular fruit and nut case, the sort you can't cure, so we have to find other ways of dealing with him. Short of castration, that is. Don't worry, we'll do everything in our power to keep you safe.'

I'm sure that's what they said last time, but I thanked him anyway and he told me when to expect this WPC, just in case we inadvertently opened the door to you know who. Mum of course was terrified at the news.

'I know he's going to come round. Today or tomorrow, he can't help himself.'

'They'll be looking out for him.'

'What if he is in disguise? Look at all the preparations he made last time.'

'Let's not panic about it. Let's wait and see what this policewoman has to say.'

It didn't help mum's nerves that WPC Nolan was more than half an hour late for her appointment, especially when she told us why.

'I'm really sorry about this; bad start I know. Just the station's been kicking off in the last hour or so 'cause there's a young woman's body been found.'

'What, round here?'

'Just out of town I think, I didn't get all the details before I came out. Anyway, let's not concern ourselves with that right now. There wouldn't be a cup of tea and a biscuit going, would there? Sorry to ask, but I've had literally nothing since I came on at seven and if I don't get something down me soon I'll pass out. It's been that kind of day.'

While we talked in the front room Abi took on kitchen duty and made a bacon sandwich for Heather, even though she's not really supposed to do cooking. (She has been brilliant since mum stepped in to stop her being fired from the cleaning company over what happened. Mum and I agreed it absolutely wasn't Abi's fault.) Tregarron was right about Heather; she was lovely and very easy to talk to, though you could tell she'd be no soft touch with the baddies. She hadn't been particularly well briefed about the case so we spent the first fifteen minutes or so filling in the details. She was quite shocked. Although she had come across stalkers before, this was the first she had heard of somebody so delusional they actually believed they were married and had set up home with the person they were stalking.

'It's more common than you'd think,' I said, 'Especially in America for some reason. It's called erotomania. I've been researching it; well, looking on the internet. Can you remember that David Letterman, the talk show host?'

'I think so.'

166

'He had some woman pestering him for years claiming she was his wife. She was always breaking into his house apparently, 'borrowed' his car, that sort of thing. She ended up throwing herself in front of a train.'

'Poor woman,' said mum.

'Oh, you're so soft. This is typical of her,' I told Heather. 'Frightened to death of our guy, but she still feels sorry for him.'

Mum defended her position. 'Well, I certainly wouldn't want him to kill himself over me.'

'No, but a good long spell in prison wouldn't go amiss. Not going to happen now, unfortunately.'

'Not for want of trying, I can promise you,' Heather said. 'Jack Tregarron was spitting chips when he talked to me this morning.'

She told us about the terms of the restraining order and showed us on a city map she'd brought where the off-limits were, drawing two rough circles with a pen she took from her notebook

'See, that's a fairly sizeable area.'

'It doesn't cover Alex's walk to university, though.'

'Don't fuss, mum. It's you that needs protection. Anyway, I can look after myself. Chucked him down the stairs, didn't I?'

'Yes, I heard he got quite a whack on the bonce,' said Heather, and we had a good laugh together.

'Pity I didn't...' *finish him off*, I was going to say, but I remembered mum's sensitivities on the subject and let it drop.

Heather winked and leaned in to me. 'I'm not supposed to say anything but... you might want to take notice of where my finger just happens to be resting on the map.'

I looked down and saw her right forefinger on an area east of the city centre. She tapped her nail on a street, Gladstone Terrace. 'Just so you know to avoid it,' she said in a sort of murmur. I realised she was telling us discreetly where *he* lived without saying it out loud.

'Thanks.'

Heather told us Tregarron had wangled approval for twice-daily police patrols of the streets around our way and around the studio for the next four weeks initially, and she gave us a direct line which guaranteed a rapid response if we needed it night or day. 'I'll pop in as often as I can over the next month or so,' she said, 'Just to see how you're coping.'

'That's great, thank you.'

'But only if there's bacon butties on the go.'

Heather started to fold up the map she'd been using to show us the no-go zones. Her attention was caught by something on the outer fold and she held it up to me. 'Oh, that's the place, look. That's where that

167

poor girl's body was found this morning. In the woods here somewhere, I don't know exactly.'

I gasped when I saw where she meant 'You're joking me.'

'What?'

'Look mum, that's the woods right next to the cemetery. See, it says *Deerholme*.'

'Oh, I don't want to look. Keep it away from me, I'll have nightmares.'

I explained to Heather. 'It's where my sister Ruth is buried. We go there regularly.'

'Sorry, I didn't mean to scare you.'

'She didn't top herself, did she? Sorry, you'll think I'm obsessed with suicide.'

'Suspected murder.'

'Oh god, how old was she?'

'I don't have the details. Probably be on the local news tonight. Keep an eye out for it.' She looked at mum, still pale on the sofa. 'Or maybe not.'

I probably wouldn't have switched the TV on if mum had been in the same room, but I happened to be in my bedroom at the time while she was downstairs playing the piano. I wasn't even looking for the news particularly, just flicking the channels on my little set for want of something better to do. National weather, then over to the local news; and there it was, the lead story. I didn't recognize that particular part of the woods - anyway there was a sort of tent erected at the spot she was found, and barrier tape strung up, so it was difficult to get a sense of it as a location other than a crime scene. It was the second part of the story that had me hurtling down the stairs yelling, 'Mum, mum. Switch the telly on. Quick, you need to see this.'

I don't even know why I did that - it was like a panic reaction. Tell you the truth I think I was as much running away from the news or running to mum for comfort as I was desperate for her to see it. Of course all I did was put her in such a state of confusion that, between the two of us and the remote, by the time we switched the main telly on downstairs they'd moved on to something else.

'He's been arrested for that murder, I'm sure that's what they said.'

'Who? What are you talking about?'

'The stalker. They didn't say his name. I probably missed his name with coming to get you. Damn. But they said a forty-three-year-old man living alone in... What was the name of the street Heather pointed out?'

168

'What... I didn't see.'

'Gladstone something. 'Cause all the streets in that block were Prime Ministers, I noticed on the map. Gladstone Terrace, I'm sure it was. They said the woman lived there as well.'

'I thought you said a forty-three-year-old man living alone.'

'They're flats though, I think. You know, like student houses. Let's see what's on text about it.'

That didn't give us any more information, but a search on-line confirmed what I'd heard including the woman's name, Jane Ogden. Just thirty-two. I couldn't find the man's name anywhere.

'I'm certain it's him, it has to be.'

'It doesn't have to be. You're jumping to conclusions. Oh, it can't be. Didn't Heather say the poor girl's body was found this morning?'

'Yes.'

'Well, he was in court this morning. And at the police station before that. So it can't be him at all. I'm glad, really.'

At first I thought mum had a point. Then I remembered the girl had been missing a few days. 'She could have been killed anytime... Oh, my god.'

'What? What is it?'

'He was there. He was at the cemetery, we know he was.'

'What are you saying?'

'The flowers on Ruth's grave. Remember? We knew it had to be him.'

'Oh, Alex.'

Mum started to cry - whether for Ruth, or herself, or the dead girl, or for what might have so easily happened to us, I don't know, but she sobbed a good five or ten minutes while I cradled her into my shoulder.

'I'm going to call the police,' I said once she had cried herself out.

'Yes, call Heather.'

But Heather had gone off shift, so I asked to speak to Detective Sergeant Tregarron.

'He's out of the station at the moment. What's this about, please? Maybe I can help.'

'I don't know, could you tell me if...' I always tried to avoid saying his name; hated it, somehow, when I had to; it made him seem creepily close. Now I had no choice. 'Could you confirm that Alex Robson is under arrest at the station?'

There was a slight pause. 'I can't confirm that, no. Are you press?'

'Oh no, I'm... Alex Taylor. DS Tregarron knows me.'

'Well, as you can imagine he's very busy at the moment, we all are.' (Thinks I'm a time waster.)

'Just that I believe I have some information that might help. About the murder, I mean.'

'Oh yes, what is it?'

'I'd rather speak to DS Tregarron.'

The man at the end of the phone sighed. Irritated.

'As I said, he's out right now.'

'Could you please ask him to call me as soon as he gets back? It's urgent.'

'If it's so urgent, why don't you tell me, Miss Taylor.'

'It's *Ms* actually. No, I'll wait to speak to Jack, thanks.' I said *Jack* deliberately so he'd know I knew him well.

The officer's tut was like a smack in my ear. 'Give me your contact details, then.'

I was thinking, as I gave him my number, there must be a bit of competition among the police about who comes up with what evidence to catch a killer. This bloke wants to be the one to give his boss a vital clue. But was it a vital clue, a bunch of flowers on a grave? The more I thought about it the more I doubted myself. Maybe I *was* just being a time waster.

It wasn't much more than five minutes before DS Tregarron rang me back on a mobile. He must have thought I was going to complain about being kept in the dark because he started off by saying, 'You've just beaten me to it, Alex. I've been meaning to call you and your mum about the arrest, but I've literally been flying about since it happened. It's great news though, isn't it?'

'So it is him that's been arrested?'

'Yeah, we've just this second officially released his name to the media. We're that confident. And this is the big one, love. I'm sorry for the girl, obviously, but it was going to happen sooner or later. Just thank your lucky stars it wasn't you or Karin. Well, thank yourself girl, it was you that had the good sense to push him down the stairs.' (He's really bubbling over with this.) 'Now we've got the chance to put him where he belongs for life.'

'Did we tell you about the flowers?'

'What?'

'I didn't think so. Listen, I don't know if this is worth anything, but he went and put flowers on Ruth's grave.'

'I'm not with you.'

'My sister. She's buried at Deerholme Woodland Park.'

The silence at the end of the phone lasted so long I thought we'd been cut off.

'Are you there?'

'I am. Sorry, Alex. I didn't know that.'

'That was where mum and I were last Thursday lunchtime when he came to the studio.'

'Hang on, I thought you said you'd seen him there.'

'No, we saw the flowers. They were still fresh.'

'My god And this was Thursday?'

'Yes.'

'You little beauty. And his name was on the card?'

'Oh no, there wasn't a card.'

I could hear the disappointment in the silence before he spoke again.

'How did you know it was him?'

'It couldn't be anyone else. Our dad's dead. We're the only relations Ruth had. Of course she didn't have friends.'

Tregarron sounded more hopeful. 'Yes, and we know Alex liked his flowers. I'll send somebody there straightaway, have them picked up. You never know, we might get a fingerprint.'

'Oh, they're not there now. I threw them away.'

'You threw them away?'

'Mum was freaked out. Maybe they're still in the bin. I don't know how often they empty them. I put them in the bin next to the seat on the mound.'

'Well, let's hope they're still there. I'm with you - they must have been left by him. But we've got to be able to prove it. If we do, though. If we do...'

Mum was very quiet that evening. I kept my eye on her while we watched rubbish TV (she didn't want to see any news channel) and I couldn't help noticing how much she'd changed in the course of a week or so. That confident, interested, graceful character I knew seemed to have deserted the body of the woman slumped on the sofa. She didn't reveal any pleasure or even much interest when I confirmed it was our stalker who had been arrested for murder. If anything it seemed to lock her more into herself. I supposed, like me, she was thinking about how close she'd been to becoming another statistic. Another woman killed by a violent man.

When the phone rang I thought it would be Tregarron calling to tell us whether they'd managed to find the flowers. But it was an unfamiliar

171

female voice that asked whether this was the right number for Mrs Karin Taylor.

'Who is this?'

'You must be the daughter. Alex, is it? I imagine you're delighted to hear about that monster's arrest today.'

'Who is this?'

'Sorry, this is Petra from The Herald. Just wanted a quick word with your mum if that's OK.'

'What about?'

'Is Karin there?'

Mum appeared at the doorway. 'Who is it?'

I placed my hand over the receiver. 'Reporter.'

She shook her head, went back into the lounge. I spoke to the woman on the line.

'How do you know about us?'

'We're very concerned about you. Just wanted to know how you feel now he's been done for murder.'

'No comment.'

'We'll make it worth your while.'

I hung up on her and went back to sit with mum.

It was late and we were getting ready for bed when the phone rang again. I wasn't sure whether to answer at first in case it was the journalist trying her luck once more. It was Tregarron. He was practically bursting with excitement.

'Alex, we've nailed him.'

'Did you find the flowers?'

'Not only did we find the flowers, he was kind enough to leave the stickers on the wrapping so were able to track them back to the store. I've even got the girl who sold them to him coming to an ID parade tomorrow morning along with the bus driver on that route. Our man's got no wriggle room this time.'

'Has he admitted it?'

'His sort never do. Don't worry, I've got a drawer full of evidence, and your flowers... they've put him at the scene at the relevant time. Well done, Alex.'

'We've had some woman on from The Herald.'

'Yeah, all the nationals are showing an interest. Did you tell her anything?'

'No. How would she get this number? We're ex-directory.'

'They have their ways. Don't worry, it'll mainly be for background to use when it comes out in court or we get a conviction. There's only so much they can publish right now. Be careful talking to them, but listen, don't piss them off, pardon my French. They make better friends than enemies, that's all I'm saying.'

I told mum it was almost certain our stalker would have to face trial for murder.

'I hope that doesn't mean I have to go to court and testify.'

'I'm pretty sure we both will. At the very least we saw him on some of the days the girl was missing, or knew where he was. Maybe even on the day he killed her.'

'If he killed her.'

'Mr Tregarron seems certain. Well, looks like he'll be going away for a long time. That's got to be a good thing.'

'I don't know,' mum said. 'I just don't like the thought that he might actually have killed somebody.'

I didn't pursue it. It was very late and she really looked in need of a decent night's sleep.

XIV

Heather called in a couple of evenings later to confirm that the case would be going to the Crown Court and that Alex Robson was locked up on remand.

'Is that the same as ordinary prison?' I asked. 'Or just somewhere to keep him until the trial?'

'It's proper jail, don't worry. And he's Cat A so he won't be getting any privileges I can promise you. It's not a soft option.'

'What's Cat A?'

'Category A. Dangerous. High risk. Prisoners who might try and escape. He'll have a screw escorting him everywhere he goes. He'll be restricted over things like classes he can attend. No phone cards - he'll have to have special permission to make a call, and that'll be monitored. In other words he won't be able to do so much as have a dump without being watched.'

'Spied on,' says mum from the sofa.

'If you like. And quite right too.'

Heather could be quite blunt beneath her friendly manner - I suppose it comes with the job. I wished she hadn't said about him having a dump. Left me with a repulsive unwanted image of him sitting on a bucket in a cell while a guard peers at him through the peep-hole. Disgusting - and what's worse it made me almost feel sorry for him. I didn't want to feel sorry for him even for a second. Nor did mum, I'm sure, but she couldn't help herself.

'I met the girl's mother today,' Heather said. 'She wanted to attend the proceedings so I got the care detail. Monica, she's called. Poor woman. Jane was her only one, and she had a husband die of cancer three or four years ago.'

'Oh, I feel for her,' mum said. 'Would it be possible to send her a... what do you call those cards you send when people lose someone?'

'Condolence. In Sympathy, sort of thing,' I said.

'Or perhaps even a letter. I'd like to let her know how sorry we are.'

'Tell you what,' said Heather. 'Why don't I mention you to Monica? She might even welcome a chat. You've something in common, really.'

I wasn't sure about this at all - had my doubts that any good would come of out it for Monica or Karin - but mum thought Heather's suggestion was a good one, so I let it go.

A few evenings later Monica Ogden rang the house phone. We'd been alerted by Heather so we were half-expecting the call, but it still gave me a strange feeling to be talking directly to a woman whose daughter had been brutally murdered, and I was at a loss for what to say because even the usual clichés of regret seemed inappropriate somehow. I managed a couple of bland sentences, but mum was already hovering at my shoulder and I was relieved to be able to pass the receiver and the responsibility across to her quite quickly.

They must have talked for half an hour or more. After five minutes anybody listening in would have imagined the two of them had been friends for years. From what I heard of mum's side of the conversation no mention at all was made of the man who was their only real point of connection. Instead they talked about their daughters - Monica about Jane, Karin about Ruth - and shared their grief over them; there were quiet tears and consoling noises at various points in the conversation. I did get a passing mention from mum but I wasn't fussed about most of the attention being on my sister - I could understand mum playing down the fact that she had one living child at her side while Monica had none, and I could see that talking about Ruth gave Karin a point of contact with Jane's mum. I could understand as well that for Monica especially there was real therapeutic value in their talking, and I was proud of mum in the end for recognizing that would be so, and putting herself forward the way she did. Still though, I was surprised to be told when she came off the phone, 'We're going to Jane's funeral.'

'Sorry?'

'Monica has asked me to go and, well, I've said yes. But I need you to come with me, Alex. I can't go on my own.'

'Mum, we're not family, we don't even know these people. We'd be entirely out of place.'

'Nonsense. Anyway, it's not all family. Mr Tregarron has told her he'll go to represent the police.'

Represent the police. It suddenly struck me that in the circumstances Jane's funeral was likely to be quite a public event. The press were bound to be there. We'd been pestered several times more by Petra and a couple of other hacks from the tabloids even though there was very little they could say about the case before the trial; they were obviously preparing to go to town on the story later. I wondered if mum realised what she was letting herself in for. But she seemed to have made her mind up without discussing it with me.

'When is it?'

'Oh, Jane's... that is, the body hasn't been released yet. Monica is going to let me know as soon as she can arrange the date, but everything else is in place. It's only an hour's drive, it won't put us out so much, darling.'

'Mum, I'm not bothered about the drive or the time. It's just, well... it might not be the quiet affair you're imagining.'

'All the more reason to go along for moral support. Monica needs all the friends she can get right now.'

'I... Well, whatever.'

I expected that at some point we'd be called by the prosecuting lawyers, and we were. They were particularly keen to have us on board, not only as witnesses to the flowers in the cemetery but as key 'bad character' witnesses. They thought it almost certain the judge would allow his stalking activity to be admissible in court because it was relevant in this case and because the guy was still insisting that he was married to Karin, so he was kind of inviting it on himself. Neither of us were keen, and mum was especially unhappy about having to act as a witness, but as Jack Tregarron explained to us we'd only be subpoenaed anyway so we might as well go along willingly.

What we didn't expect was to be contacted by the defence team, but that's exactly what happened and in a very formal manner - mum and I separately on the same day received letters by registered post from his solicitor. It was quite a polite letter in its way but I felt intimidated by it. It said they were aware that the prosecutors were talking to us and asked if they could also be given the opportunity to discuss the case before the trial at our convenience.

'I suppose it's only fair,' was mum's opinion.

'What, to help with his defence? You're joking, aren't you? What if we somehow accidentally helped Jane's killer get off? What would Monica think about it? How did we feel when he walked more or less free after our experience with him? And bad as that was, it hardly compares to murder.'

'We just have to tell the truth, that's all.'

'Sometimes these lawyers can twist the truth, mum, maybe make you say things you don't mean.'

'Oh, I don't know, darling, I'll leave it up to you.'

I still hadn't made my mind up when a call came from his solicitor's office following up the letter. I must admit I panicked and put the phone down. I really didn't know what to do, so I rang Mr Tregarron to ask if this was normal.

'It happens.'

'What do his people want from us?,

176

'Maybe looking to strengthen his alibi defence. Fat chance. Or maybe they're just playing cute.'

'What do you mean?'

'Sending letters by registered post, then following up by telephone. They're making a detailed record of when they contact you so that if you refuse to talk to them they can buttonhole you in court. It goes like this. *Can you recall receiving a registered letter from me on such and such a date asking if I might discuss this case? Can you remember putting the phone down on me on such and such a date when I followed up that letter? Have you discussed the case with the other side?* Blah, blah, blah. The idea is to try and demonstrate to the jury that you're a biased, hostile witness. Very clever really.'

'So you think we should speak with them, then?'

'I shouldn't bother, to be honest. Just shows they're getting desperate. Listen, when the jury weighs up your evidence against his, who do you think they'll believe? When they switch their eyes from that nerdy perv in the dock to a pretty girl like you on the witness stand and they hear how he was creeping up your stairs to attack you with a screwdriver like he did Jane...'

'He wasn't carrying a screwdriver.'

'No, but he had it in his pocket. He was ready to.'

'No, that's wrong. He'd taken his coat and his shoes off and left them downstairs in the lounge, like he belonged there. The tools were in the inside pocket - I remember them rattling against each other when I picked up his coat to give to the ambulance men.'

Tregarron went quiet for a few seconds, then he said something in a very deliberate tone. 'You might want to refresh your memory on that, Alex. I'm sure you'll remember telling me he had his coat on.'

I didn't reply immediately. I was thinking about what mum said. *We just have to tell the truth, that's all.* I thanked him for his advice and put the phone down.

'The funeral is on Friday,' mum told me. Jane's body had been quietly released to the family, and Monica had called again to remind Karin of her invitation.

'And I'd like you to come back afterwards,' Monica had said, 'You and your daughter. I've booked the function room at the undertakers' place, just tea and a finger buffet for a small group of us. So don't go slipping off straight after the crem.' She'd broken down after she said *crem* and mum had to go into consoling mode again. After that there was no way I could persuade her not to go on Friday.

177

I searched online for a picture of Jane Ogden. I'd avoided it before, but somehow I felt it was wrong to go to her funeral without even knowing what she looked like. If she'd ever been on Facebook someone must have made it their business to remove her account, but I did find a photo the press had been using; obviously the same one must have done the rounds as it kept popping up in the various news snippets about the murder. She looked younger than thirty-two (then again I had no idea when the picture was taken) and what I would call unsophisticated. Smiling with her mouth open. A roundness to her face and her eyes. You can't tell much from a photo but I could imagine her quite... *gauche* - I think that's the word - in real life. *Real life*. She was kind of hippyish in an old-fashioned sort of style, with her hair dyed red.

As I studied the photo I was trying to connect Jane in some way with our guy. Could he have been stalking her at the same time as mum? What struck me was the huge difference between the two women. Karin is older by a few years than him; Jane was more than ten years younger than he is, and younger-looking still if this was a recent picture. More than that, mum has a grace to her, a natural elegance and style (it's not just me that says so) while this girl... yes, *gauche*, it's the right word. What I'd read about erotomanics was that they usually go for women (or men) a bit older than themselves, usually of a higher social status, and often someone with some sort of authority, like a doctor or maybe a chief executive. I know I was jumping to all sorts of conclusions about this one picture, plus the bits I'd gleaned from mum's conversations with Monica and where she was living when she died, but it seemed to me this girl was not stalker material. *Sorry, Jane* I couldn't stop myself thinking before I realised what a stupid, absurd statement to make, even in my head - as if any woman would take the chance of being stalked if it meant she was alluringly attractive. But however awful it sounds I felt it was true about Jane, that she was *not* stalker material. And I reckoned if Alex Robson did kill Jane Ogden it was for some completely different reason.

Mum was right that the drive wouldn't take more than an hour, but we had not allowed for how much trouble it would be to actually get into the crematorium. There was far more traffic filing through the gates than it seemed the place was built for, all the official parking spaces were already taken, and when we more or less abandoned the car, bumped up on a grass verge, we had to struggle through a crowd of onlookers to get into the building before the hearse arrived; so many that I thought at first we'd overlapped with an earlier funeral, but there wasn't one. No wonder

Monica had to organize proper printed invitations - I wouldn't be surprised if there were ticket touts operating outside.

And of course the media were there, including a couple of television cameras. I suppose Jane's funeral was open season for the press, free from the restrictions of the trial process, and they were making the most of it, feeding the ghoulish appetite of their readers and viewers. No doubt Petra from The Herald was among them somewhere. I noticed as we were showing our tickets to the usher at the door that the TV crews were taking special interest in the bouquets and messages that had piled up either side of the entrance in spite of Monica's request for family flowers only. Ironic. From what I'd heard via mum about Jane she probably wouldn't have had enough real friends in life to fill a table at Nando's for a birthday party. In death she'd taken on some weird form of celebrity. What is it about the British and their public displays of grief for people they have never met or know anything about except through TV, online gossip or tabloid tat?

It had always been our intention to stay at the back of the room for the service. When we got in we found we had no other choice. In fact, apart from a couple of vacant rows right at the front that had obviously been reserved for the immediate family who were arriving behind the hearse, there didn't seem to be any seats to be had at all, and there was already a line of spectators standing at the back. Perhaps there really had been ticket touts, or more than a few strangers who'd somehow been able to blag their way in. Press, I shouldn't wonder. Mum and I joined the standing line, near to the entrance lobby. She looked demure yet almost *chic*, despite her low heels, in her tailored black suit and understated hat; I felt like a schoolgirl beside her in my black coat and shoulder bag.

Some muted organ music started up to alert us that the coffin was about to be carried through the door. There'd only been a few whispers anyway, but these died down completely, and we all shuffled to attention. Mum and I had to step back slightly to make room for the pall-bearers, all undertaker's men, who filled what little space there was at the back as they brought the coffin through. There was a tendril of flowers snaked across the top which I guessed might have spelled *Jane* but it was too high for me to see properly. The men continued down the aisle and placed the coffin carefully onto a platform to the left which had poles at each corner and red velvet curtains drawn open as if Jane was being laid to rest on a four poster bed.

The pallbearers bowed to the front and withdrew before the main funeral party came down the aisle. The woman in a cheap black hat at the head of this group was being helped in with a hand under her elbow by

179

some man in a suit; I guessed she must be Monica. I hadn't prepared for the fact that she'd be so much older than Karin - touching sixty, I'd bet - considerably shorter and, I have to say, carrying a lot more weight. The man deposited her gently on the end bench at the front and continued on to the platform where he introduced himself as the funeral celebrant.

It was difficult for those of us at the back to follow proceedings closely as only the people with seats had been provided with the Order of Service leaflets, so we found ourselves mouthing to songs we didn't know the words to, and gazing at the coffin or the celebrant at times when he invited us to follow the text for the more formalised parts of the ceremony. I noticed that during the tribute he made no reference at all to the manner of Jane's death other than it was 'so unexpected'. I suppose it would have been considered bad taste to let the ugliness of the real world intrude at an event like this. Instead we learned what a wonderful woman, daughter and granddaughter Jane was; popular with ex-schoolfriends and work colleagues; a bright and gifted girl with a promising new career cut short by tragedy, and of course a great sense of humour. Some of which may even have been true. I noticed that the celebrant had a microphone pinned to his lapel and I wondered if the service was being relayed to the crowd outside as well as to us privileged few with a ticket. I soon found myself willing it to end, though even I couldn't stop choking up a little when the red curtains finally closed on the coffin of the young woman I never once met.

We waited while Mrs Ogden, wiping tears from under her glasses, was assisted back up the aisle by the man in the suit, then we all filed silently out of the building behind the small family group.

What had started out as a bright autumn day was becoming a more typically dull one. The worsening weather didn't seem to be putting off the crowd, still hanging about to gawp, though they had drawn back, probably when the hearse had arrived, to leave a wide expanse of gravel drive immediately in front of the crematorium. Many had their eyes on Monica. She busied herself at first with a white-haired old woman with a walking stick that I had noticed among the family party - her own mother, maybe. Someone led the old woman away, and Monica talked for a while to the celebrant, thanking him for a good job, and others did too - a whole queue of them - including a thirty-something male whose tight suit and white shirt contrasted sharply with his mop of dark hair that looked unwashed as well as untidy. After shaking hands with the speaker he swung himself over to Monica and gave her a huge bear hug, almost burying her face in his broad chest, his jacket sleeve straining when he flexed his left arm to steady her hat as it threatened to slip off altogether under his embrace. I couldn't shake the feeling that I'd seen this man before, but before I could pursue the thought it was mum's turn to step forward and introduce herself.

'Oh, Karin, is this you?' Monica said. 'You look so, so lovely.' And then, strangely, 'Oh, I'm ashamed.'

'Don't be silly.' Karin had put her hand out to shake Monica's but instead she drew her into a fond embrace. 'Thank you so much for inviting us to come. The service was wonderful. You must have been so proud of your daughter.'

'I was. I was.'

She began to weep softly in Karin's arms. I could see mum looking at me over her new friend's shoulder, could tell what was going through her mind; how was she going to introduce me, her living, breathing daughter at this raw, emotional moment. But it was Monica who showed the way. She broke gently from mum to look at me and smile.

'And this must be Alex. Oh, she is exactly like you.'

'Hello, Mrs Ogden. Sorry...'

'I could have picked you out from forty yards away, now I've seen Karin. Look at the both of you. You could be in a magazine.'

At that very moment, and only for a moment, a flash brightened the dullness of the day. We looked up, startled, in the same direction. Another flash, and another from a different angle.

'Do you mind?' mum said, suddenly cross and public. 'This is a funeral.'

'No cameras,' I said, then felt red and foolish for saying it. One of the photographers grinned and turned to a woman at his side, waiting for instructions. She walked up to me with great self-assurance, held out her hand.

'Hello Alex, we've spoken on the phone. Can I just have a quick word with the three of you while you're together?'

I stared stupidly at her extended hand. Mum came alongside me, batted the hand away with more force than I thought she was capable of. 'You've been told before. We don't want to talk.'

Behind us we heard Monica yell, 'Matt, can you give us a hand here? Press.'

A few seconds later the guy with the scruffy hair barrelled past us and pushed the heel of his right hand square into the female reporter's chest.

'Out!'

'Don't you push me.'

He pushed her again. 'Out!' Grabbed her arm, swung her round, pushed her roughly in the back. 'Out! And you.' He started on the photographer, forcing him across the gravel until both journalist and photographer gave up the fight and scampered away in the direction of the car park. I saw others follow more discreetly.

'Thanks, Matt,' Monica said.

'No bother.' And he walked off after the gatecrashers to make sure they got themselves well away from the premises. My eyes followed their progress, but not really taking in the scene. I was distracted, buffeted by the sudden commotion and violence that had erupted around us.

'Are you all right?' mum asked me.

'Think so.'

'That would be Petra.'

'I guess.'

'Give em the old heave-ho, that's the way to deal with that scum,' said Monica. 'Don't let them bother you. Listen, you're coming back to Anderson's for tea and a bite to eat.'

'Yes, but we don't really know the area,' mum said.

'Just follow the funeral car. We'll wait for you at the gates.'

Fortunately there weren't more than thirty or so at the undertaker's for the buffet. One of the few people I recognized was DS Tregarron, in a black suit, who already had his chops around a cold chicken drumstick. I hadn't seen him at the crem, and I wondered where he and his colleagues were when the scuffle broke out.

Mum and I stood together, just the two of us in a corner with a cup of tea and a bakewell tart, feeling a bit out of place, to tell the truth. The function room was a large glass-fronted conservatory that looked out onto a garden of rest. We pretended interest in the view and commented on the gathering clouds for want of more interesting conversation. I was glad when Monica was temporarily free from well-wishers and we were able to go over and stand with her for a while. While she and mum chatted I looked around, working out who I'd seen at the service, and who might belong to who. The old dear I took to be Monica's mother was sitting in a chair with a drab saggy-boobed woman who could possibly be Monica's sister. The celebrant was finishing off a vol-au-vent in between jokey remarks to one of the undertaker's staff. And there was the big bloke that Monica called Matt, filling his plate at the buffet. That same feeling of familiarity came over me as I watched him. There was a break in the conversation between Karin and Monica.

182

'Who's the man you asked to get rid of the journos?' I asked Monica. She followed my eyes to the buffet table.

'Oh, that's Matt. He was Jane's ex.'

'Really? Were they together when she...'

'No, no. Oh, they lived together in the town here for two years, more, on and off. She met him in a nightclub when he was a bouncer, doorman, I should say.'

'I could see him as a bouncer,' mum said. 'The way he dealt with those two at the cemetery; gave them the old heave-ho in your words.'

'Oh, he hasn't done the doorman job for a good while. Something happened, I don't know, but he left. Has his own business now. Well, cash in hand sort of thing. Bit of plumbing, construction work, anything needs fixing round the house. Man's things I mean. He's doing all right, as far as I know.'

'You don't see so much of him these days, then?' I asked. Still watching him, sitting alongside granny now, working through his sandwiches.

'I didn't, up until recently. As I say, Jane finished with him at last. To be honest, I didn't lose any sleep over it at the time. They were forever falling out over one thing and another. He was quite difficult to live with, according to Jane, but she was no angel, god rest her soul. She had a temper on her just the same. And moody. Many's the time I've come in and her holdall has been in the passage, and she'd be there wanting her old room again. But the last time she really left him for good. That's what she said. For good. The down side of it was, it's one of the main reasons she moved away. That and the job. She was doing very well in that new job her boss told me. Very well.'

Matt was talking amiably now to Monica's mum and sister, if that's who they were.

'He's stayed friends with the family, though? Obviously, he's here. Seems to still get on well with everybody.'

'I saw him a couple of times after Jane went away. He was really, really upset about it. Wanted me to talk to her, try and bring her round, sort of thing. But that's not my place, is it? We fell out about it actually. Didn't see him... Well, I didn't see him at all for a while. Then, of course my whole world collapsed. Tell you what, he was straight round on the Tuesday when he heard. We cried our eyes out together in my kitchen. Since then he can't do enough for me.'

Monica took a hanky from under her sleeve, blew her nose on it. Her eyes were going red.

'He might not be somebody I'd have chosen for a son-in-law, but I tell you what, he's been like a son to me these last few weeks.'

Mum put her arm round Monica's shoulder, signalled to me with a slight uplift of the head that we should be going soon.

'I'll just see if I can find a Ladies',' I said. Truth is, I was beginning to feel a bit queasy.

As I weaved my way out past the tables there was a sudden crash. I turned and, to my embarrassment, everyone's eyes were on me. On the floor at my feet I could see pieces of a broken plate, and just under the table a half-gnawed chicken drumstick and a screwed-up napkin. My shoulder bag must have caught the abandoned plate as I walked by. I mouthed a general apology. Out of the sea of faces the one I could see clearly was the old woman, Monica's mother, who looked offended by what I'd done, as if I was deliberately trashing the place. I knelt down in confusion, tried to gather up the broken pieces. One of the waitresses came scuttling over.

'I'll do that, love, don't you worry about it. Just a little accident.'

I'd nicked my finger on a piece of the plate and there was a smidgeon of blood. She gave me a clean napkin to hold to it and advised me to run the finger under a cold tap. I thanked her and went on my way, feeling more nauseous, glad to escape.

The men's and women's toilets were side by side along a narrow corridor by the entrance. As I was walking along it I met Jack Tregarron coming out of the Gents'.

'Oh hello, Alex. Grand do, eh?'

I wasn't sure whether he meant the funeral or the food. He sidled past me, but as he did so he put his hand on my sleeve and leant into me, muttering.

'By the way, between you and me, we've had some fantastic news from the lab about your namesake.'

'My what?'

'Him. Alex. We've got a definite DNA match from what we picked up in the cemetery.'

'The wrapping on the flowers?'

'No, but as good as. Remnants of a spliff found right under the same bin. One hundred percent match.' He squeezed my arm and went on his way.

In the loos I ran water over my finger. The wound was nothing - it was already closing up. I had a physical sensation of the tissue knitting, repairing, because all my senses seemed suddenly heightened to an absurd degree. I could feel the impression of Tregarron's fingers still on my

184

sleeve where he'd squeezed. *One hundred percent match*, he'd said. No room for doubt. I looked at myself in the mirror. Pale as a ghost in the mirror, but my senses raging. The crashing sound. The old woman's offended stare. Monica. *Like a son to me.* From the shelf below the mirror the smell of pot-pourri was overpowering. I went to a cubicle to be sick, but I couldn't breathe for the smell of the water in the lavatory pan. Harmless, clean water, but I had to get out.

Mum was waiting for me by the entrance. In her hand were gathered two little posies of white flowers. 'Are you all right? You look so pale.'

'Fine, just need some air.'

'I've said our goodbyes for both of us, so no need to go back in.' She held out one of the posies. 'Monica wanted you to have this.'

'Mum.'

'She insisted.'

'Some of Jane's funeral flowers?'

'Her favourites, apparently.'

The posies, mine and mum's, were made up of white carnations.

'Just till we get home,' she said.

As we walked through the garden of rest the first drops of rain began to fall. It was turning chilly too. I pulled my coat collar to my throat; mum held onto her hat with her left hand, linked her other arm under mine.

'Thank you for being with me.'

'Hurry up, mum, it's coming on heavier.'

A tiny stream separated the garden of rest from the car park; two steps took us over the little footbridge. The MX-5 was parked just a few yards across the tarmac from the bridge, but we had to wait in the rain a few seconds as another vehicle was heading for the exit. I looked up to watch it go by. A plain white tradesman's van. I had a clear view of the driver in profile, head and shoulders, as he passed. He had taken his jacket off to drive, but I knew him by his untidy mop of hair and the muscled arm bulging his white shirt. Matt, from the funeral. Matt, who'd rescued us from the reporters. Matt the ex-bouncer. Matt, like a son now to Monica. Matt. Jane's ex.

How can a dream be true? That's what I was thinking as we drove home in the rain. Mum quiet. Radio off. Only the windscreen wipers swishing. How can a dream be true? The man following me across the glass roof. The man whose hair wasn't right for dad. Wasn't right for our stalker. The man with muscled shoulders, like someone who works out. The man who

185

I'd only seen for the first time today. The man in my dream was Jane's ex. Matt.

Because today was not the first time I'd seen him. Because my dream was filled with fragments, broken bits, of people and things I'd known and seen and worried about and noticed or didn't consciously notice at the time or remember since. Why didn't I remember? Because it had no importance. It was mundane, part of the background. A van comes out of the cemetery gates. A workman. Unremarkable. And later, because we weren't looking to remember him. Weren't asked to look or remember. Because they had their man. That's who we had to think about. Anything you can tell us about *him*. Build up our picture of *him*, the stalker, the killer. That's him. All the evidence is there. Stacked up. But somewhere in my unconscious brain I'd locked in what I'd seen of this other man, only the head and shoulders visible from the driver's window of the van that was just part of the background.

Except he shouldn't have been part of the background. This wasn't a worker from the cemetery. This was a man who lived and worked forty miles away. An odd-job man. On the fiddle. He had no cause to be there. No reason to be there. Unless the reason was Jane. He was with Jane. Or following Jane. Like he followed me in my dream. How long had he followed Jane till he became her nightmare?

What's Tregarron going to say about this? *One hundred percent match.* What's Monica going to say? *Like a son to me now.* And what will happen now? What's going to happen to...? I glanced sideways at mum. Hands steady at the wheel. Quiet. Serene. Just driving. Watching the road. Driving her daughter home. Maybe tomorrow or the next day she'll phone Monica again, see how she is. She'll stay in touch, because as different as they are mum cares for Monica. Because she's a caring person. She's a loving person. And with *him* out of the way she can get her life back together again. He could be out of her life forever. For life.

We just have to tell the truth, that's all.

But how can I, mum, if telling the truth means *he'll* be out? If keeping quiet means we're rid of him forever. The only way we can be rid of him. It's our chance. And if I say something now, if I throw the cat among the pigeons, he's going to be free again. And back in your life. Back in our lives. To prevent that happening, to save you from all that in the future, I don't have to do anything at all. I just have to stay quiet. Not even say anything to you.

Mum continued driving, watching the road through the rain. And I stayed quiet with her, all the way home.

186

UNDYING DEVOTION

XV

It's what they call in here 'association'. Only no-one wants to associate with me. Two prisoners are playing pool, whacking the balls so violently with their cues that one has just come spinning off the table and rolled under my chair. The TV is on a channel where the ads are in a noise level competition with the pool players. No-one is watching, but try turning it off and you would likely be murdered by a pool cue to the back of the head. Four prisoners are multi-tasking, having a who-farts-longest contest while playing dominoes at a formica table. Farting. Giggling. Clicking and knocking their dominoes on the table. Occasionally someone will scratch his crotch or dig into an ear then examine his little finger for earwax before returning his attention to the game. No-one wants to play dominoes with me. My sitting here at all is only tolerated because a screw is standing a couple of yards from my chair.

I could read if I wanted to; there's a bookcase in the dayroom filled mainly with pulp westerns from the early 1960s. I did try flicking through a couple of them once but I gave up when I couldn't be sure what the sticky stuff was on my fingers. I could read in my cell, and do, but twenty-three hours a day inside the same four pressing walls can become tedious, while having the only cell door in the wing with added cage metal makes me feel like Hannibal Lecter. So sometimes I sit here and watch my fellow-inmates exchange pleasantries.

The governor is considering a move for me to what he calls the Vulnerable Prisoners' Unit and what everybody else calls the nonces' wing, occupied mainly by paedophiles and the odd police informer or 'grass' as they're still known here - it's striking how un-21st-century prison jargon is.

Of course I've not been convicted of anything so I'm not a real prisoner, I'm a remand prisoner. The big difference is that I wear brown dungarees while most of the people in here wear blue. Still no word of when my trial is likely to start.

Another guard, whose name is Meadows (not exactly appropriate for his work environment) pops his head through the doorway looking for me. He knows he doesn't have to bother checking the groups around the room; the loner will be in his usual place.

'Visitor for you.'

This is no surprise to me or anyone here, not now, never mind the 'loner' tag. I get three visits a week, more than any of the others, and not just because I'm on remand. I don't need to ask who my visitor is because it's invariably the same person. She's been writing to me, phoning me and coming to see me since I left her at the magistrates' court. I'm starting to think Deborah Ann Peters is developing something of an obsession for me. Whether sexual or not I haven't a clue - her letters are as innocuous as a maiden aunt's. (Come to think of it, she probably is somebody's maiden aunt.) It does help to relieve the monotony of prison even if it's only exchanging one level of boredom for another. There's no mystery why Deborah Ann doesn't have a boyfriend. Not only does she lack that certain *je ne sais quoi*, she has very little of any personality from my point of view. But at least she's there for me. She's always there for me.

The screw who sought me out leads the way to the visitors' unit while a second screw tags along behind, the special privilege of my Cat A status. We have to walk from my landing at the top of the building, through metal doors, down metal stairs, round three of the four gantries of the central landing, through more doors and down more stairs to the ground floor. Along the way we pass cells, open and closed, past prisoners who see me by now as their regular freak spectacle and a chance to practise their limited vocabulary of abuse: 'weirdo', 'wanker', 'nonce', 'pervert', 'lady killer', 'lady boy' (for some reason), or just a straightforward 'bastard'. Some obscure hierarchy of acceptable offence operates here; the prisoner who just yelled 'sick psycho' at me is in for gouging somebody's eye out with his bare hands in a gang fight.

The doors leading into the visitors' unit are diagonally opposite each other, and both are heavily locked and guarded. They put every arrival through the humiliation of a search - just by presenting yourself as a visitor you are marked as a criminal's associate and automatically put under suspicion. After searching they bring the visitors into the room first and sit them at one of the green tables that look as if they've been prepared for some scaled-down version of ping pong, with a raised five inch black panel running along the middle of each table. After the visitors are seated the prisoners are led in one by one through the opposite entrance.

It's a slow day; only half a dozen of us have visitors, and I'm first in. Momentarily confused - I can't see Deborah Ann at any of the tables - then I realise with a start it's *her* sitting at the far end of the room, the only one who doesn't stare at me as I come through with the guard, but sits facing forward as if I were in the opposite chair already. Not Deborah Ann at all: it's my dead daughter Ruth.

Or the ghost of Ruth. Or not Ruth - of course not - but the girl playing Ruth in this Kafka game they've arranged to deceive and disorientate me. She looks up from the chair as I come to stand behind it and wait for permission from the guard to take my seat. The resemblance really is remarkable, I have to give them that. She's wearing the same green coat, the same Maltese Cross earrings; her hair and make-up the same. She hasn't spoken yet, but I already know. This time it's not the voice that gives her away - it's the hint of contempt, the cold expression in her eyes. Not my Ruth.

'Sit down,' the guard says.

She waits for me to sit and face her at her level. Perhaps she's expects me to speak first, but I can be as sly as they are. I'll wait for her.

'Mum doesn't know I'm here.'

'You mean Karin doesn't know you're here. You don't need to tell me that. I'm absolutely sure of that.'

She's aiming for poise, draws herself up to say the line she's clearly rehearsed. 'I've come for one reason and one reason only.'

'To try and confuse me.'

'Actually, to help you... on condition.'

She leans forward to whisper, 'I have information that could get you released,' but she barely gets the words out before the guard steps forward and barks out an order.

'Don't cross the centre line. Sit back on your chair!'

Ruth recoils, startled. Sits back so forcefully her chair legs scrape on the floor. Poise lost, for a moment she's in panic mode, looks like she might run off. With an effort she contains herself, though the rims of her eyes are ready to spill tears. I don't let my eyes leave her face, but the room has gone dead quiet and I know that everyone has turned momentarily towards the commotion. I can still smell her scent from her move towards me. She's wearing Karin's perfume.

'Sorry, miss,' the guard says, feeling guilty maybe, having seen her shocked reaction. 'That's the rule. You were told the rule.'

'Yes. Sorry, officer.'

No big deal - everyone else in the room goes back to their conversations. The girl playing Ruth takes a moment more to compose herself completely. Studies her fingers as if she's waiting for them to stop shaking, then she's back in character. Looks at the guard, who is affecting indifference. Looks at me.

'Did you catch what I just said?' She speaks softly as if she doesn't want to be overheard, though I'm perfectly aware she'll be carrying a wire. Does she take me for a fool?

'I heard you.'

'I can save you from spending the rest of your life in prison. There's only one strict condition before I give you the information I have.'

'What is it?' Though I know already what she's going to say.

190

'I want you to promise me, on your mother's life, that you will never, *ever* make any attempt to contact Karin ever again.'

'You bitch.'

I knew it. I knew exactly what their game was. This whole thing constructed to keep me away from my wife. To never, ever see Karin again.

'You scheming bitch.'

Fury takes over. I stand and launch myself across the table at her. She knocks over her chair as she scrambles to get away, cries out. The guard tackles me from behind, his weight crushing me onto the table. The central panel snaps under me. Somewhere in the roof a siren sounds. Doors clang open, I can hear the clatter of boots, and I'm dragged by two screws from the table to the floor. Pinned down, my cheek pressed against a floor tile. Distorted view of Ruth looking down at me, a hand to her mouth. A woman prison officer approaches from behind to lead her out through the door. I scream after her.

'Never! Never! Never!'

XVI

I'm in the middle of a living nightmare. There's no relief from it, no waking up to find it's all been a dream; the harsh reality of every new awful experience is seared into my brain. My first days in prison felt like a holiday compared to what's happened to me since the girl playing Ruth tried to trick me into swearing the rest of my life away from Karin. They thought they had me in a classic Catch 22: life for the murder they fitted me up for or some kind of negotiated freedom; at what price? Another life sentence out there without ever seeing my wife again. If my reaction surprised them they were more than ready to punish me for it.

Immediately afterwards, three days in a strip cell. A concrete box, empty of all furniture but a plastic piss-pot and a thin mattress on the floor. They stripped me of my prison clothes too, replaced them with a canvas rip-proof onesie - 'a monkey suit for the chimp' one of the screws said as they forced me into it. For the first twenty-four hours they locked me into a body belt with handcuffs either side. Impossible to sleep. Noisy interruptions by the guards every fifteen minutes, day and night, and a bare lamp burning in the cell which was never turned off or even dimmed.

The governor came to see me in the strip cell.

'What's going on, Alex? We can't have you attacking visitors, can we? Such a pretty girl as well.'

'She's an evil bitch.'

'You have a major problem with women.'

'Just that one - she's a devil.'

The governor folded his arms, gazed at me, considering.

'I'm going to have you transferred to another wing.'

'I'm not a sex offender. I don't want to be locked up with paedos and rapists.'

'You're not going to the VPU. I'm sending you to the hospital wing. It's the best place for you, Alex. You'll get some help there.'

'I don't need help, there's nothing wrong with me.'

'Oh, I think there is.'

At school we read the novel *A Clockwork Orange*. I remember it well because the central character was called Alex. He's put away for murder and the authorities give him injections and horrible aversion therapy techniques to condition his brain. I'm convinced that's what they've got lined up for me here in the hospital wing. Not if I can help it.

I've been here just over a week. Even before they moved me into this cell they sent me for an interview with the doctor.

'Are you feeling suicidal, Alex?'

'No, why should I be.'

'Depressed?'

'I'm in prison, who wouldn't be.'

'What drugs do you do?'

'Don't do drugs.'

'I'm going to give you some medication.'

'I don't need medication.'

'Just to help you sleep at night.'

'Tell them to turn the lights out and stop peering through the hatch at all hours, that'll help me sleep at night.'

But he gave me a prescription anyway.

This cell is more cramped and squalid than my old one. If I thought the word 'hospital' implied this wing would be more hygienic I soon changed my mind when I looked into my slop bucket just after they banged me up here. Actually I didn't need to look into it; the smell was overpowering. They hadn't bothered emptying it from the last resident of the cell. Deliberate enemy action. I also soon found out that they've put me next door to a guy with a nasty habit of smearing his faeces over the wall at regular intervals. In fact most of the prisoners on this wing seem to have one nasty habit or another, including several who spend their time in the dayroom moaning and rocking back and forward constantly, and others (or maybe the same ones) who yell and cry out loudly from their bunks half the night. Never mind *A Clockwork Orange*, I feel like an extra on the set of *One Flew Over The Cuckoo's Nest*. But I still refuse to take the doctor's prescribed medication.

There's no relief from this madness by taking frequent trips to the visitors' unit like I did before; the governor has punished my behaviour in the unit by cancelling visitor privileges, and they won't even let me write to Deborah Ann to explain what's happened. She'll think I've abandoned her, don't want to know, had her barred for no reason. Not true Debbie, none of that is true. I appreciate that you were there for me.

So I have no visitors, no association with the other inmates (by my choice as much as theirs), no classes to go to, and no work. I asked to be given a work detail: declined. Twenty-four long hours a day where the only change from mind-numbing tedium comes in spells of nerve-jarring mental torture served up in one insane form or another by medics, screws

193

or fellow-prisoners. Twenty-four long hours a day with not one word of a trial starting, not one breath.

I've been trying since I was slammed in here to conjure up an image of Karin and I can't - it's as if she is unable to penetrate the thickness of the walls to come to me. Tonight I begin quietly repeating her name like a mantra, working myself into a trance-like state to forget my surroundings and create some safe space for her to slip into. Half an hour or more of chanting. Unsuccessful - the mantra dries in my mouth and dulls my brain without opening anything up for me, for her. So frustrating. I lie with my forehead on the cold wall in a sweat of desperation. Cheap emulsion on Victorian brick. It has a smell of its own, close up, mingled with the staleness that hangs everywhere, that enters your skin and leaks, staler again, from every pore.

There's an exposed pipe for water or heat running the length of the wall under my bunk. As I lie, half-scrunched, a regular knocking starts up from somewhere along the pipe. Pay no attention to it at first - just one of the random noises like the cries of prisoners down the corridor - and I have other things to try and think about. After a while though I notice there's a regular pattern to the beat, four notes, a pause, then four notes, like a bar repeating on one piano key. Open my eyes, listen properly now. The sound travels along the pipe - it has an eerie quality to it. Four regular beats. *A-L-E-X*.

I roll off my bunk, go to my locker and find my spoon. Reach down past the edge of the bed to tap at the pipe below. Five regular notes. Pause. Repeat. *K-A-R-I-N*. The answer comes back. *A-L-E-X*. My heart starts to race. I reach down again to tap with my spoon. Fingers gripping at the end for resonance. One. Pause. Four. Pause. Three. *I L-O-V-E Y-O-U*.

For one long moment nothing comes back. Then the answering taps. One. Pause. Four. Pause. Two. Pause. Four. Pause. Three. Repeat. One. Pause. Four. Pause. Two. Pause. Four. Pause. Three. First word, *I*. Last word, I guess, *YOU*. The two letters can only be *TO*. *I WANT TO .... YOU*. KISS? Surely not the *F* word; Karin wouldn't be so coarse, even tapping out a message, though we both want it so much. Perhaps she is saying *I WANT TO FREE YOU*. I tap with my spoon. Three notes. *Y-E-S*.

Another silence, then four taps followed by a sort of scraping across the pipe. What does that signify? Some sort of punctuation, a question mark? A four word question. *WHAT? WHEN?* When? Is she planning some sort of escape for me? I don't know how to respond, how

194

to help her with the plan. As I'm trying to work out what I can communicate in taps that could possibly be useful the question comes again, followed by another. Five taps and a scrape. *WHERE?* She needs to know when and where. What can I say? But she is first with an answer. Two. Pause. Three. Pause. Six. Second word probably *THE*. First word *AT* or *IN*? At the... In the... In the yard? In the kitchen? No, six words. In the... shower? Toilet?

Oh, Jesus, I know what this is. What am I doing? I let the spoon fall onto the floor with a clatter. I feel sick. Nothing from the pipes at first then four taps and a scrape. *WHEN?* again or *ALEX?* Ignore it. The statement tapped out *I W-A-N-T T-O*... Fourth word tapped hard. Ignore it. I turn away from the wall.

More taps from the other end. Urgent. Demanding. Getting angry now. Louder and louder all the time. Very angry. Rapid, rapid taps. Bangs. Frenzied, uncontrolled, insane, and loud enough to fill the place until finally somebody bawls out from another cell.

'For Christ's sake, will you shut the fuck up!'

Karin does come to me in a dream, but not as I'd wished for. In fact it isn't like a dream at all but as if I'd been roused to full wakefulness to find her by my bed looking down at me. It's the middle of the night but there's a strange orange light in the cell with shadows leaping onto the wall behind. It takes me a moment to assimilate. Karin seems to have emerged from the pages of a gothic novel. She is wearing a full-length white shift like a Victorian nightdress. The strange, unsteady light is from a candle sputtering from a lamp-holder in her left hand. She looks terrified. I rise from my pillow.

'What's the matter?'

Karin's fingers reach to her mouth. Her lips have lost their colour and her face is drawn. She turns away from me, scampers to the cell door in bare feet. A ballet, but where are her dance shoes?

Her voice. 'Let me out. Let me out.'

'Karin, what's the matter? What's wrong, my love?'

She turns back to look at me, presses her back against the door. Her face in the candlelight is haunted, horrified. Her right arm beats and beats against the door as if she'd break it down to get out or break herself with trying.

'You'll hurt yourself, don't. Trust me, I'll get you out. I'll get us both out. Don't worry.'

I start to leave my bed. Karin wails, screams. That awful cry I've heard before. The long scream from the base of her, in the hallway after

195

Ruth died. I can't stand it. I fall back on my mattress, squeeze my pillow over my ears. Try to block out her screaming and the frantic beating against the cell door. The scream fades into the banging of the door. *Shut the fuck up!* Louder than ever. The banging of the door.

My cell door opens and two strapping guards barge in. One white, one black. What's this now?

The white one speaks, Geordie accent. 'On your pins, Robson. Stand up next to that wall.'

'My name is Taylor. Alex Taylor.'

'Call yourself what you like, marra, you're still getting a fucking cell spin.'

'A what?'

'Heard you got contraband stashed in here.'

He starts pulling the sheets off my bed. His partner rips open the door of the tiny locker.

'What are you talking about? What kind of contraband?'

'Why don't you tell us?'

'I don't have anything. Who grassed on me? It's total bullshit.'

They ignore my protests. Geordie turns his attention from the bed linen to the bed itself, pulling it away from the wall. The black guy has tipped everything from the locker onto the floor. Unscrews a tube of toothpaste and squeezes three or four inches out onto the top of the locker. Dabs a finger in the mess and licks it.

'Where would I get it from? I'm not allowed visitors. I don't talk to the others. And by the way I've got no money since I've been refused every work detail I've asked for.'

The black guy turns to me. 'Take your clothes off.'

'What?'

'Strip, right now, or I'll do it for you.'

Reluctantly I strip down to my underpants, placing my clothes on the floor. The black screw picks them up, starts searching through them with his fingers, his eyes still on me.

'I said, *strip*.'

I pull down and kick off my underpants. Vulnerable and more frightened now. He looks through the abandoned pants cursorily.

'Take a step away from the wall. Turn. Hands on your bum cheeks. Bend down and pull.'

I can't believe this is happening. I can't believe he's shining a torch up my backside.

'Put your clothes back on.'

By now Geordie has virtually completed the destruction of what little furniture and effects are in the cell. By way of a finale he turns over the slop bucket, letting piss run out under my bed. He shakes out a turd from the bottom of the pan but doesn't bother to examine it. Leaves the slop bucket on its side as he makes his exit.

'You can borrow a mop from the shit-meister next door,' he says. 'He has one permanent.'

They leave my cell door unlocked and disappear as quickly as they came. I stand watching the flow of piss come up against a dam of scattered objects on the floor.

Three hours later (more than an hour of which I've spent sluicing, cleaning and restoring my cell) they're back. I can't believe it. But one thing I'm sure of, this time they're getting the fight they were trying to provoke when they came before. My fists are clenched as Geordie approaches my bunk.

'On your pins, Robson. Legal visit.'

'My name is... What did you say?'

'Legal visit. Your brief's here to see you.'

Even the governor can't prevent legal visits. I jump off the bed, search for my shoes, fumble in putting them on.

'Buck up, can't keep the man waiting.'

We set off in convoy at some speed, Geordie in front of me, his mate behind. As we negotiate the gantries my mood changes from surprise to urgency to excitement to doubt and finally to suspicion. What is this about? Why this sudden appearance after I've heard nothing for so long? What's their game now? Is this another part of the strategy to box me in, keep me away from Karin forever? Whose side is Marks on? I'm so engaged in thinking about these questions I'm deaf to the usual insults as we march past one cell door after another.

The solicitor is waiting in a private room next to the visitors' unit. He's more genial than he's been in the past, even shaking my hand as I come in, which causes the attendant screw some concern. My suspicions grow. Why is he being so unnaturally friendly?

'Great news for you, Alex. Sit down, sit down.'

Definitely something off. Mr Marks props his elbows on the surface of the table in front of me, clasps his fingers together as if he's about to say grace, nods and smiles.

'What would you say if I told you you were going to get out of here very soon?'

'You mean they've agreed bail?'

197

'No, I mean out of here for good. Free as the proverbial bird.'

Oh no, not this again. Ruth failed the first time, now he's trying it.

'On what condition?'

'No condition. Well, the condition of the police and the CPS dropping all charges against you.'

'Why would they do that?'

'Because you did not kill Jane Ogden.'

You did not kill Jane Ogden. Words I'd almost despaired of ever hearing except in my own head. Words that hit me like fresh air, a window opening, I could fly through it. *Alex Taylor is innocent.* The optimist in me wants so much to soar again, but my recent experience dampens the urge, presses the hope down. I'm still hearing voices of caution, scepticism, doubt. In the old days when they put people on the rack they used to loosen it off occasionally, just so the poor sod being punished could feel the pain more acutely for having a moment of relief before it was tightened again. Is this what's happening here? Or is it Mr Marks that's letting himself be fooled? For all I know, as sincere as he seems now, it may be only him that has converted to the idea of my innocence and he's getting carried away with his new-found enthusiasm. Certainly he's not coming across as the straight-faced functionary I had him down for. I'm the one who's trying to stay level-headed about this.

'I know I'm not guilty, maybe you do too, Mr Marks, but the police are one hundred percent confident I did it.'

'Not anymore.'

He unclasps his fingers, looks down on the floor for his briefcase and hauls it up to the table to search for his documents.

'Forgive me, Alex, I won't keep you from the details any longer. A great deal has happened since the last time I saw you, a very great deal, and I like to think your defence team can take some credit for it.'

He spreads his documents like a comfort blanket on the table between us.

'The fact is that through a witness we have been able to supply a new lead to the police who have subsequently come up with fresh evidence to clear you and bring the right man to justice.'

'A new witness?' Still doubtful.

'Yes. Congratulations, Alex. I'm delighted to bring you this news. Didn't I always say I felt the evidence in your case was circumstantial? In my view DS Tregarron was rather gung-ho in his pursuit of you and exceeded his brief in doing so. Or perhaps I should say he let his brief remain too narrow.'

198

He means this. He really means this. Tregarron's made a balls of something. No surprise there. 'So it's Tregarron's fault. Right. OK.' Breathing hard now, trying to keep up, stay calm. 'Has he been caught planting evidence, is that it?'

'No, no. I wouldn't wish to cast aspersions on the officer's *modus operandi* in that respect. His fault was that he lacked dispassion, which made him too singular in his approach. He didn't leave himself open to other possibilities; that's always dangerous in police work, and in legal work. Our witness was able to point to another man at the scene of the crime. A positive identification, and a very interesting one.' He checks a document. 'Did Jane ever mention to you someone called Matthew Murdie?'

'No. Never heard of him.'

'An ex-boyfriend. Rather more than that, actually. They lived together for two years until she finally left him. She even moved forty miles away to be rid of the fellow.'

Now I make the connection. Matthew Murdie must have been the mysterious *M* in Jane's diary. She'd written something about not wanting to go through that again, whatever *that* was. She'd hoped I wouldn't be that kind of bastard.

'What about him?'

'It seems he was in the car park of the Deerholme cemetery on that fateful Thursday. That *fatal* Thursday. Now what was he doing so far away from home? And why there particularly? Was he with Jane?'

'Or following Jane.' I've got it.

'You're catching up quickly, Alex. Now, when we heard this, one of the things we wanted was to double-check all the CCTV footage that the police had looked through, and extend the search too. Some of this we did ourselves and some the police did, alerted by our team. We were actually looking for sightings of Mr Murdie but on the way we came across something that had been missed the first time by the police - I suspect because they were too focused on looking for you on film. One of the cameras we checked covers the main checkout tills of Morrisons supermarket. Guess who we came across making a few purchases at the checkout on Thursday morning.'

'Matthew Murdie.'

'In some ways more interesting still. It was Jane Ogden. She bought a Fresh to Go prawn sandwich, some crisps and a bar of chocolate that she packed into a little black nylon rucksack, just like the one you described.'

'Picnic for one.'

'Exactly. And Jane made another significant purchase that morning.'

I can guess what it is. I remember when I came into the store later that day they still had four or five left in the bucket, all looking pretty much identical. I offer my suggestion.

'A little bunch of white carnations wrapped in cellophane.'

'Which she placed next to Ruth Taylor's grave marker in the cemetery when she visited an hour or so later. The bunch that was later wrongly assumed to be the one you bought from Louise at the cigarette counter. If you think about it, it's only to be expected. You and Jane lived in the same property. What is the likelihood that you would shop in the same store?'

'About one hundred percent, I'd say.'

'Let's call it ninety percent, to be fair.'

Mr Marks pauses for a moment, puzzled by my half-laugh at his response. It's not him - it's partly the bubble of excitement rising in me and partly that our exchange of made-up percentages has sparked a memory of playing the same game with Cody. *No such thing as one hundred and twenty percent.* Carry on, sir.

'Now what is the likelihood that Matthew Murdie - or Matt as he's generally known - would visit that store in the normal scheme of things, given our knowledge that he and Jane were no longer together and he lives an hour's drive away?'

'About zero percent.'

'Or nought nought point nine five, if that's even a figure. And indeed we haven't been able to find him in the store on that day despite the extended CCTV search. But this particular Morrisons has an automatic number plate recognition system in operation at the entrance to its car park. Interestingly Mr Murdie's vehicle was logged as entering the car park at 9.54 am on the Thursday and leaving at 10.17 am. A vehicle of the same description was seen coming out of the cemetery gates that lunchtime, driven by a man who exactly matches the description of Matt Murdie. Either he was giving Jane Ogden a lift from her flat to the supermarket and then to Deerholme or, more likely given their estranged status, he was following her for whatever reason. He may have tracked the bus she was riding on all the way to the park. These are details that have still to emerge fully.'

'What sort of car was he driving?'

'Not a car, a van. Matt Murdie does a certain amount of odd job and handyman work. He is your classic white van man.'

'He drives a white van?'

'He does.'

I feel something like the chill I experienced when I first saw what I thought was the ghost of my daughter Ruth. Here is another ghost that's been haunting my dreams, dogging my days. *What's the white van got to do with it?* It's what Jane said when she saw the words written on the A4 sheet pinned on my door. Ironic. Prophetic. And how strange that a white van - which I thought was somehow associated with the death of my daughter, that I began to think might be pursuing me - is tied up with the killing of my neighbour. I remember being shocked by the sight of the white van cruising past Jane's window the first day I went into her room, the morning I first read her diary. Did he see me through the window? How long had Matthew Murdie been sussing out Jane's new circumstances, watching the house, checking who her new friends might be, tracking her movements, stalking and following? He was waiting for the right moment. Moment for what? What did he have in mind? Did the murder emerge out of some furious row, some anger-charged chase that blew into something he didn't really intend, or was it a premeditated, purposeful act? Spontaneous or planned? How did he come to have a screwdriver in his pocket? In his hand.

'I think I've seen that van.'

'Really?'

'Outside the house at Gladstone Terrace. I'm sure I saw it once, and I remember thinking it looked suspicious. I wish I'd reported it now.'

'We can all be wise after the event.'

I sit quiet for a minute, trying to come to terms with what Mr Marks has told me so far. I so want to believe that this is my golden ticket out of here. I so want to believe. But the doubts are still pressing down on me, and they're not irrational.

'You know, if you think about it, there's a risk in all this. What if we're in danger of doing to Matt Murdie what the police did to me?'

'You mean accepting circumstantial evidence as proof.'

'Yes. What if he did drive across to see Jane that day, maybe to try and persuade her to come back to him? Who's to say she didn't tell him about her plan to visit the cemetery? Maybe he offered her a lift, took her there of her own accord. Maybe they enjoyed a walk together, had a full and frank discussion about their relationship. Who knows, maybe they even made up. He might have started driving back home thinking everything was going to be hunky dory while Jane was still in the park, filling in all the details of the day in her diary. And maybe somebody else came along and killed her. A stranger. A random madman. It happens. Have police found the murder weapon on Matt Murdie?'

'Not yet.'

'Well, then.'

Mr Marks smiles. 'Maybe you're in danger of putting yourself back in the frame, Alex.'

'I'm just saying... I wouldn't wish what's happened to me on anyone else.'

'It won't.' Mr Marks squares up his papers on the table. 'For a couple of reasons.'

'Go on.'

'First, Matthew Murdie has denied being anywhere near Deerholme Woodland Park on the day of the murder, and has denied seeing Jane Ogden on that day. Weigh that up against the video evidence in the supermarket, the witness evidence at the cemetery, and the fact that, although he claims to have been finishing a plastering job in his home town that day as part of a house renovation, the person he was working for had gone over to the house at around lunchtime to check whether the job was finished, only to discover Murdie hadn't turned up. Much later that night he was called by Mr Murdie who seemed unusually keen to let him know that the work was completed. In fact he asked him if he wanted to come across to see it there and then. This was at a time when most people would be thinking about going to their beds.'

'OK, but maybe he just didn't want to let on he was skiving earlier in the day.'

'I think you'll find my second reason more compelling. It very much concerns you.'

'Oh, right.'

'You'd agree, wouldn't you, that somebody in possession of something missing from Jane's belongings would be a likely suspect?'

'Yes.' I didn't need Marks to remind me of Jane's bike or, most damningly, of her diary.

'Well, in that respect Murdie seems on the face of it to have been quite clever. We don't know what has happened to the stuff she had with her at the time of the attack, but an extensive search of Murdie's house hasn't uncovered anything, and his van is clean, in fact scrupulously clean for a working vehicle. No biological clues to Jane around anything connected with Murdie, not even faint traces you might expect from someone who shared the same property for two years. So he covered his tracks quite well, if not too well. But there will have been one thing bothering him over the days and hours since her death, as he considered the certainty that her body would eventually be discovered either before she was reported missing or after.'

'What would be bothering him?'

'He'd know that, in the absence of compelling evidence to point straight to her murderer, the police's first port of call for questioning, and possible suspicion, would be the people who knew her best - an estranged partner would be an ideal candidate for interviewing; so unless he did something to distract the police he could expect them to come knocking at his door sooner or later. Thinking about this, sometime over the weekend I'd guess, he decided that he had to cast the shadow of suspicion somewhere else. Alex, did Jane have a key to your room?'

'No.'

'Murdie would have Jane's keys from her rucksack so he could get into the house, and certainly into *her* room whenever he wanted.'

'It must have been him that took my flowers. Funny, it's OK for him to kill his ex-girlfriend but not for me to send her flowers. Jealousy. That's why he'll have destroyed them.'

'Possibly. My supposition is a little different - it was because your note made it obvious you'd written it after she disappeared from the house and you knew nothing of her whereabouts. He left the letters addressed to you in her drawer - wanted to make sure the police were immediately aware of your connection with Jane. I'm wondering though how, without a key, he gained access to your room without breaking in. There were no signs of forced entry.'

'You mean to plant the diary in the toilet cistern?'

'Yes.'

I try to imagine how he might have managed to get in. Close my eyes, aiming to picture my room as it was the last time I saw it. That was the Tuesday I'd been released from the court, the same day that Jane's body was discovered. I was only there a short time - the gas was off and it was cold. It was cold.

'I left the window open.'

'Sorry?'

'I opened the sash window in my room on the Friday morning and forgot to shut it again.' (I don't want to complicate things by telling Mr Marks I was hiding in Jane's room while Mr Chatterjee was waiting in mine, and dashed straight out with Jane's bike because he'd made me late for Abi.) 'Yes, the window was open from Friday until after I was released from the police station on Tuesday. I shut it when I arrived back at Gladstone Terrace. Murdie could have got in through the window anytime he chose between times.'

'And obviously did.'

I have no idea what Matt Murdie looks like, but in my mind now he's a burglar in black skulking through my flat, dropping Jane's diary into my toilet cistern. No, he tore the pages out first, didn't he, screwed them up and dropped them into the bowl. I know why he did that - because he's in there, captured in Jane's words. I only saw the one entry about her leaving him, but I bet if I'd read properly through the earlier entries I'd have learned a lot more about Matt Murdie than I know now. So would the police, if they'd got hold of Jane's diary before he ripped out the pages. I bet he read about me in the diary as well, and that's what gave him the idea to make me the fall guy. His revenge for taking his girlfriend away; maybe that's how he saw it. Quite clever, to use the diary as a weapon against me, fingering me as the killer at the same time as destroying it as evidence against him.

'Mr Murdie is a plumber among other skills, I hear,' says the solicitor. 'Perhaps that's why he chose the toilet cistern as the hiding-place he knew would be discovered in a police search.'

'I was just thinking, quite clever.'

'Well, yes, but it led to his downfall. I've finally got to the nub of my second reason we can be sure of his guilt, Alex.'

'What's that?'

'During the initial search the SOC officers tested for fingerprints. There was nothing at all around the bathroom area. Obviously whoever put the diary there was careful about wiping down afterwards, but he couldn't wipe what he couldn't reach. On the inner surface of the cistern, just at the rim, they found a single, unidentified fingerprint. Naturally they checked with the records database, which came up with nothing, so they dismissed the print at the time, assuming it belonged to a previous tenant or perhaps a workman. The thing is, Matthew Murdie has never till now been charged, never mind convicted, of a crime, so he had never had his fingerprints taken. However, we have subsequently found that he was dismissed from a previous job as a nightclub doorman following his increasingly heavy-handed behaviour with customers he'd chosen to eject. There was a particular incident that should really have landed him in court for assault which was the last straw for the management. Murdie is a body-builder and a heavy steroid user - a recipe for cultivating a violent temper.'

Another image from the recent past comes to me as he talks. Is that where Jane got that bruise that was still showing below her panty line the night she slept in my bed?

Mr Marks finishes his explanation. 'I'm sure you'll have worked out by now, Alex, that when Matthew Murdie was fingerprinted on arrest his print was found to match exactly the one found under the lid of your cistern. He tried to claim that he'd once done a plumbing job at the house but your landlord Mr Chatterjee has confirmed to the police that Murdie will have been a boy in school the last time that particular bathroom unit had any attention.'

Mr Chatterjee's neglect of routine maintenance sounds about par for the course. The solicitor's mention of it seems like a comic coda to Mr Marks' story, but it doesn't mask for me the seriousness of what I've just heard. Jane Ogden was killed in a frenzied attack, probably with a screwdriver, by her former partner. The images of her mutilated body come back to me, make me feel physically ill again.

'You're very quiet,' says Mr Marks. 'Do you trust me now when I say that in a very short time you are going to be free?'

'I can hardly believe it, but I'm starting to think that's really going to happen, yes. Thank you very much indeed Mr Marks, You and your team have done a fantastic job.'

He smiles modestly enough, but with a glow of understandable pride.

'We might as well get the process started. I have a few forms for you to sign right now.'

This is more like the Marks I know. The ultimate bureaucrat. As he moves papers on his desk to find the appropriate forms I notice a handwritten document among the pile.

'That looks like Karin's handwriting.'

'Karin Taylor's? Indeed. It's her statement.'

'You mean Karin was...?'

'The witness who came forward, yes.'

'Not Ruth?'

'Alex, you know Ruth Taylor is dead.'

I shrug my shoulders, wait for him to continue.

'We had written to Mrs Taylor because we knew she would be called as a witness for the prosecution in your case. We wanted to find out what she was likely to say in the witness box, and what her manner, her attitude was likely to be. Towards you in particular of course. She didn't respond to our request and we thought we'd lost our chance, then she called us out of the blue. Having seen Matthew Murdie in his van at Jane Ogden's funeral, her chance encounter with him at the cemetery came flooding back to her. Apparently he'd almost driven into her car at the cemetery gates; he will have been in quite a hurry to get away, as you can appreciate. Karin didn't want to go directly to the police with this new information - between you and me, Alex, I don't think she has a great deal of respect for DS Tregarron - and she was very anxious when she came to us, didn't want us to tell her daughter, who was firmly against helping your defence, but Karin felt that the truth had to come out whatever the consequences.'

I sit back and drink all this in. Of course, that's just my Karin. And how clever of her, how resourceful, to find a way of freeing me from this torment, this madness, after I had failed so spectacularly on my own. Thank you, Karin, I love you.

I cheerfully sign Mr Marks' forms and he tells me he'll aim to facilitate my release by the end of week. He shakes my hand again and delivers me to the guard who'll escort me back to my cell for what will be only the shortest of stays now.

The guard is Geordie, of course. He'd been in the room throughout my interview with Mr Marks, though the solicitor had insisted he stay well away from our table; 'client confidentiality' he'd reminded him. I'm not so naive, though, to think Geordie hadn't picked up a fair chunk of what was being said. Halfway back to the wing he hands me proof of it when he halts on the landing, turns and puts his face uncomfortably close to mine.

'Seems like we're going to be losing you then, Robson. Shame. Listen, I don't know whether you are a sad psycho killer bastard or not. Tell you one thing I do know, though. You're still a fucking knob head in my book.'

I smile at him, and keep smiling after he turns and we resume our three-man convoy, walking at a fast clip back to my cell. The tune from *Karin's Song*, locked out from me since my transfer to the hospital wing, has returned. Plays in my head as we walk.

XVII

I wish I'd asked Mr Marks to provide me with some better clothes to go
out with - a new suit would have been nice; worth the expense for a
special occasion. Instead I'm given just what I stood up in when I was
arrested outside Gladstone Terrace. All my clothes have been in a sealed
bag since I was transferred here from the police station but somehow
they have the prison stink on them. They feel slightly big on me; I guess
I've become even skinnier on a prison diet, especially since I usually
scraped most of it into the waste bin at the canteen. (I always suspected
somebody might have gobbed into my food, and in the hospital wing it
was probably laced with whatever drug the medics wanted to steal into
me.) My pockets are empty but I'm told the rest of my property will be
waiting for me to sign for at the gate.

Also waiting at the gate - or rather the building nearest to it - is Mr
Marks himself, and a male colleague I've never seen before who is about
the same age as me. Marks is my nominated discharge escort (upmarket
security) and he helps me with the formalities of ID checks, release
papers and the return of my property, basically just the few pounds and
pence I had in my pocket at the time. 'If you'd served a proper prison
term you would have been eligible for a Discharge Grant of around fifty
quid,' he said. (The word 'quid' sounds strange coming from Mr Marks -
he's generally so formal in his language.) 'Ironically, because charges were
dropped you're entitled to nothing. But at least we've arranged some
transport for you.'

'Can we sue the police for wrongful arrest? Get some
compensation.'

'Probably not, but I'll look into it if you wish.'

He hands over my cash sealed in a small plastic bag, which makes
me think about the day of my first discharge: how Tregarron returned my
tools still in their plastic exhibit bag, and how I got rid of them later.

'Did they ever find my screwdriver and tuning hammer?' I ask Mr
Marks, who shakes his head. I wonder if the bag is still stuck in the
middle of that hedge, or if the house owner has found it and quietly
added the tools to his own collection in his garage or his garden shed.
Imagine if I really was the killer - he'd be unknowingly harbouring crucial
evidence.

'Now, listen Alex,' Marks says. 'The press have got wind of your
release, and there's a pack of them around the gate and in the visitors' car
park. I guessed something of the sort would happen so I've made some

contingency arrangements. Unless of course you wish to become a media celebrity, have your fifteen minutes of fame.'

'Er, no.'

'I thought not. Which is why I've asked Stephen along, though we've travelled here separately. Stephen, this is Alex. Alex, Stephen.'

'Hello,' we say together and shake hands.

'You'll see Stephen is about your age and build. In fact he would have been a good candidate for your ID parade.'

'No, he looks too much like me for that.' A joke, but Marks just nods his head briefly. He's more interested in telling me his cunning plan.

'Stephen and I are going to leave first, with Stephen's coat over his head like so.' Stephen demonstrates on cue. 'The media will assume it's you. They'll pester us and possibly follow our car, and/or they'll vacate the car park as soon as we've gone. I want you to stay here ten minutes after we've left, then go alone to the car park, where you will see a driver in a green Peugeot waiting for you. I'm sorry I couldn't have provided you with a more prestigious vehicle but I did not want to draw attention to it. The driver's name is Thomas and he will take you home, but please do watch out for possible door-steppers at the other end. Does that sound like a good plan?'

'It's an excellent plan, Mr Marks. Thank you.'

That faint glow of pride again. I do believe Mr Marks has enjoyed himself more over the last few days than he has ever dared to before. From his inside pocket he produces a gold fountain pen - with a hint of a flourish, it seems to me.

'Then we just have one last form to sign and the action can commence. If you could sign here first, Alex... Thank you. And I sign here.'

I watch him add his signature below mine. I look at it again when he's done.

'Is that an x?'

'Of course.'

'I always assumed you were a k-s.'

'Interesting. Well I can assure you, that's the correct spelling.' He puts his pen back in his pocket. 'No relation.'

I hang around in the discharge area for ten minutes, as instructed, after Mr Marx and Stephen disappear through the gate. It seems much longer; I can't wait to be shot of this dreadful place. The shadow of it falls cold across the yard as I take the long walk to the main entrance (or exit in my case). The prison gate is huge, but there's a little door set in it which a guard opens for me. He directs me to the visitors' car park at the side of the building and I set off to look for the green Peugeot. Mr Marx's plan seems to have worked - there is no media presence as far as I can tell. I only have the vaguest idea what a Peugeot looks like, but the driver sees me first anyway and emerges from the car to wave me over.

A few rows away from him someone else also opens their car door to stand and look at me as I walk into the car park. She hasn't been fooled by the solicitor's ruse; she obviously knew that wasn't me under the coat. Somebody must have told her I was being released today and she's driven over specially to see me. More than that, she wants to be the one to drive me home; she's beckoning now like Thomas did, though perhaps a little less confidently, half-hidden behind the door of her Mini.

Do I stick to the plan, or go with her? There's no real dilemma for me. I'm sorry, Deborah Ann, I really, really appreciate the kindness you've shown but, let's be honest, I don't want to encourage you. Don't want to mislead you. There's no future in our relationship. End of.

I give Debbie what I hope she recognizes is a cheery wave as I take the route away from her and towards the Peugeot. A thank you very much and goodbye wave. She drops her hand and I turn my attention to Thomas.

'Sorry to keep you waiting.'

'No problem. Looks like everybody's gone. I was a bit worried about that one, though.' He nods in the direction of Deborah Ann's Mini. Debbie herself has given up and sat back in the driver's seat.

'No, it's fine, I know her. She's not press. Just somebody from Social Services.'

I climb into his front passenger seat and in a few moments we're off in the direction of the motorway. We chat for the sake of saying something - the weather, some football on the telly that Thomas saw last night and I know nothing about - then lapse into silence until we reach the outskirts of the city.

'Where to from here?'

I give him the address and he asks me to keep him right as he doesn't know the area very well. We're near home when I remember what Mr Marx warned me about door-stepping journalists. I have Thomas drop me at the end of the street so I can check if anyone's hanging around before I go in.

'Looks pretty quiet. I'll get off, then.'

'Yes. Thanks for the lift, Thomas. Appreciated.'

The Peugeot drives off and I walk carefully along the street. Pretty quiet, as he said. I stop for a moment or two under the canopy of trees, just to be sure. I can feel my heart beating now. The excitement has been growing for me since we came off the inner ring road. Now I've seen the MX-5 parked outside the house it's all I can do to remain calm. It's OK, I keep telling myself. After what she's done for you, you know it's going to be all right. It's going to be perfect.

It's time. There's not a soul in the street. I step out from under the trees, walk across the road, up the drive and up the three steps to the front door. I can't help smiling, thinking, I must remind her to get me a new key. All in good time. I ring the doorbell once and wait. Stay calm. Glance up and down the street as I'm waiting. A Mini passing by, that's all. The quiet click of the lock pulls my attention back to the house. She's opening the front door. Not Abi. It's Karin. It's really and truly my Karin.

Biography

David Williams grew up as one of seven children in a mining community in the North East of England, a childhood he has written about with humour and affection in his popular collection of short stories *We Never Had It So Good*, published by Zymurgy.

While pursuing a varied career in teaching, entertainments, marketing and management development, eventually leading to the formation of his own successful company, David has also been a prolific free-lance writer, with many plays broadcast by the BBC, books and plays published by top education publishers in the UK, Australia, Germany and Scandinavia, and many credits as a writer and format creator for popular TV and radio quiz and game shows.

A member of The Society of Authors, David Williams is a regular contributor to the Society's magazine *The Author* and writes occasionally for other magazines and periodicals. He has also written and produced educational and training videos, DVDs and software. David often performs at public readings, festivals, workshops and seminars.

As Close As You Are To Me is David's third novel for Wild Wolf. His thriller *11:59* and his historical novel about the railway pioneers *Mr Stephenson's Regret* both reached the semi-final stage of the Amazon Breakthrough Novel Award and have garnered high praise from critics and readers alike. The Kindle version of *11:59* reached Number 1 spot in the UK thriller charts and Number 4 in the USA.

David Williams has been married to schooldays sweetheart Paula 'for years and years'. The couple have three grown-up children and three grandchildren, with more on the way. When not deep in writing or research David indulges his passion for snooker, demonstrating without shame a huge gap between enthusiasm and ability.

Lightning Source UK Ltd.
Milton Keynes UK
UKOW04f0026171114

241720UK00001B/26/P